under-
ground

under-
ground

CRAIG SPECTOR

A TOM DOHERTY ASSOCIATES BOOK

TOR® NEW YORK

UNDERGROUND

Edited by Pat LoBrutto

Book design by Nicole de las Heras

A Tor Book
Published by Tom Doherty Associates, LLC
175 Fifth Avenue
New York, NY 10010

www.tor.com

Tor® is a registered trademark of Tom Doherty Associates, LLC.

ISBN 0-765-30660-3

EAN 978-0765-30660-9

First Edition: April 2005

Printed in the United States of America

0 9 8 7 6 5 4 3 2 1

For Vera

ACKNOWLEDGMENTS

The writing of a novel is always such a strange bargain—for all the solitude and obsessiveness implicit in the act, it cannot be done (at least not in my case) without the love, help, support, friendship, and goodwill of a great many people. It is, for this writer, a curiously collaborative act. To the following people I offer my gratitude and appreciation.

To Patrick LoBrutto, editor, ally, and friend; to Melissa Singer, Tom Doherty, and Tor Books/St. Martin's Press; to Anthony Gardner, literary agent; to Richard Christian Matheson, the brother I met along the way; to Peter Atkins, world-class pal; to Diana Mullen and Dana Middleton, for standing by their men; to Dr. Leib Lehmann, for the running dialogue; to Pete and Gail Clough, for thirty years' worth; to Peter and Tanya Hopps, Anna Nikichina, Jeff and Lena Goodman, Kimbra Eberly and Kenny Graham, Donna Ebbs, Preston Sturges, Jr., Karling Abbeygate and Donnie Whitbeck, Steve Patterson, Bob Malone and Karen Nash, Jim and Diana Gibson, for friendships old and new; to Danya and Deb Gonzalez, with love and a prayer; to Lance Bogart, Wayne Alexander, and Nikki Chippetta, for various and sundry life-support; to Dan McGuire and Ed Yashinsky, for exercises in character; to Lubov, Alexander, and Denis Vasilenko, and Maya Federenko, for doma; to Ray and Evelyn Covert, for fighting the good fight; to Ashley and Jake, with love and hope; to Eileen Addison, ever intrepid; to only sister, Kim, Barbara Spector, and Dotsy Broaddus, for familia; and to John M. Skipp, for the protean vibe.

Special thanks to Smash-Cut, the Monks of Love, and Soul Circus, for the musical interludes.

Last and never least, to my lovely wife, Vera. For everything.

My thanks to you all.

Craig Spector
Los Angeles, CA
Thanksgiving 2004

A man's character always takes its hue, more or less, from the form and color of the things about him. The slaveholder, as well as the slave, was the victim of the slave system. Under the whole heavens there could be no relation more unfavorable to the development of honorable character than that sustained by the slaveholder to the slave. Reason is imprisoned here, and passions run wild.

—Frederick Douglass

part one
capture

1

Tuesday, August 26. Stillson Beach, VA. 4:26 p.m.

It began with a word: six letters plucked from the Roman alphabet—two vowels, three consonants, one used twice—that, when combined just so, spelled *war*.

Justin Van Slyke squinted through gargoyle shades at the heat shimmering off the parking lot as a groundskeeper arrived and quickly prepped roller and pan to erase the vandal's taunt from the neat wooden sign. The word shone black against a field of purest white, jarring graffito under the elegant script that announced WELCOME TO CUSTIS MANOR, and in smaller serif, COURTESY OF THE CUSTIS HISTORICAL PRESERVATION SOCIETY. Justin watched as the offending letters were masked by the first pass of the roller, only to bleed back ghostly gray. The word lingered stubbornly, like it just didn't want to go away.

A lawnmower droned somewhere beyond the tree-lined drive at the edge of the lot where the shuttle tram waited; a faint breeze wafted, bringing the smell of fresh-cut grass, mixed with the barest hint of magnolia and dogwood, on the thick summer air. It was heart-attack hot, even for August: the kind of sodden, surly weather that promised thunder but delivered only stinging sweat.

Justin checked his watch. 4:29. It was time to go. As he picked up his pace, he cast one glance back at the workman laboring so diligently. The word was gone.

The word was *Nigger*.

The tour guide looked all of twenty. She was perfectly blond, perfectly Southern and genteel, with perfect teeth, perfect skin, and a perfect aquiline nose. She radiated helpful wholesomeness. A little yellow name tag on her navy blazer read HI, MY NAME IS BAMBI!

Of course it is, Justin thought, doubting that an imperfect thought had ever creased her smooth suburban brow. The tram got under way, quiet electric motor carrying it effortlessly past the wrought-iron gates that marked the entrance to the estate grounds. Justin hunched his six-foot frame into the last row of seats, keeping very much to himself: seeing everything, trying not to be seen, doubting that either was likely.

"I'd like to welcome y'all to our last tour of the day," Bambi said with practiced cheerfulness, clutching her mike like a game-show hostess, her voice slightly tinny through the tram's speakers. "Custis Manor is a fine historic landmark and one of the few completely restored antebellum plantations left in this part of the country."

The other tourists nodded and craned necks and autofocus zoom lenses, snapping pictures of the outbuildings coming into view on either side of the drive. The group was a random assortment of blue-haired matrons and Hawaiian-shirted retirees, a sunburnt midwestern family, some Yankee hipster yuppie honeymooners, a gaggle of Japanese exchange students with T-shirts emblazoned *Old Dominion University* . . . and three young black men, whose somber presence seemed to set Bambi a wee bit on edge.

Justin was not surprised. He knew that the truth about this place wasn't anywhere in the history books, but with the approach of Greek Week, the tour guide's unease was hardly unwarranted. For years, students from black fraternities across the nation had descended on Stillson

Beach to party away the Labor Day weekend. In the last several years, though, this influx of rowdy youth had led to violent clashes between police and partiers, this last year edging into full-scale riot and virtual martial law. Now, in the wake of budget-slashing, social program–gutting measures proposed by Senator Elijah J. "Eli" Custis—and the rabble-rousing rhetoric of his eldest son, independent gubernatorial hopeful Daniel "Duke" Custis—things were edgier than ever. Duke's bid to unseat the black incumbent, Governor Raymond Langley, was exceeding all expectations, both in the polls and in mudslinging negative campaigning. Many feared that last year's riots were just a pregame warm-up for the weekend about to unfold.

Bambi pressed on, extolling the virtues of the painstaking restoration of this archetypal microcosm of early nineteenth-century Southern life: kitchens, dairies, washhouses, henhouses, smokehouses, gristmills, and drying racks for the tobacco that was once its staple crop. The whitewashed wood structures presented an idyllic 3-D still life and, as Bambi assured all, were second only to Colonial Williamsburg in historical accuracy.

With one somewhat glaring omission, Justin thought, as he fingered the long and jagged scar that ran across his cheek. Still, it had changed greatly since the last time he was here. In a way, it was deeply ironic—the very years that had etched their cruel mark into his rugged features had resurrected this place; the two decades that had been sucked into a seemingly inexorable downward spiral of state pens, back rooms, and dank alleys had here rendered new that which was once crumbling and rotted. The last time he was here, it was the darkest of nights. But now, the sun was shining. Everything was pristine and sanitized.

And no one was screaming.

"And here we are," Bambi said. A collective murmur sounded as the tram rounded the last bend and rolled into a wide traffic circle. Three flagpoles dominated the center of the circle: the center pole reserved for Old Glory, flanked by smaller poles from which hung the rich blue state flag of Virginia, two Confederate regimental battle flags, and that ubiquitous blood red Confederate icon, the Southern Cross. They fluttered lazily in the breeze. A cardinal perched atop the center pole, regarding the tram with quizzical indifference, then flew away.

The big house was stately and serene, tall white Doric columns punctuating a broad-beamed front porch suited to sipping iced tea and surveying domain. The tram hissed to a stop and Bambi ushered the group up the wide stairs. As Justin ascended, he caught a glimpse of the charred stubble of a massive barn at the distant fringe of the estate: the one part of Custis Manor left neglected. In the shadow of the manor, its scorched timbers and rough-hewn stone foundation were strangely haunting.

Then they were inside, with the splendid staircases and balustrades that dominated the sprawling entrance. To the left, a magnificent mirrored ballroom. To the right, a voluminous sitting room and library. And directly before them, the great hall, in which the portraits of the family patriarchs hung. There was Senator Elijah, nearest and most recent. There was Elijah's father, Vance, another important statesman, dead now some twenty years. There was Vance's great-grandfather, Emmanuel, the noted Confederate colonel who steered the family fortune through the turbulence of the Civil War and Reconstruction to the Gilded Age at the dawn of the last century.

And at the end of the line, the portrait of Silas Custis: true and founding father of the lineage. It was he who built the manor and the family fortune upon which his heirs had relied. It was his distinctive countenance—high, arching brow, deep-set eyes, gaunt and severe features—that the rest of the clan had genetically replicated. He had been dead for over one hundred and fifty years. But not nearly dead enough.

I'm back, motherfucker, Justin hissed under his breath, staring up at the portrait. The portrait stared back, impassive and imperious. Justin glanced at the three black youths, exchanged a terse nod.

Suddenly, the men sprang into action: two whipping out spray-paint cans and defacing the paintings while the third launched into a fiery tirade.

"THIS HOUSE WAS BUILT ON A FOUNDATION OF LIES!" the black man roared, addressing the horrified crowd. "BUILT ON THE BLOOD OF THOUSANDS OF AFRICAN BROTHERS AND SISTERS WHO WERE PLACED IN BONDAGE AND SENT HERE TO BE SLAUGHTERED!"

Bambi screamed for Security as the chaos mounted. Two more paintings bit the dust. The black youths continued to rage as a pair of blazered goons entered the room. One grabbed a spray-painting youth by the arm; the kid turned and sprayed him in the face, then kicked him in the crotch. The goon dropped in ruddy blackface, moaning.

Justin looked around. The window of opportunity was fleeting. He quickly slipped to the back of the panicked crowd and raced through the library to the servants' stairway he remembered so well . . .

. . . and for a moment everything seemed as it was twenty years ago: the narrow staircase leading to wide corridors upstairs, flanked by open doorways to many rooms. The shattered furniture had long since been restored or replaced. The huge gilt mirrors were crystal clear and unbroken, reflecting him at every turn as he hastened toward his destination.

On the second floor, at the far end of the east wing, Justin arrived at the master suite. He stepped inside, locking the door behind him, and looked around. *No blood.* A voice in his head. The last time he was here, there'd been plenty. Heart pounding, he crossed the bedroom to the far doorway that marked the entrance to the bathroom. He entered, locking that as well, then beelined for the pedestal sink, a late-nineteenth-century upgrade courtesy of Emmanuel's reign. A small antique mirror hung over the sink, a larger gilt-framed full-length one off to the side. Justin turned the faucets on and emptied a small black pouch full of herbs into the basin, then produced a small black candle, lit it, and set it on the rim. Then he shoved his hands and arms into the churning pool, ran the water through his hair, dousing his face and soaking his skin. He stood there, dripping, and gazed at his reflection in the smaller mirror.

Now, said the voice in his head. *You have to do it now.*

Justin produced a razor and pulled open his shirt, buttons popping and plinking on the hardwood floor. Taking a deep breath, he began methodically slicing into his chest. Pain blossomed as the blood welled thickly. Justin sliced again, crossing the wound, then again, etching a cryptic pattern into his quivering flesh. Justin turned to the larger glass and, touching his trembling fingertips to the wounds, began to paint a similar pattern on its surface. The air began to charge: a terrible, potent buzz crackling in the closed atmosphere of the room.

Outside, the bedroom door crashed open. Justin began to chant low, in the magick's tongue: a language he barely understood, for a ritual he had only recently been trained to perform. As he chanted, other voices seemed to join his, a low, ghostly chorus. It filled the room, but its source came from somewhere behind the mirror.

As he chanted, bodies slammed against the heavy wooden door. Hinges creaked as screws split wood. Justin ignored it, focusing all his attention on the pain and the ritual. He chanted, the sound of his voice droning and hypnotic, the ghostly chorus rising in his head. He felt dizzy, nauseated. Justin focused on his own eyes staring back at him from the mirror, his pupils black and wide.

He watched in amazement as the surface of the glass suddenly rippled, turned black and shimmering as an ocean at night. His reflection went murky, diffuse. Justin bit back his fear, reaching forward with bloodied fingers. His left hand met the surface, touching its shadowy twin . . . then went in. Something began pulling him forward, into the rippling surface of the glass.

Behind him, the guards hit the door again. This time, it gave. Justin turned and saw their faces glowing in the strange light radiating from the mirror. Their expressions were alarmed and horrified. But not surprised.

THEY KNOW! he realized as he pressed forward into the shimmering portal, shuddering against the cold that enveloped him, gripping him from the other side. He sucked one last gasp of air and closed his eyes, submerging fully. For a moment he felt unmoored, floating in a swirling void; the sounds became muffled and indistinct. Justin exhaled and took a desperate breath: the air that filled his lungs was chill and laced with a strange, pungent scent. His body moved languidly, as though underwater. He turned and opened his eyes, saw the room now visible through the portal of the mirror, the daylight surreal and glowing. He drew his left leg in, then his left arm . . .

. . . and suddenly other hands were upon him—hot, living hands, seizing him by the wrist, yanking him back. The guards strained to pull him out; in the strange light of the other side, their fleshy faces were rendered monstrous, grotesque, their mouths ragged gashes, their eyes like black, soulless pits. They pulled on his arm, dragging him back; Justin screamed as the heat of the world washed back over his exposed flesh. For one excruciating moment he was the subject of an interdimensional tug-of-war. The force on the other side of the mirror was pulling him almost fully into the darkness as one of the guards fought to hold him and the other roared into his walkie-talkie. In their struggle, they knocked over the altar. Justin screamed as the portal slammed shut . . .

. . . and in an instant the mirror went solid again, slicing off his right hand just above the wrist. Blood sprayed the faces of his assailants as Justin disappeared into the shadows. The mirror rippled, went clear and hard again. And Justin was gone.

Except for his right hand, which lay, still twitching, on the bathroom floor.

2

Wednesday, August 27. Baltimore, MD. 5:47 p.m.

Caroline Tabb Connolly wheeled her white Toyota Land Cruiser into the narrow driveway of her North End townhouse. The truck was a plush and comfy ride, with oversized tires, an oversized car payment, a cowcatcher grill, and a Greenpeace sticker on the back bumper. A best-selling self-help audio book, *Mine Is Not A Four Letter Word!*, was playing on the CD player. Caroline keyed off the ignition in mid-affirmation, then grabbed a thick file off the passenger seat, her stainless-steel Sharper Image coffee mug from the console cupholder, and her cell-phone from its charging cradle. The coffee was cold leftovers from this morning's crack-of-dawn commute; the papers were de rigueur dead-lines that could not wait . . . or so Ellen, her account manager, had just made painfully clear. Caroline was bone-tired, nerve-jangled, and quietly seething. As she struggled to climb out of the truck, the heel of her new Via Spiga pump got caught in the steel mesh of the step.

"Shit!" Caroline hissed. As she turned to free it, the heel snapped off just as the little dangling wire to her Nokia headset caught on the gearshift, the earpiece hooking on her Pasquale Bruni earring and jerk-ing her back. Caroline lurched, off balance, then went down. As she did, the lid came off the travel mug: sales contracts, color brochures, and day-old caffeine went flying, soaking the leather interior, the scattered files, and the front of her new Donna Karan silk blouse.

Caroline let out a barely muffled scream and threw the rest of the file across the neat lawn, then fought like hell to keep from crying. It was just that kind of day. A big client at Ethan Allen was inches from closing: five beds and four baths; living, dining, and den; some hotshot VP from Towson and his wife redecorating their entire house—a "starter castle," as it was known to the trade—some five thousand square feet of upwardly mobile opulence. Caroline had been working them all month, matching earth tones to accents until her eyes glazed over, catering to their every vague yet entitled need. She had taken countless late-night inspiration calls and countless more meetings with the exec's wife—a taut Prada princess with nothing better to do with her days than buff her abs and imagine new ways to spend hubby's quarterly bonus— smiling and nodding as the prissy little skank went from nuevo to retro to country classic to postmodern and back again with nary a clue. Caroline had pressed on like a trouper—coordinating contractors, making every conceivable arrangement—until finally she had them pinned down: a revolting mélange of styles that violated every aesthetic atom in her being. But screw it—it was worth the nine grand in commission when they finally got off the fence and signed. Which they were supposed to do at nine forty-five this morning.

Which they then did not do.

Caroline had watched with mounting panic as the clock ticked by ten, then eleven, then noon. The contracts were neatly laid out on her desk. The clients did not return her calls. Finally she tracked down the VP on his cell, on the ninth hole at the Golden Horseshoe in Williamsburg. He sounded chipper—like nothing in the world was amiss—and thanked her for all her hard work. He said they'd opted for a little getaway. But when Caroline tried to pin him down, he finally fessed up: they had decided to "go another way." Thank you, and buh-bye.

And that was that. No further explanation, not even the grim satisfaction of knowing she had been gutted by a margin-slicing competitor selling Chinese knockoffs of high-end product at 30 percent under her cost, or some big-box discount joint dealing direct and screwing them all. She was simply dismissed, adding injury to insult as nine thousand badly needed dollars sprouted little angel wings and flew away.

When Ellen had found out about it, she had summoned Caroline into her office. Caroline had gritted her teeth and dutifully gone, trying hard not to mind the fact that the twenty-two-year-old who had once been her assistant was now her twenty-nine-year-old boss. Ellen had smiled and cautioned Caroline that regional was looking at cutbacks and she had best bring her accounts up to speed in the next quarter; when Caroline had protested, Ellen had pretended to listen and then had abruptly cut her off, told her to just do it.

Don't forget, she had told her, *you're expendable.*

"Expendable," Caroline muttered bitterly for the five hundredth time, like a bad sample loop replicating endlessly into the core of her self-esteem. It was the first time in her life she had ever been called that, and it burned. She felt degraded and humiliated, emotionally downsized.

It wasn't supposed to be like this, she thought morosely, the sentiment extending beyond this latest incident to encompass her entire adult existence. *I was going to do something important. I was going to be an artist.* She was thirtyish—stopped officially counting at the decade's midmark—and attractive enough, with auburn hair, sharp, clear eyes, and the all-around superstraight air of the reformed wildass. But it gnawed at her—the years of schooling, the degree from Parsons, the frustrated ambitions that gradually gave way to the encroaching demands of marriage and motherhood and mortgage and the sundry other trappings of a normal life. The life she never planned on having. The life that now, more than ever, felt like a drowning tide slowly closing over her.

"Shit," Caroline said again, sitting in a frustrated heap, wallowing in her own personal whirlpool of middle-class torment. It was ten to six;

Kevin would be home soon. There was barely time to get a tasty and nutritious din-din nuked and on the table.

Caroline gave a deep sigh, then picked herself up and set about containing the damage.

Muted laughter and the low thud of trip-hop filtered down from upstairs, followed by the smell: dank and sweet, like a sinister vapor trail.

No, Caroline thought, sniffing. *No way in hell. Not in my house. Not today.* She ascended in stocking feet—ruined shoes kicked off at the foot of the stairs—and recoiled as sound and scent grew stronger. She came to the door at the end of the hall, twisted the knob. Locked. She banged on the door.

On the other side, the laughter stopped, followed by the urgent sound of bodies flailing in hasty search of garb. A beat later the door cracked open and Zoe appeared, dark hair disheveled, shirt misbuttoned, jeans unzipped. A vaporous scent wafted around her like an alien atmosphere.

"What?" Zoe said, her tone dripping with nineteen-year-old contempt. Her blue eyes were red rimmed, pupils irised wide, hugely stoned. *"What?"*

"Can I talk to you?" Caroline said with barely mustered civility. It was not really a question. She looked past her daughter and caught a glimpse of a young man hunkered on the edge of the unmade bed, pulling on his boots even as he tried to blend into the woodwork. He stood, flipping long, braided hair back, and turned. His shirt was open, revealing smooth chocolate skin. He looked at her and smiled sheepishly.

Zoe saw the look on her mother's face and instinctively stepped forward to block the view. "Could you come back later?" she replied, also not a question. "I'm kinda busy right now."

"Now," Caroline said flatly, eyes flaring. Zoe rolled her eyes and sighed grievously. She might have taken after her father in many ways, but she had her mother's sighs.

It was thirty minutes later when Kevin Connolly opened the back door, stripped off his leather Harley jacket, and walked in on domestic Armageddon. The air reeked of Glade. In the living room, the battle was still raging.

"*I can't believe you!*" Zoe cried. "*You're such a hypocrite!*"

"*That has nothing to do with this!*" Caroline spat back. "*I will not have you smoking dope and screwing in my house!*"

"*It's my house too! I'm not a child anymore! You can't tell me what to do!*"

Kevin sighed. *God, not again.* When Caroline's zero-tolerance approach collided with Zoe's equally intolerable teen defiance, the last thing Kevin Connolly could hope to be was neutral Switzerland. Both his wife and stepdaughter were stubborn and strong-willed, but this close to home, his professional training was no help at all; the resulting paralysis just aided and abetted the slow-death dissolution of his nuclear family unit. He glanced back at his leather jacket, a distant thought urging him to just head back out, hop on his hog, and ride.

Kevin headed for the fridge instead, wishing against his own hard-won better judgment that there was a beer in there, or a wine cooler, or even an NA-style malt beverage. Alas, and thank God, no. He grabbed the pitcher of iced tea and poured himself a glass, then eased his bulky frame down in the cozy breakfast nook. The kitchen, like the rest of the house, was an exercise in contemporary casual perfection, like Martha Stewart on steroids. Caroline had seen to every tiny detail, from the neat black-and-white checkerboard floor tiles to the whitewashed pine cupboards and black granite countertops, the herb box in the oversized window over the big double sink, the hanging delicate crystals sparking refracting prisms of light, the cutesy Pennsylvania Dutch plate that read BLESS THIS HAPPY HOME. The décor was part wish fulfillment, part heavily reinforced false advertising . . . as at the moment, their abode was anything but happy.

Kevin groaned. His job at the Upper Baltimore Self-Help Center left him drained enough as it was: eight hours an underpaid day of overseeing addicts and victims of domestic violence in an endless stream of damaged humanity, not to mention coping with the latest round of politically fashionable budget cutbacks. Bad enough he had to lay off three counselors this week, and more than doubled his own caseload in the process, and he still wondered if his own head would be next on the proverbial chopping block. Worse still was that Caroline was perpetually overworked and overstressed, *and* the primary bread-winner. The disparity in their respective earning power was a fact she often invoked at moments of peak anxiety. But to come home to his own private drug war . . . it was just too much.

Just then Zoe stalked in, in a flurry of homegrown homegirl fury, Caroline following hot behind. The air crackled with outraged estrogen. "Don't you walk away from me!" Caroline barked.

Zoe ignored her, grabbing a Snapple from the fridge. As she turned, Caroline saw Kevin, caught squarely in the crossfire. He smiled uneasily.

"This isn't funny!" she said, pointing to her daughter. "She was smoking pot! With some . . . boy!"

The pause was a naked edit; the B-word was out there. Zoe picked up on it in a heartbeat. "He's not a 'boy,'" she said. "His name is Trey . . ."

"Really!" Caroline whirled, righteous parental indignation on over-drive. "Well, Trey isn't welcome here anymore!"

"Like he ever would be?" Zoe shot back. "What bugs you more, Mom—that we were fucking, or that he's black?"

And that was when Caroline slapped her: a short, sharp smack that shocked all three of them with its ferocity.

"Jesus, Caroline!" Kevin blurted out. "What the hell are you doing?"

Zoe's cheeks flamed red against pale skin; her eyes went wide, welling tears that she would not let fall. Caroline, for her part, looked horrified: her offending hand hanging before her like a suddenly inno-cent bystander. "Oh God, sweetie, I didn't mean that!" She reached out imploringly; Zoe recoiled, then her eyes went steely cold.

"This is bullshit," she hissed, slamming the Snapple bottle down. "I'm outta here."

She pushed past Caroline, moving toward the back door. Kevin started to stand.

"Zoe, don't . . . ," he began. "Let's talk about this . . ."

"Fuck you, Kevin!" Zoe snapped. "You're not my father!"

Kevin stopped, stung. Zoe turned and stormed out. The back door slammed. Caroline and Kevin were left staring at the door, the floor, each other.

"Well," he sighed. "That was fun . . ."

"Tell me about it," Caroline nodded morosely. "This day has been from hell. I don't know how it could possibly get worse . . ."

Just then the phone rang. They both looked at it warily. It rang again. Though she was physically closer, Caroline made no move to answer it. Kevin shrugged and picked up.

"Connolly residence," he said officiously. A pause as he rolled his eyes. "I'm sorry, she's not available right now . . ."

Caroline looked at him, mouthed *Who is it?*

Suddenly the pace of the conversation quickened. "What?" Kevin said. "Whoa, slow down . . . What kind of emergency?"

Caroline moved toward him, suddenly concerned; Kevin muffled the phone to his chest as he cast her a baleful glance.

"It's Josh," he said. She looked at him, like *Josh?* Then it clicked.

"Oh shit," she said.

Kevin sat flopped on the microsuede camelback couch in the living room, absently channel surfing the big-screen Samsung TV with the sound turned down and the closed-caption on, trying to not hear the muted strains of Caroline's voice in the kitchen. He could hear her pacing and feel the tension vibrating through the walls. He tried to imagine the effect Joshua Custis would have on Caroline right now, didn't even want to think about it. It rankled him too, his own instant demotion to emotional second-class citizen the moment the call came through.

Kevin sighed; it had ever been thus. Josh, the great love of Caroline's life, long since banished along with the rest of the relics from her reckless youth, yet still somehow—maddeningly, occasionally—*around*. They had remained friends, close in a way that belied explanation . . . or, at least, none was ever offered. And even though Caroline spoke very little of that period, she guarded it zealously, part of the vast, uncharted expanse of her past. It was like some great secret had transpired between them, some personal demon that had marked her forevermore. Kevin wondered if Joshua Custis might be the one to finally pry the lid off her past and let those demons loose.

And he wondered where he would be were that ever to happen.

Caroline, for her part, wasn't a happy camper. In the best of times, once every couple of years was more than enough for a call from Josh; a quick update to know he was okay, an even quicker trundle down a truncated memory lane. She had a continuing interest—no, make that *need*—to know he was all right, less from any residual romantic baggage than a simple affirmation that gravity still worked and her own hard-fought reality was still intact. But listening to his crazed ideas about the world and how it worked was enough to drive anybody a little nuts; understandable, given the past they shared, a past that few even knew about and most would not believe if they did. Now, with Zoe's transgression—and her own—so fresh in her mind, Caroline didn't know if she could handle it. At that moment she was more than ready to write Josh off for good.

Right up until the point that he told her Justin was gone.

"What do you mean, 'gone'?" she said, a seed of genuine dread suddenly blossoming in her heart. "What are you talking about?"

"It happened yesterday," he said. *"He was back at the house . . ."*

"What house?" she said, but the dread in her heart told her: there was only one house. The only one that mattered. Her voice lowered to a hushed urgency. "Jesus, Josh, what was he doing there?" she asked, not entirely sure she wanted to hear the answer.

"I can't explain right now," he said, his own voice dropping to a near whisper. *"Something happened . . ."*

Caroline listened to the rest of it as if from a great distance. The news hit her like a wrecking ball, making the seemingly solid firmament go suddenly rubbery beneath her feet. She asked what happened. *An accident,* he said, and did not elaborate. Josh told her that the funeral would be held this Friday. He begged her to come. And all the sweet reason and common sense in the universe meant nothing as twenty years of heavily buttressed mental walls cracked open.

"Yes", she answered, amazed at the word even as it left her lips. "Yes, I'll be there."

Caroline hung up. She stood for a moment, quivering. Then, very quietly, started to cry.

3

Amy Kaplan's battered CD boom box sat by the threadbare Salvation Army mattress along with a stack of discs from notable indie women artists—Ani DiFranco, Aimee Mann, Karling Abbeygate. Music played low in the background, an ethereal female voice with a lilting English accent set against pulsing, sinister backbeat:

> *There's something terrible about Ellis*
> *He's not who he pretends he is*
> *No, he's not a penniless poet,*
> *In fact, he's ruled by cosmic forces . . .*

A small fan whirred in the close confines of the Avenue D room as Amy sat cross-legged on the mattress, a silk scarf wrapped tightly around her exposed calf. The little fan didn't cool so much as rearrange the stultifying air, still close and heavy even after nightfall. The miles of concrete, brick, and pavement absorbed heat during the day and radiated it back until the wee hours like some giant kiln built to bake nine

million souls to a disagreeably ripe disposition, basted in soot and dump-
ster juice and served on a bed of wilted dreams.

On the boom box, the music continued.

When Ellis listens to these cosmic forces
He says baby contact is being made
But I caught him rolling the baker's wife
He's a devil, a charlatan
He says he's lying low . . .

The room was small and spare but clean, with not a trace of the usual
haphazard squalor of a junkie squat—no fast-food wrappers, empty
bottles, rancid cast-off clothing or crumpled bits of foil. Rather, it was
ascetic—spartan, even. Her few clothes were neatly folded in an old
wooden milk crate; one pair each of sandals, sneakers, and boots were all
lined up against the far wall. A battered biker's jacket hung on the back
of the door. A small collection of cosmetics and aromatic oils was neatly
arranged around a flea-market vanity draped with Indian-print scarves;
a street-scavenged table and chair sat by the tiny kitchenette, done in
early Dinner for One. No TV. No radio. No computer. No telephone.
Just the little CD player and a small pile of dog-eared books on Tarot, I
Ching, the Kabala, and other esoteric and bizarre subjects.

The music swelled.

Lying low, he's lying low,
He's lying, lying, lying,
Must have been around
for a hundred years,
a hundred years or more . . .

Amy blinked back perspiration and focused on the task at hand:
namely, finding a serviceable vein beneath the Celtic tattoo around her
ankle. She tapped the inked skin until a faint bulge appeared. Good

enough. Then she tapped her works with a well-chewed fingernail and jammed the ten cc's of temporary heaven home. A curl of blood appeared in the hypo's chamber—always a good sign. Amy pressed the plunger and the hit sluiced in; she withdrew and placed the works in a Starbuck's cup containing a dollop of Clorox. She was good to go.

Amy loosened the scarf and let a whole other kind of warmth wash over her—a tingling orgasmic rush that flooded her senses in the space of two heartbeats and filled her with chemical bliss. As she leaned back into the high, the music swelled and refrained:

Must have been around
for a hundred years,
a hundred years or more . . .
Must have been around
for a thousand years,
a thousand years or more . . .

Somewhere outside, a gun went off, two quick pops like firecrackers. Maybe a backfire, who knew? Tires screeched. A dog barked. Somebody screamed. Someone was almost always screaming. In her head, anyway.

Amy's head lolled, dark hair spilling back in a mass of unbound curls. From the far side of the rumpled covers came a sigh and a shift of body weight, revealing blond hair and smooth skin. A sprinkle of tiny moles dotted the curve of her back from sacral dimples to shoulder blades, like a distant constellation. A delicate tattoo graced the base of her spine, filigreeing the wide expanse of her hips. Cindy something. NYU undergrad from someplace nice and harmless in Connecticut. Currently taking a walk on the wild side, soon to be heading home. Amy's lovers always did, after a month or a week or a night. Amy preferred it that way.

After years of soul-searching, occult studies, and desperate longing for the answer, punctuated by periods of state-mandated medication and treatment, Amy had arrived at her own way to make it through the long nights. To quell the screaming in her head that began one night some twenty years gone, and hadn't really stopped since.

By the next beat of her heart, the smack hit her brain. The light from the overhead bulb went starry and diffuse.

Amy nodded out.

It was well past midnight by the time she picked her way down a dark and scummy section of Avenue D, stepping over derelicts and dog crap, dodging a knot of crackheads clustered on the sidewalk. This part of lower Manhattan was suited as much to her philosophy as it was to her social station: anonymous and transient, the sheer magnitude of its collective pathos forced her not to care.

A garish neon sign proclaiming THE REAL ORIGINAL FAMOUS RAY'S PIZZA shone at the corner like a greasy Valhalla. She was down now and craved the carbs of a post-high slice, maybe an orange whip for the vitamin C.

Amy's life was a precarious balancing act. Remaining a low-maintenance addict meant never having to break into apartments or descend into full-fledged criminality, a burden she could not abide, though in her younger days she was not beyond trading the occasional sexual favor for a choice bag. Her habit was only twenty bucks a day, not too much more than a two-pack-a-day smoker at Manhattan prices; of course, she was also a two-pack-a-day smoker, so the advantage effectively canceled itself. She only scored from known suppliers, kept her kit scrupulously clean and did not share needles, and otherwise had learned to live frugally, artfully carving out an existence on the jagged-edged underbelly of the city: picking up odd jobs, handing out flyers for clubs, doing sidewalk Tarot and flea-market fortune-telling, hawking Dove Bars off St. Mark's Place or World Trade Center gewgaws near Ground Zero, or anything else that could hustle a buck with a minimum of expense and no paperwork.

This week her choice item was "Magic Rear-View Shades." The *"As Advertised on TV!!!"* tag was well over a decade old, but no one was counting; she got them from a similarly spurious capitalist pal who got a free boxload from a disgruntled job-lot stocker in exchange for two rocks and a dime bag of beat weed, which in turn was scored for a slightly used and freshly hot MP3 player, all in the free barter flow of trade that characterized bohemian bottom-dweller subsistence. Amy was wearing a pair of the glasses now, despite the night's entrenched darkness. Against her pale complexion they looked hip and sinister and projected just the right amount of *fuck-off-and-die* vibe.

Moreover, the shades really did allow her to see behind herself, due to a miracle mirror-coating on the outer edges of the lenses. Not a bad thing to have when you were a single, thirty-something psychic druggie dyke on the dark side of Avenue D.

Famous Ray's glowed garishly, dead ahead. Amy was almost there when suddenly a shadow loomed right behind her . . .

Amy's heart skipped a beat. She gasped, turned. There was no one there. She looked down the block at the clot of wasteoids. None had followed.

Jesus, she thought. *That's some bad shit.* A shudder rolled through her reedy form as she wrote it off to strong drugs and stronger hunger.

But the tiny hairs on the back of her neck continued to prickle, and the feeling didn't fade. She turned again, peering carefully into the reflective shades. A dark, cloaked figure stood by an empty tenement doorway. As she watched, it reached inside its cloak and withdrew its hand. The fingertips glowed a pulsating bluish white as the hand touched the wall and began to write.

"What the fuck?" she gasped, and turned to face it, heart thundering now. There was nothing there. She turned back, peered out the corner of her eyes. Again, the figure was there, writing in swoops and swirls.

J . . . U . . . S . . . T . . .

Amy gasped as the swirls continued.

. . . I . . . N . . .

Just in? she thought, conjuring some mad newsflash from beyond. Then it hit her.

Oh God. Amy gasped again as the screaming in her head welled up, a mad chorus of despair forever burned into her neurons. Cold sweat formed despite the New York heat. She turned. The shadow figure was gone. Dull brick loomed, unmolested. She turned again, looked through the slender reflections. The graffiti shimmered, spelling a word. A name.

JUSTIN . . .

Amy began shivering uncontrollably. For years, she had been waiting for just such a sign. Waiting for the payoff on an obscure pattern laid some two decades before. In her mind's eye, the writing dripped ominously.

"Justin . . . ," she murmured. A name she hadn't spoken in a long, long time, which had never really left her mind.

Four hours and forty minutes later, Amy was at Penn Station, using the last of her cash to score not drugs but a one-way ticket on the morning train, bound for that which once laughingly qualified as home. She had sent Cindy-something packing, then spent the better part of the night packing what mattered (very little), dumping what didn't (everything else), and throwing the I Ching over and over and over again. She had to: it kept coming up the same.

The I Ching, the *Book of Changes,* was a five-thousand-year-old method of divination from China and generally regarded as perhaps the oldest book in the world; it was also, to Amy, the clearest and most sublime of the divination forms. Throwing Tarot cards may have made for great flash in Washington Square Park—and scored more cash from tourists and passersby—but when Amy wanted a straight, no bullshit answer to a burning cosmic question, she went straight to the Ching.

It was a remarkably simple technique: focus your mind on the question or object of your query and then throw the coins. Three coins thrown six times, yielding solid or broken lines depending on how they fell, then stacked neatly in two trigrams from bottom to top to form one hexagram.

This she had done tonight, again and again. Again and again, it had come up the same. It looked like this:

She had done it a billion times before when she faced a big life decision—*should I try to get a real job?*—or a million smaller day-to-day ones—*should I hit on that cute waitress at the B Bar?* But tonight, with one question burning in her mind, and with each new throw of the coins, her blood had run that much colder: two heads, one tail; one head, two tails, in perfect staggered sequence, again and again and again. The mathematical odds were so astronomical as to guarantee her a high-roller's suite and a showgirl on each arm if she were in Vegas. It just wasn't possible.

But there it was: hexagram 29, *K'an.*

Danger.

Amy didn't need to read the corresponding text; she knew it all by heart. It had become her mantra these last few hours, which even now she murmured under her breath.

"This situation is one of real danger, caused and manifested by the affairs of man," she whispered. *"Your desires have led you to danger again and again . . ."*

Two hours ago she had found Josh's number scratched on an old bookmark. She had called him collect. He told her very little, but it was enough to put her here.

Amy bought her ticket, paid for it with the last cash to her name. The ticket agent looked warily at the wired woman with the ratty backpack who seemed, if not high, then otherwise altered. Amy ignored her, counting her meager change, and headed for the track.

"You have become accustomed to evil influences and no longer fight them," she murmured. *"You must now meet and overcome them . . ."*

An MTA cop eyeballed her suspiciously as she stood on the empty platform; only then did it dawn on her that she had left in such a hurry she had forgotten her backup stash. Amy groaned, envisioning the ghost of jonesing yet to come.

"Great," she muttered. "This'll be fun." A nine-hour ride lay before her, and then . . .

She sighed. Oh well. Josh said he would cover her once she got there. If she was lucky, she just might live to scrounge the return fare.

4

Thursday, August 28. Titillations. Stillson Beach. 8:17 p.m.

Seth Bryant watched the bar from his perch near the door, dark eyes scanning for trouble from behind even darker shades. Seth's preferred approach was to see it coming and convince it that it really didn't want to make the trip; at six-two and two-forty, Seth could be very persuasive—even the most alcohol-addled hard-on wilted when one of his broad hands landed gently but firmly on a wayward shoulder. For the more re-calcitrant hardass, a black belt in Kenpo sufficed to communicate where words fell short.

Titillations billed itself as "A Gentlemen's Club," "gentlemen" being a highly generous term encompassing horny salesmen, redneck con-struction workers, buff fratboys sporting fake IDs, sailors on shore leave, and pudgy tourists packing traveler's checks and dreaming of get-ting lucky with one of the dancers. The club was gearing up for the ap-proaching holiday weekend, and already the crowd was double its usual Thursday night load: some thirty patrons lining the stools flanking the main drag, with another fifty or so packed into the tufted vinyl settees that lined the walls to either side. The smoky air was chilled to peak erectile efficiency and dense with hopeless pheromones as a total of eight girls worked in steady rotation—four on stage, grinding toned flesh against gleaming chrome poles and undulating in ersatz boudoir bonhomie as the other four slinked through the crowd, hawking private dances and overpriced drinks.

The sound system cued up Ashanti's "Baby" as the new girl tottered onstage, balancing precariously on three-inch heels as she navigated the narrow runway. Her stage name was Sasha, and she hailed from one of the lesser former Soviet nations whose principal export in the post-Communist era seemed to be killer cheekbones and estrogen. Sasha's manager, a pocked and vulpine Slav in an Armani knockoff who called himself Yuri, sauntered up to Seth. He nodded cheerfully; Seth nodded back, vaguely wondering what was the Russian translation for "pimpstick."

"How you like my girl?" Yuri said. "Isn't she hot?" His accent leaned heavy on the *e*'s and *h*'s, sounding like *Eezn't she haht?*

Seth nodded absently. Truth be told, Sasha was almost disturbingly beautiful: long and lithe, with shy, dark eyes that projected a sensual and very human vulnerability far from the brittle-edged perfection of the other girls. She was clad in a tiny thong bikini bottom and waist-length sequined jacket, which she held closed as she swayed to the beat, dark hair falling to obscure her face. Seth liked her, not in the bone-jumping sense of some Eastern Bloc booty call, but as a very nice—dare he say it, even sweet—girl. Sasha hadn't been dancing long, maybe six months, and this was her first night back after a six-week absence. When she'd taken off, Seth had privately hoped and prayed that she had dumped this place, and Yuri, and moved on to better things.

"Check it out, bro," Yuri said. "New assets . . ."

Something about the way Yuri said "bro" and "assets" made Seth want to punch him; instead he followed his gaze to the stage, where Sasha was throwing her head back and stripping off her little jacket to reveal freshly augmented, almost comically enlarged breasts. The crowd cheered; Sasha smiled and dipped down to let the resulting flurry of dollar bills slide into her thong strap.

Seth rolled his eyes as Yuri leered. "Not bad, eh, bro?" he said. "Like I tell her, bigger cups make bigger bucks." He cupped his hands in front of his chicken-bone chest. Seth rose from his stool, towering over the sleazy Svengali.

"Don't call me 'bro,'" he said. He didn't raise his voice; he didn't have to. Yuri looked up at him and visibly shriveled.

Seth let it slide; at the moment he was more concerned with reading the crowd. The reaction to Sasha's new hydroponic equipment ranged from Cro-Mag hooting to the moon-eyed equivalent of a Margaret Keane painting—for all but the two men sitting at the far end of the bar. Seth hadn't seen them come in, but he noticed them now. They were dark skinned and somber, quietly nursing drinks, not tipping the girls, barely even watching them, seemingly immune even to the pounding pulse of the music.

Something about their pointed indifference tripped his radar. The whole strip was braced for incident, while craving a much-needed infusion of end-of-season cash; if they wanted to start something, Seth resolved it would not be here and not on his watch. Seth left his post at the door and made the stroll across the room, the crowd parting before him and closing behind.

As he approached them, Sasha moved down the line and another girl came up, a young black girl who went by the name of Angel. Seth positioned himself between and behind them, hands crossed casually before him. He leaned forward. "Having fun?" he said.

The two men turned. It was then that he recognized them: a pair of local homies from Hood Street who had gone away on low-grade felonies and came back calling themselves Mohammed and Rajim. They were clad entirely in black, wore matching crocheted skullcaps and large metal Star of David necklaces on heavy link chains. The smaller one, Rajim, looked up at him.

"Terrible thing to see a beautiful African sister debase herself for the Man," he said. Up on stage, Angel arched her back and shook her moneymaker, oblivious. Seth leaned forward, big hand resting on Rajim's shoulder.

"If you don't like the show," he said, "perhaps you should just go."

"Relax, brother," the larger man, Mohammed, said.

Seth looked at him. "Last time I checked, my mom had two girls and a boy," he said. "I don't recall any of 'em being you."

Mohammed glared back and reached inside his jacket. Seth instinctively moved in, gripping his wrist tightly. But when the man's hand emerged, it contained nothing but a small and innocuous piece of paper.

"What's this?" Seth said.

"A message," Mohammed said cryptically. "From a friend of a friend."

Seth released his grip, read the note. His expression soured, then went steely.

"Outside," he said. "Now."

The three men stood in the alley behind the bar, the distant thud of music rumbling behind them. Seth pulled out a Kool Light, lit it.

"Okay," he said, blowing an acrid plume into the night sky. "One of you knuckleheads want to tell me what the fuck is going on?"

"Says what it says, nigga," Rajim replied.

Seth whirled and straight-armed him, grabbing Rajim by the collar and slamming him back into the brick wall. The sheer speed of the movement took Mohammed off guard; as he moved to intercede, Seth's left leg cocked back, clipping Mohammed's knees from behind and knocking his legs out from under him. Mohammed pitched backward and smacked into the pavement, the full weight of impact cracking his head against the pavement. Rajim squirmed like a bug in a science project against the massive hand now pinning him.

"I abhor violence," Seth said levelly. "But I promise you, if you don't start giving me some very straight answers very quickly, bad things are gonna happen."

"I don't know, man! I don't know!" Rajim sputtered, eyes bugging. Seth tightened his grip, hiking the man up until his feet barely touched the ground. Suddenly Seth felt a cold ring of metal press against the base of his skull, heard the soft but foreboding click of a hammer cocking.

"Let him go," Mohammed said. He pressed the gun barrel into the nape of Seth's neck for emphasis. Seth released his grip and raised his hands; Rajim dropped, sucking wind. The moment he did, Mohammed backed away, the gun still leveled at Seth's head.

"Now, you can be stupid and dead," Mohammed said, "or you can be smart and do like the man says."

Seth looked at the crumpled piece of paper again. It was short and blunt:

> Seth—
> Justin is gone. Mia is alive.
> Friday, Church of the Open Door.
> I need you.
>
> —Josh

Seth's heart pounded. The message was a bomb lobbed in his lap, catching him in the blowback from his own past. And much as he might desire, he could not escape its emotional shrapnel range. For Seth too had a secret buried some two decades past. And he owed what life he had to Justin Van Slyke.

The message left lots of questions unanswered. Like, for example, just exactly what Josh was doing with Mohammed and Rajim, and vice versa.

"Just a friend of a friend, man," Mohammed said, lowering the weapon. God only knew what that meant.

Seth thought about his life. He had a wife for whom the word *love* was not nearly strong enough and a baby on the way. He had a deep and personal relationship with God that was exactly that: personal. He had a small greenhouse, spent his days making things grow; he had his moonlighting gig, bouncing rowdies with raging boners, to make ends meet. And the scars had pretty well healed over. The physical ones, anyway.

"Well?" Mohammed spoke calmly. "What should we tell the man?"

"Tell your friend of a friend," Seth said, "that I'll be there."

5

Thursday, August 28. Stillson Beach. 9:00 p.m.

Wallace Jackson made his way down the basement corridor leading to the Medical Examiner's office, a low-slung cinder-block building several blocks away from police headquarters and far off the main drag of the beach. In the normal course of events, it was a way station for human tragedy: from traffic fatalities and drug ODs to simple heart attacks and other, more mundane causes, along with the occasional drowning or boating accident that came with any seaside community and the somewhat less occasional homicide or suicide. The mayhem ratio swelled proportionately in the on-season months, from roughly May to September; the off-season calmed considerably, as the town winnowed down to its local population and the rhythm of life became as dull and predictable as the tides. In his eighteen years on the force, including the last five as chief, Jackson had seen his fair share of death, natural or otherwise, but he still shuddered as the doors hissed shut behind him and salt sea breeze gave way to the cloistered scent of air-conditioning, disinfectant, and formaldehyde. It was one thing to view the sundry sad cases of human demise as a procession of paper, forms, and photos, quite another to visit one in the flesh.

This case in particular he was not looking forward to at all. By any stretch of the imagination, Jackson was having a very shitty day, the last forty-eight hours serving only to deepen the mystery. They had gotten exactly zip out of the three spray-paint perps from Tuesday's incident at Custis Manor. Their presumed leader, a lowlife by the name of Henri Hayes, was particularly eloquent in his silence. Hayes had a criminal file over a half-inch thick and knew the drill by heart—he shut up, asked for a lawyer, and waited. The other two henchmen followed his lead, though whether out of loyalty to Hayes or fear of him was up to debate. In Jackson's view, either was likely.

There was no question that Hayes knew far more than he was saying, which was nothing. There was also no way Jackson could tie any of the suspects to the bizarre scenario that had unfolded upstairs. Everyone interviewed at the scene had placed the trio downstairs the whole time; aside from the coincidence of timing, there was not a scrap of evidence to connect them to the other, far more mysterious, incident. They were booked and arraigned on misdemeanor charges and held as long as possible, but when their bail was made, Jackson had no choice but to set them free.

To compound his joy, Jackson's superiors had spent the better part of the day chewing off his not-inconsiderable ass. They wanted answers and assurances: the holiday weekend was upon them, and there was no telling what news of the protests might do in an already charged atmosphere. Fortunately for all, the Custis people had effectively squelched any leakage to the press, presumably at the behest of the estimable Senator Eli. The story had made page two of the papers and had barely blipped on the local news stations, partly due to endless coverage of some new wrinkle in the war on terrorism and the upcoming elections, but also due to the Custis Foundation refusing to allow news crews on the property. It was a small mercy, but Jackson found it strange.

Not nearly as strange, though, as what the media and the good citizens of Stillson Beach didn't get to hear about—the upstairs bath, or "voodoo room," as it had been christened in-house. Indeed, given the lockdown effected by the manor's tight-lipped security, it was only by sheerest chance that the officers responding to the scene were made aware of the bizarre scenario courtesy of a tour guide named Bambi Walsh. Ms. Walsh was hysterical when the officers encountered her, and given their subsequent grisly discovery, her reaction was entirely warranted—she freaked out, quit, and promptly holed up in her tiny apartment on Bayview Avenue.

Jackson sighed and pushed open the doors leading to the morgue. Elizabeth Bergen, the Chief Medical Examiner, was seated on a rolling stool at the lab counter, munching on a Subway sandwich, red hair pulled back in a ponytail, glasses pushed up on her forehead, feet barely touching the floor. Bergen pushed back from the counter and stood. At five foot two, she barely reached his chest, but Bergen made up in attitude what she lacked in altitude.

"Took you long enough," she said.

"Day sucked," Jackson replied.

"Wanna trade?"

"No thanks. What you got?"

"Catch of the day," she said. She tossed him a pair of disposable latex gloves; as he slipped them on, he and Bergen moved to the bank of stainless-steel drawers that dominated the sterile room. Bergen swung a door open and hauled out the man-sized tray on rolling glides; inside, a body lay wrapped in an opaque plastic zippered bag. Bergen opened it, revealing a young Caucasian female.

"Harbor patrol found her on this morning's tide. We ID'd her off dental records." Bergen checked her tag, cracking deadpan, "Wallace Jackson, meet Bambi Walsh."

Jackson looked at the dead girl and grimaced. Her tan skin was puckered and pallid, face and torso chopped into an unrecognizable hash and scored with hundreds of smaller, shallower wounds. She smelled faintly of seaweed. "What's the cause of death?" he asked.

"Officially? Drowning," Bergen replied. "There was water in the lungs, anyway. The deeper lacerations are postmortem, most likely a propeller; the rest look like barnacle abrasions from bumping up against a hull."

"Accidental?"

Bergen shrugged. "Hard to say. Her BAC was point eight-five. Could've had one too many and took a long walk off a short pier. Could've had help . . ."

Bergen zipped the bag and slid the drawer back into its recess.

"Great," Jackson muttered. "Just great."

"Hey, don't order yet," Bergen said. "You also get a free set of steak knives." She motioned to the microscope. A wafer-thin slice of matter lay pressed on the little slide under the lenses; Jackson regarded it warily, then leaned forward and squinted into the eyepiece.

"What am I looking at?" he asked.

"Tissue sample. It's fresh."

"And?"

"Consider the source," she said. Bergen gestured to a small steel tray adjacent to the scope. Jackson peered inside. The severed hand lay palm up, fingers folded loosely over like the legs of a dead crab. She looked at him gravely. "We get our share of parts down here, Chief," she said. "But they're usually not still *moving*."

Bergen looked at her quizzically. But before he could say anything, the damned thing twitched.

"Whoa!" Jackson blurted. "W-what the . . . ," he stammered. "How the fuck . . . ?"

"Good questions," she said. "Been asking them myself all day."

Jackson looked again. As he watched, the hand twitched again, a weak spasm.

"This is a trick, right? Like that thing with frog legs . . ."

"Galvanic response? You wish." She shook her head. "We first noticed when we tried to print the thing. Had it in the meat locker to stave off decomp, but then we noticed."

"Noticed what?"

"There *is* no decomposition," she said. "The stump's severed so clean it's like it's been cauterized. I took a tissue sample about an hour ago to analyze it, and that's when it started. Like it woke up or something." She paused a beat. "Go ahead and touch it."

Jackson looked at her like she was nuts. Bergen rolled her eyes. "Relax, Jackson. It won't bite." She took his hand and placed the fingers lightly upon the severed wrist. "Notice anything?"

"It's still pliant," he said, curiosity overcoming revulsion. He felt again, then jerked his hand back suddenly.

"Jesus, is that . . . ?"

"Yup." She nodded gravely. "Fucker's got a pulse."

Jackson sat back on a stool in naked shock as Bergen reached around him. "I wanted you to be here when I did this. Borrowed this rig from EMS." She reached for a pair of wires with a small plastic clip on one end, placed the clip carefully on the tip of the index finger, then reached over to a small life-systems monitor and flipped it on. The screen lit up, a glowing green line scrolling. It blipped, scrolled some more, blipped again.

"Whatever it is," she said, "it ain't dead yet."

Jackson stared at it, dumbfounded. "Liz, what the hell's going on here?"

"Beats me, Chief," Bergen said. "But if you find the guy this belongs to, ask him if he wants it back."

6

It was just after nine when the Land Cruiser swung into the narrow gravel drive, tires crunching stone as the headlights illuminated the modest ranch-style split-level home surrounded by a thick grove of trees and a large, unmowed yard. It had been a long, tense trip, the crush of beltway traffic gradually giving way to secondary highways and a vast suburban sprawl of strip malls, fast-food joints, and faceless neighborhoods. As darkness fell, the scenery faded to long wooded stretches of state parkland dotted with glimpses of beaches, marshes, tidal flats, and inlets, and all of it punctuated by the complete absence of conversation within the vehicle. Caroline had refused to leave Zoe behind, and Kevin didn't dare leave them without a referee.

Caroline had felt the knot in her stomach tighten with each flat and passing mile. And as the road whipped by, she felt herself transported back through time as well as space to a night long ago and a younger version of herself, younger even than the sullen shadow of her daughter slumped in the back seat: a young Caroline Tabb driving down these very same roads in a beat-up VW Beetle, long hair wafting in the slipstream, the Police's *Ghost in the Machine* wailing on the stereo, a roach clip smoldering in the ashtray. A young girl dreaming of a mysterious and gleaming future in New York or Paris or London, far beyond the tidal pull of this place. A young girl dreaming of one day escaping and never, ever coming back.

The truck pulled up in front of the garage and stopped. As Kevin keyed off the ignition, the sounds of crickets and cicadas swelled oppressively in the night air. Caroline checked her makeup in the visor mirror and gave a practice smile. "Well, we're here," she said.

"Big whoop," Zoe muttered. Caroline glared at her daughter in the mirror. She knew full well that Zoe hadn't seen her maternal grandmother for years, collateral damage from a mother-daughter blowout shortly after the death of Caroline's father; the resulting years had led to an escalating estrangement, familial bonds winnowing down to holiday phone calls and the barest of contact. It was only reasonable to expect that Zoe's grandma would be a peripheral figure in her life. But at the moment, Caroline was not feeling reasonable.

"Behave," she said. Their eyes locked for a moment; then Zoe looked away in defiant resignation.

Outside, the porch light went on. A silhouette appeared in the kitchen doorway: Doris Tabb, waving. Caroline waved back. And for better or worse, she was home.

Zoe looked on in surprise as they entered. Her grandmother's house, like Grandma herself, was a genetic one-eighty from her mother's carefully coiffed domestic ambience: a cluttered clash of cast-off flea-market fare interspersed with tumbling piles of newspapers, magazines, and junk mail, all buttressed by plastic shopping bags from designer discount chains like Ross and T.J. Maxx. Elvis and Beatles memorabilia covered the tabletops, some still in their original packaging. It looked pack-rat pathological, like an Alzheimer shopaholic.

"Never mind the mess," Doris said, waving it all off. "I cleaned out the guest room for ya, and Zoe, sweetie, you can have the couch. Just throw your bags in and take a load off. Y'all want some iced tea?"

Doris ushered them in as Kevin smiled and humped the luggage upstairs. She was a rumpled dumpling of a woman in an oversized denim shirt and workout pants, silvered hair cut short, with dangly earrings and bangly bracelets and a perpetual cigarette between her fingers. She hugged Caroline, who stiffened and tilted her head, not so much returning the gesture as enduring it. "Good to see you, sweetie," Doris said, patting her back.

"Hello, Mother," Caroline said, then disengaged. "I better help Kev." As she retreated, Doris turned to Zoe, beaming. "And look at you, baby girl," she said. "I haven't seen you in ages. Come give your ol' gramma a hug."

Doris threw her arms open and enveloped Zoe, who hugged her back awkwardly, looking over her shoulder. "Wow, check it out," Zoe said, teen angst ceding to momentary wonder. The dining room table had been overtaken by an elaborate rig of laptop computer with an extension flat panel LCD monitor, multifunction fax/printer, flatbed scanner, and cable modem; wires snaked off and draped down onto the floor in tangled piles. A digital camera sat on a tabletop tripod. "Damn, Grandma, are you like a hacker or something?"

"EBay, baby." Doris winked conspiratorially. "When your granddaddy died, he didn't leave me a pot to pee in. Thank God for the Internet—do you realize how much money you can make selling *crap?*"

"No way," Zoe said.

"Way." Doris smiled and ducked into the kitchen, returned with two glasses of iced tea. She handed one to Zoe, clinked glasses, and took a sip. "I was a sixty-five-year-old widow with no visible means of support, and I didn't know a computer from a Coupe de Ville. But I took a couple of courses and figured it out."

"You make a living doing this?"

"Hell, sweetie," Doris said. "I cleared sixty grand last year. I got fifty auctions running round the clock. I go to flea markets, swap meets, yard sales. Buy low and sell high. I'm Dick Cheney's wet dream come true!"

"Damn," Zoe said, frankly marveling.

Doris took another sip of tea and looked at Zoe. "So what y'all come down for? Not that I'm not glad to see ya, but your momma don't tell me squat."

"Some guy died." Zoe shrugged. "She's been all freaky ever since."

"Who was it?" Doris asked.

"I dunno," Zoe said. "Justin something . . ."

Doris heard the name, and her face fell.

"Oh, hell," she said.

Caroline sighed grievously as Kevin placed their bags in the corner of the tidied guest room: bed freshly made, dresser, bookcase, and night tables dusted and smelling faintly of Pledge. Even the spines of the books were dusted. "It's not that bad," he said, conciliatory.

"Are you kidding? It's worse," Caroline replied. "Do you see this?" She gestured to the neat room. "It's like she did it to spite me."

"Don't you think you're exaggerating just a little bit?"

"Am I?" Caroline huffed, then sat on the bed. "I don't know," she confessed miserably, then added: "Sorry. I just really don't want to be here."

"Then why are we?"

"Because," Caroline started, then stopped, thinking, *Because I owe him . . . Because I need to know if I made the right choices with my life . . . Because I need to know if I ever really had a choice at all.* But all that came out was, "Just because."

From downstairs, a burst of laughter sounded—Doris's raspy nicotine cackle—followed by a rare accompaniment: Zoe's laughter, uncharacteristically girlish and delightful. Caroline looked at Kevin, dejected.

"Great, they're bonding," she said sarcastically, then, softer: "Sorry. Go on down. I'll be there in a minute."

Kevin nodded and kissed her on the forehead, then moved to the door like a man tiptoeing through an emotional minefield. Caroline watched him go, feeling a thousand hairline cracks spread through the thick shell of defenses that constituted her psychological Kevlar.

As the downstairs conversation swelled to a cheerful burble, Caroline's gaze fell upon the bottom shelf of the bookcase; she reached down and pulled out a thin hardbound edition of the *Stillson Beach Sentinel,* her senior yearbook. The sea green leatherette cover was faded, but the embossed logo—a pre-PC Indian brave in full feathered headdress and stoic, chiseled profile—was still visible. Caroline ran her fingers across the image, remembering the contest amongst the student body for the new design that would grace the cover, remembering Doris goading her into submitting a drawing, Caroline feigning disaffected disinterest while secretly excited. Remembering the day they announced the winner and hearing her name reverberate through the halls as she hunkered in the girl's bathroom with Amy Kaplan and Mia Cheever, blowing a joint in one of the narrow stalls.

Caroline opened the book, its laminated pages stiff and crackling. She paged quickly past the *T*'s and her own younger self until she came to the *V*'s and the little black-and-white picture of the roguishly good-looking kid with the dark and soulful eyes, a sly little bad-boy half smile on his face, peering out from another lifetime ago. The name beneath the photo read *Justin Van Slyke.*

Caroline looked at the picture; she felt fragile, vaguely resentful, but weirdly exhilarated, like there was a strange sense of completion to this, some long-neglected loose end about to be tied at last.

"Because I owe him," she murmured. Then put the book away.

After dinner, Doris and Zoe were seated at the kitchen table as Kevin and Caroline bid an early good night; Caroline wavered a moment at the door, then gave Doris a stilted hug.

"'Night, Mother," she said.

"'Night, sweetie," she replied, and patted her back. "Y'all sleep tight."

Caroline nodded and looked at Zoe, who was lingering at the table. "You going to bed?" she asked. Before Zoe could answer, Doris interceded.

"Y'all scoot. I want to spend some time with my only granddaughter," she said, waving them off. Zoe looked at her, then back to Caroline.

"It's okay, I'll hang awhile," she said, smiling. "I'm still pretty wired from the trip."

"All right," Caroline said awkwardly. "G'night, then."

"G'night," Zoe replied serenely. They did not hug. Doris and Zoe watched as they retreated; then Doris winked at Zoe conspiratorially.

"Hot damn," she said impishly. "Wanna drink?"

Zoe's eyes widened as Doris went to the kitchen cupboard and produced a bottle of Jack Daniels. "I tucked this away out of respect to Kevin, but after an evening with your momma I damn sure need one."

Zoe giggled as Doris returned with the bottle, a pair of gold-rimmed shot glasses, and a fresh pack of smokes. She lit one and looked at Zoe. "How old you say you were again?"

"Nineteen," Zoe replied.

"Close enough," Doris said, and poured. The two women clinked glasses and downed the shots. Zoe felt the liquor burn and exhaled sharply; she looked at Doris. "Gotta tell ya, Grandma, you're like the anti-Mom."

"Oh, hush," Doris said, waving it off. "Your momma ain't that bad. She just needs to lighten up a little."

"Tell me about it," Zoe said. "Was she always like that?"

"Lord, no," Doris exclaimed. "She was a little hell-raiser once upon a time."

"Wow," Zoe said, having trouble conjuring the requisite mental image of her mom being anything but, well, *Mom.*

"You know," Doris continued, "Caroline was about your age now when she had you. Fresh out of high school. Your Granddaddy about had a heart attack."

There was a long pause as Zoe suddenly grew quiet. "Did you know my dad?" she asked. Doris sighed and poured another round.

"She never said," she confessed. "We tried everything to get it out of her, but she wouldn't give it up. She just said it was a mistake." Zoe winced ever so slightly at the word, and Doris instantly backpedaled. "Not you, dear. Him."

"Oh," Zoe said, nodding. "What about the dead guy?" she asked. "Justin whatsisname . . ."

"God, I hope not . . . for your sake." Doris looked at her. "That boy was nothin' but trouble."

"Oh well," Zoe murmured and downed her shot. As she swallowed, she looked at the glass more carefully. It was inscribed *Down the Hatch!* with an African native dancing around a cooking pot as another readied himself to place a comely white girl inside and a third gnawed a human bone.

"Whoa," Zoe said, looking at the glass. "What up with that?" She put the glass down as if it were suddenly contagious. Doris looked at her askance.

"Relax," she said, holding hers up. "I got burned on a buy; guy said they were period, but it turned out they were fakes from Taiwan. Worth less than I paid for 'em . . ."

"You sell these?"

"'Black Americana,'" Doris explained. "Big thing now. Check it out . . ."

Doris got up and went to the pantry door, produced a key. "I keep this locked, for obvious reasons." She opened the door, motioned Zoe to enter. Zoe peeked inside, eyes widening.

"Holy shit," she murmured.

The pantry was six by four, with shelves on all sides, filled floor to ceiling with figurines and memorabilia, dolls, toys, banks, old advertisements, tea cozies, and kitchen aids: all of them featured characters ranging from painterly to garish, bright eyed and black skinned, with bright white or ruby red lips. A mint condition Aunt Jemima ad, circa 1944, exclaiming *WHOO-EE! My tastifyin' AUNT JEMIMA PAN-CAKES sure perks up appetites!* stood next to a Little Black Sambo serving plate inscribed *Dat's MIGHTY FINE Eatin'!;* a tin package of spot remover called Carter's Inky Racer, with a little black boy running around a horse track, was propped next to a ceramic mammy holding a little sign that read *Ain't No Bitchin' In Mammie's Kitchin!* And of course the ever-popular "jolly nigger" mechanical coin bank: a hinged iron casting of a black boy in a watermelon patch with his hand jutting out, ready to pop a dime into his leering, toothy mouth.

"Goddam, Doris," Zoe said reproachfully. "Who buys this shit?"

"Collectors, historians," Doris answered, shrugging it off. "I don't really care, s'long as their money's green."

"I guess," Zoe said. She gazed at the collection: wall-to-wall images plucked from the fabric of everyday life over one hundred years or more: mammies and sambos, toms and picaninnies, coons and brutes and golliwogs. The figures were all smiling. It was all in good fun.

But none of it was very funny.

7

By the time Amy arrived in downtown Norfolk, she felt like a paper cutout of herself, soaked in sweat and diesel fumes and ready to crumple. The first leg of the trek—three and a half hours from New York to DC—had been only mildly discomforting, the morning crush of inter-city commuters traversing the Northeast Corridor being no worse than your average midtown subway at rush hour. She had scored a seat by mer-est chance and sheer chutzpah, but her victory was short lived as she spied the No Smoking sign plastered to the thick Plexiglas window. She sighed and hunkered down for the ride, trying to hypnotize herself with the mo-notonous view and the rolling motion of steel wheels on rails. By the time she got to Union Station in Washington, it was all she could do to avail herself of the two-hour layover by exiting the terminal. Outside, she paced the exhaust-clogged street and sucked down smokes, her nicotine jones slated, another, more demanding one looming on the horizon.

When she detrained in Newport News, the sun was just beginning to set and Amy was feeling wobbly and hollow. There was still an hour to go, this time by bus, and as she waited to board, her senses had hyperat-tenuated, sounds and scents becoming oppressive with each ticking sec-ond: the cheap perfume of the woman in front of her and the crinkling of cellophane as the boy behind munched Doritos conspiring with the odors of oil, tire rubber, and axel grease to make her vaguely want to vomit, were her stomach not already empty and feeling like a shrunken walnut. As the bus chugged east down I-64, she felt her insides lurch with every shift of the gears; the light of the setting sun glinted off the waters, stabbing at her eyes, as they made the slow crawl through the Hampton Roads Bridge-Tunnel, each of the submerged portions feeling like a slow-motion descent into a claustrophobic, fluorescent hell. She leaned back and tried to nap, to think of anything, or nothing.

The conversation with Josh replayed maddeningly in her mind, long on mystery and short on answers. It bothered her that though they hadn't spoken for more years than she cared to count, he hadn't sounded the least bit surprised to hear her voice, like he had been expecting her call. Weirder still, like he knew what she had seen, even though she hadn't told him.

Just come, he had said. *I'll explain when you get here.*

That would be nice, she thought. She wanted answers. She wanted resolution. But at the moment, she wanted something else a little more.

The bus stopped, doors hissing open. Amy opened her eyes and climbed out of her seat on legs that felt like sticks of balsa wood. She paused at the door to the terminal, wavering, when a deep voice sounded behind her.

"Amy Kaplan?"

She turned. The man was in his late thirties, clad in a somber dark suit and shades, with mahogany skin, chiseled features, and long braided cornrows pulled neatly back. She nodded warily.

"This way," he said and turned, walking. Amy clutched her backpack and followed him to a black Ford Explorer parked by the curb. The windows were tinted. A remote chirped as the door unlocked. As the man climbed into the driver's side, Amy hesitated, urban hackles rising. The man looked up, head cocked. "Relax, lady," he said. "How you think I know your name?"

Amy nodded and climbed in. As he keyed on the ignition, the doors automatically locked, sending another ripple of anxiety through her.

Amy fought it back and settled herself into the plush leather interior. "So," she said, "you're friends with Josh?"

"Not exactly," he said, but offered nothing more.

"You work together?"

The man shrugged noncommittally. Amy looked at him, annoyed.

"Okay," she said. "Got a name?"

"Louis," the man replied, then, almost as an afterthought, "Hillyard."

Amy nodded as if trying to nudge the conversation forth with the motion. "So, Louis," she said, starting over, "you mind telling me where the hell it is we're going?"

"Josh told me to pick you up and to see to it that you're comfortable."

"I see," she said. "Did he tell you anything else about me?"

Louis glanced at her with what seemed like disdain. "Glove compartment," he replied.

Amy looked at the dash, thumbed open the glove box; it opened to reveal a plain envelope with "Amy" written on it in Josh's handwriting. She opened it and saw a half dozen thin glassine packets; her fingers trembled slightly as she pulled one out, dabbed her pinky in the contents, and touched it to her tongue. "Damn," she murmured. It was enough for an extended stay . . . or one fat OD on a major high.

"Not here," Louis warned. "I assume you can wait . . ."

Amy dipped her fingernail into the packet, brought it to her nostril, and snorted. "Now I can," she said.

She pocketed the envelope and leaned back in her seat, relief coursing through her, with the promise of more to come. As her head cleared and her craving abated, she realized that though he said next to nothing, the vibe she sensed coming from Louis was palpable. It was disapproving, with an underlying edge of superiority. It was also starting to grate on her nerves.

"I take it you have a problem?"

"My people have a problem," he said, his tone civil but cool.

"What," Amy said sarcastically, "people who talk like hit men and dress like undertakers?"

Louis looked at her, fierce but dismissive. "I don't like drugs," he said. "I don't like drug *addicts*." He stopped, checking himself.

Amy looked at him; there was something else in his tone, a further unspoken condemnation that he did not, or would not, voice. Her mind turned over the variants—*women drug addicts? . . . gay women drug addicts? . . . gay women drug addicts from New Yawk?*—when suddenly it clicked.

"White drug addicts," she said. "You don't like white drug addicts."

Louis said nothing.

"Great," Amy sniffed. "My tour guide is a racist . . ."

"Hardly," Louis said. "In order to be racist one must be in a position to dominate and wield the powers of economic and legal sanction over the dominated race. We have never been in a position to enact such repressive strategies; we've always been the victims."

"Wow," she said caustically. "Did you make that up all by yourself, or did someone program it into you back at Robo-Bro Central?"

Louis glared at her from behind his shades; Amy glared back, fatigue and trepidation giving way to an anger that overwhelmed her own instinct that pissing off this angry brother was maybe not the brightest idea in the world. She held her hands up in supplication.

"Sorry," she said. "No offense."

"None taken," Louis said. "I don't expect you to understand. You see racism. I see righteous fury." He said it calmly, like it was the most natural and obvious thing in the world.

Just then Louis wheeled the Explorer into the entrance of a nondescript Econo Lodge, then parked in front of a room in the back. As he climbed out, Amy caught a glimpse of a gun in a holster tucked into his waistband. She felt a cold spike of not anxiety but fear as it occurred to her that between the snort and the sparkling conversation she had not really been paying attention to where they were going and had no idea where they now were. Amy reluctantly followed as he produced a key, unlocked the door, and entered.

The room was bland but clean: bed, dresser, TV, table, chairs, crappy prints on the walls, all anonymous by design, the kind of room that made no impression and left no trace. "Stay here," he told her. "Don't go out any more than you have to, and keep a low profile when you do. I'll be back to pick you up in the morning."

He laid the key on the dresser and turned toward the door. Amy stepped forward; it suddenly dawned on her that the only thing more uncomfortable than being around Louis was being alone.

"Is Josh coming?"

"Tomorrow," he said. "Get some rest."

"Look, Louis," she said, "I know I'm tired and bitchy and a little freaked out right now. And I know Josh has a fucked-up sense of humor, putting the two of us together. But if you don't mind me asking"— she paused as though waiting for his go-ahead—"what the hell am I doing here, and what are you doing hooked up with Josh Custis?"

Louis turned and removed his sunglasses; his eyes burned with something beyond attitude and rhetoric. "We have mutual friends," he said. "And mutual interests."

Amy met his gaze, and for the first time felt like the "we" included her, if only a little. Louis nodded to a newspaper lying on the table; Amy picked it up. It was a day old and open to page two, where a small headline read "Vandals Hit Historic Landmark." She read it quickly, taking in the scant details, but the name alone—*Custis Manor*—was enough to chill her blood. She felt suddenly weak.

"I-is this where"—she stammered—"where Justin . . . ?"

Louis nodded.

Amy sat down on the edge of the bed, her head spinning with the sounds of distant screaming. "Holy hell," she murmured.

Louis looked down at her, his eyes betraying if not compassion at least wholly human empathy . . . and something deeper, darker.

"Holy hell," she said again.

"Something like that," he replied.

8

It was just after midnight when a gust of chill air stirred the doors to the morgue.

Elizabeth Bergen had just come down from the upstairs snack machines, a Coke and little bag of Cheetos in her hands, fingertips yellowed with dusty imitation-cheese coating. To the best of her knowledge, she was the last living soul in the joint, and she liked it like that; it was quiet, and she could concentrate without distraction, devoting herself fully to the task at hand. And tired though she was, her brain was firing in high-rev mental overdrive. Her body might have needed to—*might; yeah, right,* she thought—but her mind just didn't *want* to sleep. It wanted to keep going until she had plumbed the depth of the mystery. The question, of course, was as obvious as it was inscrutable: *What the hell is that hand, and why is it still moving?*

She yawned. Her chest felt like someone had strapped a wet cinderblock to it, her stomach burbled from caffeine-and-junk-food overload, her eyes burned from staring into microscopes and at her computer screen. She didn't care. She wanted to know.

Even on the most normal case, Bergen liked to get to know her dead. She routinely spent hours sifting through their guts; it seemed only fitting to spend a few minutes crawling into their skins, trying to see the world through their eyes, imagine those last few moments as they shuffled off the mortal coil. Sometimes it helped piece together the puzzle.

And this . . . this was beyond strange. She couldn't resist.

"Why were you in the bathroom, Justin?" she murmured. At least she knew his name now: the prints had come back belonging to one VAN SLYKE, JUSTIN A. His rap sheet showed the chronological descent of a small-time loser, a social misfit who had bounced in and out of jail since high school, running juvie to county to even a stretch in the state pen. Nothing special there; every trailer park in the county contained a dozen Justin Van Slykes; certainly not the kind of person to foment a political and racial crusade. "You wanted something . . ." she continued. But what was it?

Bergen sat at her desk, a crowded gray metal government-issue monster crammed into the anteroom adjacent to the examination room. The glow from her computer monitor and a little halogen desk lamp cast a small circle of light against the shadowed expanse of the room; the only other illumination being the hallway lights refracted through the windows of the big double doors. She leaned forward in her chair and looked at the digital photo JPEGS on her screen: close-ups of the hand from every angle, CSI shots from the scene. Once she had decided to crack this, she had put the hand safely away under a John Doe tag; though it still showed no signs of lividity or decomp, it was cool to the touch, even below room temperature, and Bergen didn't want to risk losing it.

She studied the images. The glass fragments from the mirror were simply that: plain mirrored glass, antique vintage—indeed, virtually the only glass in the manor that was period accurate and not restored at a later date. Some of the frags were bloodstained, type A positive, but she found it interesting that the spatter pattern corresponded with the pattern on the floor and was consistent with a vertical distance of at least five feet.

"You were standing when it happened," she continued. "And you didn't use the glass to cut yourself. So what did?" This was a total mystery; the incision at the stump was cleaner than could be made by the sharpest surgical steel.

She clicked her little optical mouse and zoomed on another image. There was a small tattoo at the juncture of the thumb and forefinger: crude, obviously self-inflicted. Jail tat. A name, etched with little curled and spiky vines: MIA.

Missing in action? she thought at first. *No.*

"You had a girl," Bergen murmured. The tat was old, the ink bled into surrounding tissue. "You thought about her a lot . . ." She zoomed the photo, comparing ink depth in the skin. "And you kept going back to it, adding little things, embellishing her name . . . You had time to kill, didn't you, Justin? Lots of time. And you thought about her . . ." Bergen sat back.

"So where is she now?" she wondered.

The breeze stirred the doors, making a little *whuff-whuff* sound. Bergen looked up; no one was there. The room was silent save for the quiet hum of the massive refrigerator compressors that fed the meat lockers. Bergen turned her attention back to the screen, flipping through the digital images. The shattered door. The bloodied floor. The closed window. No signs of tampering.

"You were locked in; you were bleeding," she continued. "You checked in, but you didn't check out." She snickered, punchy with the image of some antebellum roach motel. "So where'd you go, Van Slyke?"

Out in the main room, the big double doors stirred again—*whuff-whuff, whuff-whuff*. Something fell over on a lab counter—a small, sharp crack. Bergen sat up, suddenly alert. She reached into her desk drawer, pulled out a small container of pepper spray. Morgue break-ins were a rarity, but last year some stray brain-dead tweaker, his few functioning brain cells fired up by an old *Six Feet Under* episode on HBO, broke in looking for embalming fluid to soak his weed in. Anything was possible.

Bergen gripped the spray and rounded the corner, taking in the whole of the room at a glance. Empty examination tables gleamed dully, their steel surfaces scrubbed clean. The counters were tidy and bare. Everything was in order.

Not everything, she thought. Something was off. Just then she heard a small grating sound, hard glass on harder surfaces. She looked over and saw a specimen jar tipped over and slowly rolling toward the edge of the counter.

"Shit," she hissed, and raced toward it. Her hand snatched out, caught it in free fall.

"Gotcha!" Bergen said, clutching the jar. She stood and turned, relieved.

Someone was standing right behind her.

Bergen gasped, heart pounding. A cold rush of adrenaline flooded her senses, snapping the room into harsh focus. The man was tall and steeped in shadow, in dark nondescript garb. She could not see his face. She fumbled for the pepper spray, brought it up. The man's gloved hand snaked out and grabbed her wrist like cold iron, backing her into the counter. Bergen swung her other hand—the one holding the specimen jar—in a wildly arcing roundhouse, smashing against her attacker's temple. Glass shattered, raining bits of transparent shrapnel; the man howled an inchoate wail and released her. Bergen turned to flee.

And that's when she realized he was not alone.

A second figure loomed before her, blocking her escape. Like the other, he was tall and conservatively dressed, but she could make out his face—thin lipped and hollow cheeked, utterly devoid of expression.

Just then Bergen felt hands grip her from behind, locking her elbows and pinning her shoulders back. The second man smiled and reached up, ripping open her lab coat and blouse, exposing her chest.

And as Elizabeth Bergen struggled, the man raised his hand, pulling off the glove to reveal pallid skin. His cold fingers came to rest on the hollow between her breasts, where thin skin met the thick concave of her sternum. She watched in horror as his fingers pressed into her flesh and then passed through, worming their way inside her. Bergen gasped, icy tendrils gripping her as her heart thudded wildly like a caged bird trying to escape. There was no pain, only cold, terrible cold. Her violator leaned forward, smiling grimly.

"Shhhhh," he whispered, a sibilant hiss. "Shhhhhhh . . ."

Bergen gasped again, and once more, a last hitching, desperate breath. Her attacker's breath frosted the air, smelling of something long decayed. Then the cold overtook her, and her heart fluttered, and spasmed, and stopped.

Bergen's eyes rolled back as her body went limp, sagged. As the first man eased her to the floor, the cold man withdrew his hand. There was no blood. No wound. The cold man looked up.

"Find it," he hissed.

And with that, the shadowy figures searched for the location of the mysterious severed hand. It was critical that it be returned to Custis Manor; the master had been adamant on this point.

So it was with great alarm that the stalking servants found the drawer marked VAN SLYKE, JUSTIN A. empty.

"FIND IT!" the cold man roared.

They literally tore the morgue apart, searching every locker, dumping bodies off gurneys and out of their slots. They knew all too well the horrors that would await them if the master learned of their failure. The Great Night was ruthless in its power and unforgiving of transgressions. And it would not rest until it possessed the man who went through the mirror and left his hand behind. The Great Night remembered Justin all too well. And it would not rest until it devoured him at last. *All* of him.

Finally they reached the last locker, marked JOHN DOE 8.25 CM. They threw the door open, slid the tray out: the metal container sat in the middle, a towel laid over it. They threw back the towel expectantly.

But the hand was already gone . . .

9

In an auto body shop ten blocks from Custis campaign headquarters, a gathering was taking place. A dozen men in suits sipped Pabst Blue Ribbon and smoked, trading joking banter. One of them called out.

"What do you call a nigger in a three-piece suit?"

Another answered back. "The defendant!

A raucous chorus of laughter. Just then the steel entrance door flung open, banging hard against the cinder-block wall, the clang echoing off the cavernous space.

"All right," an angry voice sounded, *"which one of you limpdick chicken-shit assholes wants to tell me what the hell just happened?!"*

The men turned en masse to see Jimmy Joe Baker thundering through the doorway, pausing only to wipe his Bruno Maglis on the threshold. Jimmy Joe was sleek and lethal, with a face like a Doberman pinscher, a backwoods drawl, and a big-city rhythm. He was the team leader and Duke Custis's whip hand, and had been a part of their machine from the start. He was also colder and more twisted than two snakes fucking in a snowstorm, and he suffered no fools.

The men clammed up as Jimmy Joe surveyed their ranks. *"You,"* he said, pointing to the comedian, singling him out. "You were there, right?" The man nodded. Jimmy Joe stepped closer. "So tell me, how could y'all fuck it up so bad?"

"It wasn't our fault," the man waffled, thin lips grimacing. "It was already gone . . ."

"Duh," Jimmy Joe replied, then grabbed the man by the throat, squeezing mercilessly. "My big question is, where the hell did it already go *to*?"

The man grimaced as Jimmy squeezed harder. Suddenly a calmer, mellifluous voice sounded behind them.

"Let him go, Jimmy."

Jimmy Joe did as he was told, instantly releasing his grip. The comedian collapsed, gasping. The others turned as Jimmy Joe faded back and Daniel "Duke" Custis entered. Forty-two, boyish and charming, impeccably clad in Armani, Duke looked at the fallen man and extended a neatly manicured hand.

"My apologies," he said, just a trace of old Virginia in his accent. "Sometimes Jimmy gets a little . . . passionate."

Duke smiled warmly, his hand still outstretched; the man regarded him with a mix of relief and suspicion. Duke helped him up and patted him on the back, dusting him off. "I'm sure you did the best you could," he said, and let him return to the group. Duke turned to the gathering.

"I'd like to welcome you all here," he began. "I know some of you have traveled quite a ways to be with us, and not all of you have had the privilege to meet before tonight." His polished voice notched up to carry the room.

"You men comprise an elite group," he continued. "Each of you was originally culled from the ranks of the Klan, Aryan Brotherhood, White Aryan Resistance, the Order, and other like-minded organizations. All of you have exhibited great skill and commitment to the cause, but more: you have all learned to mainstream your ambitions"— Duke paused and smiled—"to trade the white robes and brown shirts of our brethren for gray flannel and pinstripe, for the greater good."

The collected men nodded as Duke continued. "But whatever our individual or fraternal differences, we have all united to our common purpose. And all of you"—and Duke rounded back to place a brotherly hand on his wayward servant—"all of you have pledged yourselves, body and spirit, to that cause. And for that, you have my thanks. And the thanks of my family."

The men smiled, pleased and relieved. Duke smiled back. He had reason to: his positioning in the polls was excellent, courtesy of his latest round of commercials attacking Governor Langley. The incumbent was maneuvered into a squeeze play: if he came down too hard on the incoming fraternities this weekend, he risked alienating a significant portion of the black vote. If he didn't take a tough stance, he risked appearing soft on crime. To make matters worse, Langley had holed up in the governor's mansion in Richmond, having taken suddenly ill, while Duke's visibility on the firing line was helping hone his image as the courageous "can-do" candidate. Even if nothing went wrong, Langley looked bad; God help him if the unthinkable happened.

Which was precisely what Duke was thinking about.

This was a delicate time. Daddy Eli was flying down this weekend for a very important ritual at the manor. The changing of the guard, so to speak, when Eli would pass the legacy fully to Duke. And Duke Custis would come fully into his own.

Duke smiled. Everything was proceeding wonderfully, with one little problem: the little matter of their ongoing surveillance, and what it revealed. The attack on Custis Manor was definitely pulled off by an organized group. Duke's estranged brother, Josh, was still running with this group. They were trying to crack the secret of Custis Manor.

But why? The question remained. *What does he hope to accomplish?*

Duke looked at Jimmy Joe. To provide the answer to these and other nagging questions, Jimmy and Co. had gone to the trouble of calling in one of their informants. Jimmy was a little worried; the informant's reliability was being called into question.

"Is our friend ready?" Duke asked. Jimmy looked to the other men, who nodded.

"Well then," Duke said, "let's not keep him waiting."

Duke gestured to the men, who turned and ushered him deeper into the garage.

And thus did Duke Custis meet Rajim.

The black man was duct-taped to a chair in the middle of the floor, another piece of tape covering his mouth. A tarpaulin had been spread beneath his feet, to keep from making a mess.

There was a case of Perrier on the floor. Duke Custis casually lifted a bottle and hefted it. "Drink?" he asked pleasantly.

Rajim shook his head, bug-eyed with terror.

"I abstain from alcohol myself," Duke said. "It dulls the senses."

He uncapped the bottle, took a refreshing fizzy swig. "You know, interrogation is tricky business," he explained. "Fear is the key. Fear is a prime motivator. Frighten a man badly enough, and he will abandon all pretense to loyalty, to friendship, even to love."

Duke circled around Rajim as he spoke, his tone perfectly calm and casual. "The trick is," he continued, "how do you make absolutely sure that you're getting through? Primal fears are best. Elemental dreads. Burn a man, and he fears fire; dangle him from a great height, and he fears the air; put a man in a hole in the ground, and he fears the earth. See what I mean?"

Rajim nodded, nostrils flaring, breathing hard.

"As for water," Duke continued, "did you know that a little carbonated water up the nose induces all the sensations of drowning? Suffocation, blindness, deafness, paralysis . . . a man will shit himself, cry like a baby, maybe even lose his mind. You can do it again and again, all night long if necessary. And it doesn't even leave a mark."

Duke nodded to Jimmy, who ripped the tape from Rajim's mouth. The black man sputtered and gasped. "You're fuckin' crazy, man!" Rajim cried, squirming against his captors. "I told you I tell you everything I know!!"

Duke leaned forward, grinning. "Boy," he said, "by the time we're done, you'll tell us shit you *don't* know."

And with that, Jimmy grabbed his head and held it as Duke shook the bottle and jammed it up Rajim's nose.

The first blast took Rajim so totally by surprise—rocketing through his skull, sealing him into a very private universe of agony—that he blacked out almost instantly. He returned to a world of howling, swirling pain. His lungs felt as though he'd inhaled liquid sandpaper, his nose as though they'd shoved a live wire up his nostril and cranked the voltage to the redline. He coughed and sputtered desperately, sucking in his own ropy saliva.

"I don't know nothing," he gasped, retching. "I don't know . . ."

"Really?" Duke replied.

Jimmy grabbed his head again. Duke shook the bottle. They did it again. And again. And again. The sixth or seventh time, Rajim began to spasm uncontrollably, as if they'd shorted out his entire nervous system. The eighth time he pissed himself. He told them everything he knew, as well as things he thought they might like to know and things they weren't even interested in. By the ninth time, he opened his eyes to find the room skewed and distorted, as if he were tripping. Time and space, physical sensation, the fundamental fabric of reality itself felt altered. Rajim looked up, eyes spinning and half-blind with terror, and gazed into the faces of his tormentors.

Gone were the clean-cut profiles, the tailored yuppie personae. In their place were nightmare visages: lumpen and humpbacked hell-things, monstrous deformities of the spirit made flesh, their oozing sores glistening in the funhouse refraction of light from the bathroom as they shuffled on gnarled and twisted limbs.

One particularly hideous creature loomed before him. *You belong to us,* it said. The voice belonged to Daniel Duke Custis. *Now, and always.*

Duke Custis smiled as the black man writhed. Smiled as the vision gripped him. Smiled as he saw the spark go out in the black man's eyes.

"So now you know," Custis said. *"Now here's what we want you to do . . ."*

Rajim vomited as he was given his instructions. Jimmy Joe asked him if he understood; Rajim nodded. Duke told his minions to cut him loose and send him home.

Jimmy Joe did his master's bidding, making sure to stuff some money into Rajim's pocket on the way out.

For services rendered.

10

Friday, August 29. Church of the Open Door. 12:00 p.m.

The service convened in a little hole-in-the-wall church in a depressed and depressing section of town. The weather was humid, the sky overcast and brooding, hinting at storm; the streets neglected, festooned with potholes and junked cars; bars covered the windows of half of the seedy-looking homes. The building itself was an old clapboard structure with peeling paint and a crooked steeple; indeed, the entire structure seemed to sag under the weight of collective indifference, as if God Himself had taken one look at it and departed for classier digs. A weathered sign out front read CHURCH OF THE OPEN DOOR, and at least that much was true: the high arched doors were flung back, the low sound of staid organ music filtering outside.

Caroline looked around nervously as they parked by the broken curb and got out. Kevin made his way around and took her lightly by the hand, Zoe following reluctantly behind.

"Nice neighborhood," she muttered sarcastically. Caroline sushed her, but even Kevin tilted his head skeptically.

"You sure this is the place?"

"That's what he told me," Caroline said, clutching the note from her day planner, the address Josh had supplied her scrawled hastily upon it. "At least, I think it is," she amended.

Zoe rolled her eyes. Kevin looked around. "You know, I checked the paper this morning. There wasn't any listing for a service." He paused. "There also weren't any listings in the obituaries this whole week."

"So?" Caroline snapped, then softer: "Sorry. Let's just go in, okay? We'll know soon enough." She squeezed his hand lightly; her palm was damp and cool. Kevin nodded.

They ascended the creaking wooden stairs. Inside the church, empty pews faced an equally empty pulpit; a plain pine box lay on a white-draped altar, the flowers flanking it providing the only hint of color in the otherwise bereft interior. No one sat at the organ; a small CD player supplied the mournful music. Caroline looked around and saw five very serious-looking black men standing: one at each corner of the room, another at the entrance to the rectory. The men were dressed in somber suits and positioned near the smudged and flyspecked windows; they regarded Caroline and her family dispassionately, then went back to watching the street. It looked more like a mafia meeting than a paying of last respects; Caroline smiled at them nervously and whispered to her husband and daughter.

"This can't be it," she said. "I must've gotten the address wrong."

Suddenly the stairs creaked behind them, and they turned to see Louis Hillyard and Amy entering. "No, you got it right," Amy said. "Welcome to the party, Caroline. Long time no see."

Caroline looked at them, surprised. "Oh my God," she blurted. "Amy . . ." The two women embraced quickly and somewhat awkwardly, like there was some long-buried thread of tension there. "You haven't changed a bit," Caroline said.

"And you're still a lousy liar," Amy countered and hugged her back, this time more genuinely. Caroline smiled, tears welling despite herself.

"Jesus, Amy, what are we doing here?" she asked. Just then a long-forgotten but familiar voice sounded behind them.

"Damn good question. I wish I knew."

The two women turned to see Seth standing in the doorway. Amy and Caroline both stared, slack-jawed, then cried out simultaneously.

"SETH!"

They rushed to embrace him; and while there had been a distinct emotional distance between the women, their friend was an instant and uniting force. Kevin and Zoe watched as Seth took one in each arm, lifting them both in a massive three-way bear hug, then set them down gently. Amy beamed.

"Damn, dude, what happened to your hair?"

"It went away," Seth replied, smiling. Amy reached up and touched his shaven dome. "I tried to reason with it for a while," he said, "but then I figured, fuggit!"

"Still a smartass," Amy said.

"Still a bitch," Seth countered. Amy punched him on the shoulder, and they hugged again. It was a fleeting respite: old friends sharing both the joy of seeing each other and the pain of their mysterious circumstance. Then Louis stepped forward, muting it.

"You all should take a seat," he instructed, gesturing inside. The group nodded and obeyed, moving down the aisle and into the worn wooden pews. As they did so, introductions were hastily exchanged—Seth and Kevin shaking hands as Caroline presented Zoe to her friends. Amy and Seth both looked at her as they shook hands, then back to Caroline, who spoke, her tone hushed.

"This is so terrible. Did Josh call you too?"

Amy and Seth nodded uneasily. "Something like that," Seth replied. "Can't say I'm wild about the company he keeps." They looked around at the brothers manning the windows—along with Louis, there was Henri Hayes and his two young accomplices from the incident at the Manor, and Mohammed and Rajim. "Those two mooks I know from the club. The others . . ." Seth shrugged. "I dunno. But if they're hangin' with those creeps, it can't be good."

The others nodded, a ripple of anxiety passing between them. As they tried to piece together what happened, it quickly became clear that not one of them knew exactly how Justin had died. It was also clear that Josh had manipulated each of them into coming. The more they talked, the more agitated Amy in particular seemed to become.

"Yeah, well, this is all swell," Amy said, her voice rising pointedly, projecting out to the room. "But I still want some goddam answers."

"Be careful what you wish for, Amy," a voice suddenly answered. "You just might get it." They all turned as one, as the rectory door creaked open.

And Josh Custis entered at last.

Like the rest of them, it was Josh but not Josh, the passing years etched into every fiber of his being, but not as they might have expected. The wild and unruly mane of his youth was cropped close and shot with premature gray, rendering his prominent features all the more piercing. He was tall and lean, dressed entirely in black, and looked clear eyed and fiercely focused. An ethereally beautiful mulatto woman with ice blue eyes accompanied him, her presence both riveting and oddly unsettling. Josh came forward and embraced them one by one, then shook hands with Kevin. When he came to Zoe, he smiled.

"You must be Zoe," he said. "I've heard so much about you." He held out his hand graciously.

"Hi," Zoe replied, and hesitated a moment before taking it. Caroline watched protectively, as Josh turned to her.

"She's beautiful," he said, then turned and addressed them all.

"My friends," he said, his genuine warmth punctuated by an undercurrent of intensity. "It's been a long time. I thank you for coming." He hesitated a moment, then added, "Justin does too."

Caroline and Seth glanced at the coffin, but Amy continued to watch Josh suspiciously. "You said, 'does,'" she said. "Don't you mean 'did'? Or 'would'? I mean, he's dead, right?"

Josh looked at her and smiled. "Not exactly," he replied. The others looked from the coffin to Josh to each other, uncomprehending.

"Whoa, whoa, whoa," Amy said. "You said he was dead."

"No," Josh countered. "I said he was gone."

"Mother*fucker!*" Seth exploded, rising up to tower over him as the street rose in his voice. "We all know you a crazy fuck, Custis, you always was, you and your whole damn family. But since you dragged us all down here and scared the shit out of everybody, you mind explaining what the hell we're doing here?"

Caroline and Amy visibly winced; they knew from experience that when Seth started cussing and calling people by their last names, it was time to duck.

Around the room the brothers shifted, suddenly wary; Josh waved them off and stood his ground, calmly looking up at his friend.

"It's okay," he said. "He's right. I owe you all an apology, and an explanation. You deserve no less."

Josh met Seth's angry gaze; Seth grudgingly backed off. As he did, Josh nodded to Louis, who in turned signaled the men. Then he turned to the shocked and shaken congregation.

"Once upon a time, there were seven good friends," he began.

While behind them, the doors of the church were quietly shut and locked . . .

11

Once upon a time, there were seven good friends. They were the baby broth-
ers and sisters of the Big Chill generation, born in the turbulent year that the
flames of Watts lit the City of Angels; the year that Martin Luther King
trekked twenty-five-thousand strong from the streets of Selma to the capitol
in Montgomery to end segregation and Lestor Maddox led two thousand
white hooded hopefuls through the heart of Atlanta to preserve it; the year
that Malcolm X fell to assassin's fire in Harlem and napalm first kissed the
war-torn skies of Vietnam. When their elder siblings were slogging through
the Mekong Delta or storming the Chicago Democratic Convention, they
were just coming out of diapers and heading off to kindergarten; when the
Beatles broke up and Janis and Jimi took a header into the hereafter in '70,
they were navigating the perils of first grade: just a bunch of little kids grow-
ing up in a culture rending itself asunder at the seams. But when the first
shots were fired at Kent State, a hefty chunk of the revolution grabbed their
Frisbees and hightailed it home; when the peace signs of Woodstock were
traded for the pool cues of Altamont, it seemed that the dawning of the Age
of Aquarius was perhaps not all it was cracked up to be.

By the time the seven friends entered the crucible of high school, Reagan
was in office and the Moral Majority was laying claim to God, Nixon was
an uncomfortable memory, and the baby boomers had mutated to a disco beat

as hippies became yuppies, corporate raiders became superheroes, and America ushered in an unparalleled epoch of immolated idealism, profound self-absorption, and greed. The defining moments of a generation—the assassinations of Kennedy and King, Vietnam, Civil Rights, and the Summer of Love—were little more than something they had seen on TV. "Give Peace a Chance" gave way to "Give Me My Piece of the Action," as John Lennon rolled over in his grave. Even rock and roll had gone bloated and corporate, ingesting everything in its path: the raucous, anarchic anger of punk had morphed into a moussed and manageable New Wave, Michael Jackson was urging everyone to just beat it, and the New Age was effectively toast.

For the forgotten baby brothers and sisters of the boomer wave, the rapid segue from "we" to "me" left them effectively in the lurch, with nothing but cultural hand-me-downs to tide them over. Drugs and music, bad fashion and empty attitude, combined with boundless cynicism and a deep yearning for something that really mattered, were all that remained.

And then they found each other.

They called themselves the Underground. They were seven suburban teens caught in a tidal pool of fractious cliques and social subsets that multiplied like bacteria in the petri dish of public education—freaks and jocks and straights and stoners, geeks and dweebs and punks and preppies, all swirled together in perpetually warring factions. The name was pretentious, but it managed to alienate the Stillson High administration, not to mention the straighter segment of the student body, so it couldn't be all bad. They also had a little radical newspaper, which they used for fun and generally raising hell. That publication, Subterranean Rumblings, *began as young Josh Custis's vehicle for shouting back at the world. He specialized in blistering essays of opinion, taking on everything from government-backed Nicaraguan death squads to the legalization of drugs to the rules against kissing in the halls between class. It kept him in constant trouble, both at school and at home. Many generations down from Silas, the original Custis patriarch, Josh was the youngest son of up-and-coming State Representative Eli Custis. Eli didn't much* like to see family members making trouble with the authorities and generally crapping on the family name.

"This family is everything," Eli told him on more than one occasion. "You violate that, and God help you, boy, because I won't." Josh fought back by digging in even deeper, consolidating his black-sheep reputation, becoming more of a rebel and loner. He despised his family, hated everything they stood for. They punished him for it. He got exceptionally good at withstanding pain.

But by Issue #3 of the little 'zine, in the middle of his junior year, Josh was no longer entirely alone. His little Xeroxed rag had proven a weirdo-magnet, attracting misfits like moths to a klieg lamp. The result was a proudly outcast circle of souls. Josh's best friend—and the person he loved most in all the world—was Mia Cheever. She was beautiful, with green eyes and raven hair and a sly, crooked smile. Her folks were upscale professional types, but being a daughter of privilege didn't turn her into a snotty, self-absorbed little princess. She had a mind like a bullwhip, was idealistic, caring, warm, passionate, and outspoken in her egalitarian beliefs. That last quality had gotten her canned as editor of the official school paper when she bucked the system and ran a story on racial harassment in the classroom. From there, it was a short leap to Josh's camp, where her tough, meticulous viewpoint was the perfect balance for Josh's iconoclastic rants. For while Josh's style was assault and bombast, Mia was at heart a peacemaker; even after the racial incident, she could still sweet-talk the powers-that-be better than anyone he'd ever known.

Josh and Mia grew incredibly tight. She could tell him things that she couldn't tell anyone else. They got each other's jokes, understood each other's problems, and were inspired by each other's ideas. Together they conspired, commiserated, and cried on each other's shoulders, tying up the phone lines for hours on end. The bitch of it was that Josh virtually worshipped the ground Mia walked on, a fact that he was constantly trying to hide, most importantly from himself. Not that it would have made a difference.

Because Mia was totally head over heels in love as well. Only not with Josh. The man of her dreams was a young and rowdy kid named Justin Van Slyke. The moment she confessed it to him, Josh knew he didn't stand a chance.

Justin didn't actually work on the paper, but his influence could not have been more deeply felt. He was a walking adrenaline buzz, a nonstop rush of swashbuckling charm and rebel energy. Reckless and handsome, sensitive and wise beneath his street exterior, he was the kind of dangerous boy that girls spontaneously lubed for and authority figures longed to crush beneath their heels. It wasn't bad enough that Mia loved Justin; he compounded the tragedy by falling for her too. It was one of those everybody-knew-it-couldn't-last-but-God-was-it-intense relationships: doomed from the start, and for that reason all the more determined to survive.

Watching nearly broke Josh's heart. Not just because of his unrequited, un-requitable love, and not just because he knew that he was the one who could truly make her happy, if only she'd let him. It was also because he liked Justin too. They were rivals for her affections, yes; but in time they also came to be like brothers, in a way that Josh and his big brother, Duke, had certainly never been. Josh found unexpected reservoirs of support in Justin, was aston-ished to learn that Justin genuinely admired Josh's way of looking at things. It was weirdly flattering, and good for his confidence, to be looked up to by someone so much cooler than himself.

So when both Mia and Justin starting coming to him for advice, Josh fi-nally had to swallow three bitter pills: one, that he would never be Mia's guy; two, that her friendship was the best he could hope for; and three, that he could still help bring her happiness just by really being a friend. To them both.

In the course of all that, Josh got himself tangled up with blond-haired, blue-eyed Caroline Tabb. It was a stormy romance, at best, though not with-out its high points. Caroline was at her party-hearty wildass peak, kicking up against her eccentric but ultimately middle-class upbringing. She loosened him up sexually and managed the business end of the paper with a steady, practical hand. That two-pronged earthiness grounded him, kept his project solvent and his fantasy life in perspective. Only problem was that, though he liked Caroline, he was still in love with Mia, and all the great sex and com-mon sense in the world couldn't change the way he felt. It tortured her. It haunted him. It tainted their relationship, turned it into a turbulent on-again, off-again proposition.

Obviously, this was a problem Josh couldn't take to Mia. He turned instead to Amy Kaplan, the paper's resident spooky dark-eyed poet chick. When it came to discussing those feelings too humiliating or painful to bear, Amy was the one to call. Her uncanny grasp of the underside of feeling made her everyone's confidante.

But it also kept her at an odd emotional distance, which Josh quickly learned when he tried to make a move on her. She shielded her inner workings well, as well as the knowledge that when it came to the sexual clinches, Amy preferred girls.

The only one Amy seemed to open up to was her best friend, Seth Bryant. Seth was a brilliant, black, athletic, disenfranchised Art Jock from Hell. He'd been a State All-Star fullback, but the combination of his genius IQ and his undeniable talent for pissing people off alienated jocks and brains alike. Like the others, the only place he really fit in was amongst the freaks.

The last of them was a skinny, volatile bundle of screaming nerves named Simon Baxter. He was Justin's best friend—another working-class powder keg, with a much shorter fuse—and his racy, psychotic shock-tactic cartoons were the paper's most popular feature. They also drew the most administrative flak. Because, even more than Josh and Seth, Simon was heavily into confrontation. His enemy was complacency; Simon was always first out of the trenches in any battle. And if there wasn't a fight, he would happily invent one; Simon couldn't get in enough trouble to satisfy his need for controversy.

Because of this, Josh and Simon got along great: they lived to push the limits. It also helped cement Josh's friendship with Justin, bringing the whole thing full circle.

Together, these seven friends negotiated the madness that was public high school: struggling to make sense of a time and place where the old values had been thoroughly thrashed but no new ones had arisen to take their place.

When graduation rolled around, the last days of their group were at hand. Soon they would be separated, pursuing their divergent destinies; in a couple of years, they wouldn't even recognize each other in line at the 7-Eleven. So it was that, in the last fateful days of summer, they found themselves greedily squeezing every second of time together that they could. By Labor Day weekend, there was just enough time to throw one last party for themselves. The only question was, where?

Then Simon found out that Josh's Grampa Vance had recently keeled over dead, leaving spooky old Custis Manor temporarily uninhabited. Simon had just happened into a dozen hits of high-quality purple windowpane. And when he suggested to Josh that they might want to party at the mansion, Josh had readily agreed. What was not to like about that? It would be fun. It would piss his father off royally. It was the ultimate familial fuck-you, and soon enough Josh would be free of his oppressive upbringing forever.

12

Friday, August 26. Twenty years ago. Stillson Beach, VA.

It was just past eight as the Underground motored out to Custis Manor in Justin's cruisemobile. The car was a '72 Chevy Monte Carlo, a hulking coupe with a small block V-8, Rochester 4-barrel carb, turbo 350 transmission, and power everything, a growling behemoth, once black but now mostly done in rust and primer gray with a peeling vinyl top. Seven bodies were packed sardine tight inside: Justin driving, Mia by his side, and Josh riding shotgun, Caroline, Amy, Seth, and Simon smushed into the back. The trunk was stuffed with two cases of Bud, bottles of Boone's Farm and Bali Hai wine, and assorted munchies, all courtesy of Simon's five-fingered discount from the local Be-Lo and Giant markets, plus Amy's cassette player and plenty of tapes. Carlos Santana's soaring and soulful guitar was playing on the car stereo, mixing with the sweet scent of primo Colombian bud that laced the interior as they passed a fat joint. There was a sense of palpable expectation in the air—once out of the environs of the beach, the road hooked inland, flat and winding and lined with thick, sandy pine woods that swallowed the lights of the car.

Amy pointed out the side window, where thousands of lightning bugs hovered and twinkled between the dark trees; she made a sarcastic reference to their officially entering boonieville. Josh assured them it wasn't much farther, but there was a hesitance in his voice; he confessed that Grampa Vance had been a hermit of sorts in his latter years, and Josh hadn't been there since he was a little kid. The others groaned.

Justin and Mia remained quiet; for them, the night was particularly poignant. Mia had dutifully applied to college in the spring, partly at the urging of her parents but also with the deeper knowledge that she needed and wanted to do something with her life. Three weeks ago she had gotten the notice: she had been accepted at UCLA. She was simultaneously excited and horrified; the liberation of escaping her family matching the heartbreak of what that would mean about her and Justin. For the better part of the month, the news had hung over her like an emotional death sentence; the Cheevers, being practical and loving parents, had accepted Justin's presence, and Mia's feelings for him, with a nervous reservation that had spanned their daughter's senior year. But as the summer progressed, they made it clear that they weren't about to go for the notion of their baby girl hitched to a dead-end teen romance fresh out of high school. Finally they told her in no uncertain terms: she had her whole life ahead of her. They would not let her squander her future. She was going. Period.

She had broken the news to Justin only yesterday; they had told the others as they headed out for the night's festivities. She was leaving Monday morning. The others were surprised but appropriately congratulatory, with the possible exception of Simon, who didn't say much. As for Justin . . .

To put it mildly, Justin was still in shock. Mia snuggled deeper into him as he drove, as if they could somehow absorb more of each other and store it up.

Simon, meanwhile, popped another beer and stewed in the back seat. He was getting trashed, well ahead of schedule. And though he tried to keep it to himself, it was clear that he resented Mia.

They rounded the next bend, and Josh pointed to a small and narrow side road marked by a NO TRESPASSING sign. They had arrived.

It was dark as they pulled down the winding drive: the estate was empty, the outbuildings crumbling and decrepit. As they drove, Amy noticed more weird lights in the distance: furtive greenish glowing dots interspersed amongst the thousands of twinkling fireflies like lanterns bobbing in the woods. But neither Caroline nor Seth saw them, and Amy shrugged it off to her overactive imagination as they continued down the half-mile stretch of private road that led to the mansion itself.

The big house was a faded antebellum monument to the Old South, and even in its sorry state was testimony to the fact that Josh's family was a lot better off than any of them had ever realized. As they ascended the wide wooden stairs, everyone turned to Josh, waiting for him to produce keys to let them in. Josh shrugged; he had none. Seth spoke for the group, voicing the obvious: *How are we supposed to get in?*

Josh picked up a rock, smashing it into one of the big front windows lining the porch. The glass shattered, leaving a gaping rectangular maw. Simon immediately whooped and took the lead, kicking out the stray shards in the sill and disappearing into the darkened interior. As the others looked around warily, the front door unlatched from the inside and Simon appeared like a demented butler.

Always good to start a party with a felony, Justin remarked. Mia looked at Justin. *Should we be doing this?* she asked. Justin shrugged. *Too late now.* The others had already entered. Justin gave her a comforting hug. *Relax,* he said. *It'll be all right.*

And in they went.

Inside, the great hall loomed before them, vast and cavernous and smelling of old men and dust. The portraits stared down disapprovingly, a stern and silent audience. Huge antique gilt mirrors hung on the walls, reflecting back shadows and silhouettes. There was a light switch on the wall, a turn-of-the-century addition, wires snaking down to the baseboard. Justin flipped it, flipped again.

No juice, he announced as Seth and Caroline came back hauling their stash from the trunk; Amy was nonplussed, courtesy of fresh batteries in her boom box. Just then flickering light appeared in the doorway at the end of the hall; Simon came out grinning, holding a blazing candelabra.

Bloo-ha-ha-ha, he cackled.

They set up camp in the grand ballroom, built a fire in the massive fireplace, and lit more candles, filling the room with a flickering glow that heightened the vibe and enhanced the proceedings. They broke out the brew and the pot; Amy popped in a Peter Murphy tape, his sinister baritone reverberating throughout the interior. It was fun for a while, everyone getting pleasantly buzzed in the spookhouse vibe.

But Simon wanted more.

It was just after ten when Simon called the group together and unveiled his stash. It was time to trip, he informed them all solemnly. It was a very important occasion, the last gasp for the Underground, and they needed to do it right.

As it turned out, not everyone shared his ardor. While they all liked to party, Simon was a veteran of hardcore hallucinogens, almost evangelical in his avocation of them; by his own proud estimate, he had tripped over one thousand times by the age of eighteen, as if he thought by deep-frying his neurons he could get closer to the mysteries at the heart of the universe.

Josh was up for it initially, and Justin. But Caroline chickened out on general principles. Amy was dissuaded by the manor's brooding vibe. Seth was simply cautious and not in the mood. And Mia . . .

Mia, as it happened, was an acid virgin. For all of their wasteoid rebellion, all the lost nights of their willfully wayward youth, she had contented herself to kick back with milder things and to stay within the limits she had set for herself. A little drink, a little smoke, nothing heavy, no needles; she didn't even boost her mom's prescription pills. She just wasn't into it. And she wasn't about to start now.

Simon was pissed, as if her choice was a personal affront. But his jaw dropped when Justin then offered to forego the acid as well if she was uncomfortable. This was the last straw for Simon.

Fucking princess! he hissed bitterly. *I knew she'd screw this up!*

Back off! Justin warned. *She doesn't have to if she doesn't want to.*

Justin and Simon squared off; for a moment, it looked like they might seriously come to blows.

I can't believe this shit! Simon cried out. *You're siding with her, and she's fucking dumping you!*

Shut up, Simon, Justin growled.

Fuck you, Justin! Simon shot back. *Open your eyes, man! She doesn't love you, she's just slumming!*

You're full of shit, Mia said. *I love him!*

Oh yeah, right, Simon scoffed, getting up in Mia's face. *A year from now you'll be with some preppie asshole and you'll break his fucking heart!*

And that was when Justin punched him: straight-arming Simon in the chest and knocking every ounce of air out of him. Justin had six inches of height and thirty pounds of muscle on Simon, and even though he instinctively checked the blow, the force of the contact sent Simon flying to land flat-assed on the hard wooden floor.

The rest of the group was aghast. Justin stood his ground, feeling pissed and guilty; Mia quivered with rage and indignation, and started to cry. Amy and Caroline rushed over to comfort her. Seth and Josh stood exchanging uncomfortable glances, not knowing exactly what to do. Simon scrabbled to his feet and gave them all a wounded look.

You all SUCK! he cried bitterly. *This is BULLSHIT!*

Then he ran out of the room, disappearing into the shadowed interior.

Simon raced upstairs and through the many hallways, knocking things over, smashing dusty curios and forgotten knickknacks, hot tears streaming down his face. He was angry and ashamed, seething with misery and self-loathing. Partly because Justin was the best friend he had ever had, more like a brother, and he knew he was right about her. Partly because he also knew that Mia was right too: that escaping this place was the right thing to do, and that she would go on to do major things with her life, while any future he could imagine held only trouble for himself and Justin both.

And in no small part because, deep down and secretly, Simon had always wanted Justin for himself.

Simon reached the third floor, came face to face with an enormous mirror that graced the end of the hallway. It was nine feet tall and matched with another at the opposite end, creating a refracted and skewed hallway of seemingly infinite proportion. Simon stood, panting, as he faced a hundred panting Simons, extending out into oblivion. His blood roiled, heart pounding. And he knew he was right about something else: their much vaunted Underground was bullshit too. The one thing Simon had ever felt a sense of belonging to—the one thing that had ever made him not feel so screamingly, bitterly, alone in the world—was over.

On the other side of the mirrors, something was watching. It was a corrupt, voracious force wedded to a vile, once-human personality, neither fully living nor truly dead. As such it was simultaneously native to this swamp-kissed plantation and old as the Earth itself, a soulless spirit of evil imbued with all the passions and prejudices of that which had once been mortal man. It was once in the body of a man, but it had always and forever gone by another name. It was the Great Night, and this place was its prison; and its domain.

It watched, enraged, as these disrespectful children made mock of its sovereignty. *It wasn't bad enough that they had come to defile this place,* it thought. *No, they had brought along a Jewess. And worse, they had brought along a nigger.* As it stared into the eyes of the weak and willful boy before it, it saw an opportunity: for escape, and for vengeance. They had to be punished.

And so they would be.

Simon stared into the mirror, seeing something ripple across his own reflection, until the eyes staring back at him seemed not wholly his own. As if he were staring at something more than himself, yet not him at all.

And just like that, a seed of thought blossomed in his brain, fueled by alcohol and weed and frustration and passion, and maybe just a little bit of hate. And as he stared, the thought took root and grew, coiling through him. A plan of sorts. A wonderful idea.

Simon reached into his pocket, withdrew the wrinkled baggie holding his stash: a dozen tiny squares of purple-tinged paper, each containing a single drop of lysergic acid diethylamide. He pulled one free and placed it on his tongue; it began to dissolve almost instantly.

Simon swallowed the hit.

And then he did another.

Downstairs, Seth stirred the fire as Josh returned with another six of tall boys, took one, and passed the rest around. The others sat glumly on the velvet sofas, feeling hugely weirded out. They had listened to Simon's rampage from afar for the last twenty minutes, not knowing what to do. Now it was quiet, and everyone was freaked.

Maybe we should go look for him, Amy said.

Maybe we should just go, Caroline countered.

He'll be all right, Justin said, taking a seat beside Mia. *He gets like this sometimes. He just needs to chill.*

Mia said nothing. She leaned her head against Justin's shoulder. An air of heaviness weighed over the party, which was beginning to feel more like a wake.

Just then Simon appeared in the doorway, a bottle of wine in one hand, looking utterly contrite. He looked at them all.

I'm an asshole, he confessed. He laughed nervously. *Maybe I just freaked because I suddenly realized that being a professional burnout doesn't look so good on a resumé.* He apologized to everyone—lastly, and most pointedly, to Mia. Simon held out the bottle of wine as a peace offering. Justin eyed him suspiciously, but Mia got up, facing Simon.

I'm really sorry, Simon said.

Mia nodded and took a swig, then passed the bottle to Caroline, who drank and passed it to Amy, who continued the ritual. To Seth. To Josh. To Justin, who took a big guggling gulp and passed it back to Simon, completing the circle.

Sorry, bro, he said, and hugged him. *Seriously . . .*

Me too, Simon said, hugged him back.

Simon took the bottle and finished off the dregs. Everyone breathed a massive sigh of relief at the fragile détente, and when Simon tossed the bottle to smash into the fireplace, they whooped and cheered.

Josh grabbed a dance dub tape and popped it in the player. The music swelled and filled the room, and the party started again.

They had no idea, and indeed would never have dreamed, that Simon had spiked the bottle with the other ten hits of acid. They never even knew what hit them.

13

Justin had wandered out on the porch and was seated on the steps, smoking a cigarette and staring into the night, when Mia appeared in the doorway. Inside, music and muted laughter sounded; outside, fireflies glowed in the trees like some distant imaginary city.

You okay? Mia asked.

Yeah, Justin replied. It sounded not at all convincing. Mia sat beside him, taking the smoke from his hand and taking a drag.

This place sucks, Justin sighed.

Yeah, it's kinda creepy, she said.

No, I mean here. Justin gestured widely. *This town. This whole place.* He hesitated. *You're doing the right thing,* he said. *We should all get out.*

I'm sorry, Mia said quietly. *I love you . . .*

I love you too, he replied.

They talked—about visits to California, about coming home for Christmas, about how one day maybe he'd come out and they'd get a place eventually. Beautiful dreams, all. But real was still real. And they both knew what the simple force of attrition could do.

A breeze rustled through the trees, making their skin tingle. Mia suddenly shuddered, curving into him.

Wow, she said. *I'm like really high . . .*

Me too, Justin replied. They looked at each other: in the dim light, they seemed to sparkle, the barest halo of light outlining their forms. Mia touched Justin's hair, smoothing it back.

She kissed him. He kissed her back.

As they did, an electric rush passed through them. It was a moment of perfect freefall, her soft skin and softer lips radiating heat and exquisite hunger. Mia shuddered as Justin's hand glided up and under her shirt to graze the curve of her breast; she shuddered more as his fingers found her taut nipples and caressed them. Mia arched her head back and took a deep and trembling breath. For that fleeting moment, Justin thought that the trembling was because of him.

And then it turned violent.

Upstairs, Caroline sat at the edge of the bed buttoning her blouse as Josh pulled on his pants. Twenty minutes before, she had grabbed him and led him off to one of the bedrooms, driven by simple drugged lust and something darker, infinitely more complicated. The sex was manic, rushed, and not that satisfying, less a meeting of bodies and souls than a release of bodily fluids and pent-up angst. Portraits of dead ancestors frowned down on them throughout the act, making Josh feel profoundly watched. To compound the weirdness, as Josh withdrew they both realized that the stale condom pressed into his wallet had broken, casting a pall over the postcoital vibe. Josh reached over to her and she twisted away. He asked if she was okay.

Fine, she told him curtly and continued to dress. Josh didn't buy it; he pressed her for a real answer.

Nothing, she told him, meaning anything but. He pressed harder, wanting to know the truth.

And that was when Caroline snapped, pushing him away, telling him to fuck off. But the truth was, she couldn't tell him, because she wasn't sure herself. Part of it was simple jealousy: of Mia's happy news, of the fact that she was escaping, whereas Caroline felt trapped. Part of it was jealousy of Mia herself: beautiful, perfect Mia, whose very existence made Caroline feel like sloppy seconds. And though she projected it onto Josh, deep down she knew she had only herself to blame.

Now they faced a broken rubber and a nagging uncertainty. Caroline told him not to worry about it. Josh promised her that it would be all right. Somehow.

Amy was in the library when she heard Justin's scream reverberate through the halls. They ran down and saw Josh and Caroline scrambling downstairs, looking equally freaked out and alarmed. Just then Justin came crashing in clutching Mia, who was shaking uncontrollably. Justin looked up at them, his pupils huge and black and terrified. As he laid her down on the couch, he looked at his hands and saw trails rippling off them like an aurora borealis.

Oh God, he gasped. Justin looked at the others, who were starting to feel it too. It didn't take long to figure out what was happening, or who was responsible.

Simon, Justin said. He looked at the others. *WHERE IS SIMON?*

Deep in the woods, Simon ran, brambles tearing at his clothes and scoring his skin. The woods seemed to glow and writhe, tendrils snaking out to claw at him. He could dimly feel the pain, but it didn't matter: he was in the thrall of the Great Night. It had arisen to slap his soul from his body like a rotted tooth, and now the boy was firmly in its possession. And it had much to do.

Simon came to the edge of an inland waterway, where a crumbling dock stood. An old and worm-eaten skiff lay banked in the dank and sticky muck at the edge of the shore.

Get in, said the malevolent voice in his head.

Simon pushed it out into the black and murky water and climbed in. There were two oars lying in the bottom of the boat.

Row, it commanded.

Simon rowed, pushing out into the mist, to a tiny islet barely visible in the night, where a little shack stood. Simon entered and saw a weed-choked and forgotten altar upon which sat a rusted iron pot. A faint and putrid scent filled the close air of the shack; Simon lifted the rusted iron lid and stared down at its source.

The *nganga:* the cauldron of souls.

The stench that arose from its depths was overwhelming; beetles, worms, and centipedes writhed in the foul paste that coated its interior.

Simon had a Zippo lighter in his pocket; the Great Night bade him to light a fire under the pot. This he did, the scent of woodsmoke mixing with the odor of death and decay. Simon looked down, saw a pitted knife in his hand—the one the Great Night had bade him to take from the kitchen. He dropped it in the dust.

Pick it up, the voice said. The boy hesitated. *PICK IT UP,* it ordered, booming through his skull.

The boy did as he was told. The cauldron hissed before him.

Feed it, the voice said.

Simon was sweating, wanting not to hear. His hand was shaking as it came up, the knife brushing against his cheek.

Simon's eyes rolled back in his head.

Bloody strips of meat fell into the pot, hissing as they made contact with the heat. The smell of cooking flesh merged with the smoke and crisping insects. Simon moaned and sliced, feeding the boiling mass. The Great Night savored the scent, and the pain. And the appetites it awakened.

Back at the manor, Justin threw his keys to Seth and told him to get the car. They had to get out of there, now.

Seth raced outside, his heart pounding wildly. He stopped, staring in shock. The tires of Justin's car were slashed into steel-belted fillets.

They were trapped.

Justin and Mia were huddled in the great hall as Seth returned. By then they were all chemically and psychically pried open, their nerves jangled and twitching. Escaping on foot and on massive drugs was out of the question; they had no choice but to hunker down and ride it out.

Josh looked around. *Where's Amy?* he asked. No one knew. She had wandered off. Mia had stopped shaking and was semicoherent but fragile; she reached up and touched his face with cool and clammy hands.

Make it stop, she said. *Please make it stop.*

Justin looked at her tearfully. *I can't,* he said. *It's just a bad trip. It'll be over soon . . .*

But, of course, it was only just beginning.

Amy wandered the uppermost floor, searching for the source of the sound: a high, keening wail, faint and furtive at first, growing louder as she reached the attic door. Someone, or something, was crying. As she touched the door, the sound became louder and was joined by another voice. And another. And another. The cries from the other side grew in intensity, and she heard a scraping sound: fingernails desperately clawing at the wood. They were wretched, pitiful, tormented. Their voices filled her head.

Let them out, Amy said, twisting the knob. It stuck stubbornly, unyielding. She began to pound on the door. *LET THEM OUT!*

From the other side, the cries stopped. And then the shrieking began.

There were ghostly flames leaping from the husk of the burned-out barn. Seth was back outside and stood transfixed in the drive, watching

95

it burn. He knew he was tripping, knew it was a hallucination. He knew that barn was already burnt and gone; he had seen its charred remains. But still, there it was: engorged and aflame, the fire etching its long-fallen form perfectly against the night.

It was one thing to see it, another to feel its heat radiating outward or hear its crackling roar. Even tripping by surprise and against his will, Seth was not a virgin to the experience; he knew the sensory tricks the mind played as the drugs did their synaptic mix 'n' match on his senses, and knew that even though riding it out was a little like trying to tell time with a Dali clock, it was the only thing to do. As hallucinations went, this was pretty thorough and, he had to admit, more than a little bit fascinating.

And then his fascination became horror as he saw the bodies in the flames.

Oh my God, Seth gasped. *They're still moving . . .*

There were hundreds of them trapped within the barn, writhing and twisting as the fire consumed them. Men, women, children: still alive, eternally dying, caught in the grip of an inferno. His senses scrambled, he could smell their suffering and taste their terror. He could not move, could not turn or look away.

Seth watched as their screams melded with the smoke roiling upward. It became a cloud, began to swirl. All around him, leaves and twigs and tiny stones tumbled into its center and swept up into the gathering mass. A funnel began to appear. Corkscrewing inward.

Moving inexorably toward him.

Seth instinctively ran and dove for cover behind Justin's car as the whirlwind gained strength, a swirling vortex like a tornado tearing through the manor's drive. As the howl of the wind reached its peak, he suddenly heard the thunder of horses and looked up to see ghostly riders flitting in and out of the vortex, wraithlike, eyes glowing red. The ghost riders thundered past him, and the whole mad vision disappeared, swirling, into the night sky.

He stood, stunned. *Fuck me,* he gasped, then turned to see Simon

standing way too close. Even in the shadows, Seth could see that something was very wrong with Simon's face.

Hey, bro, Simon said. *Like the show?*

Before Seth could say a word, Simon stabbed him once, then twice,
in the chest.

Justin carried Mia up the stairs, looking for a place where she could feel
safe. The walls looked skewed now, the mirrors yielding funhouse re-
fractions, distorted and grotesque. As he made his way down the hallways the walls seemed to expand and contract, bowing out toward him,
then sucking back. Like they were breathing. He knew it wasn't real,
that the walls were still walls, mere wood and plaster and paint. It didn't
matter.

Justin? Mia murmured. Her voice was a thin wisp. *I'm s-scared . . .*

You're okay, Justin whispered. *You're okay . . .*

He found an open door leading to the master bedroom. A large
canopy bed dominated the dimly lit interior; Justin laid Mia down gently on the musty covers.

Just then, they heard Amy screaming. Mia looked at him, her pupils
huge and black.

Go, she said.

Justin looked at her, heartbroken and torn. He nodded and promised
he would be right back. At the door he paused. Mia looked at him.

I love you, she said.

Justin nodded, not realizing it was the last time he would hear her say
those words.

Justin found Amy huddled on the stairs, shaking, her eyes wild, hands
clutching at her ears.

The women, Amy said. *In the attic . . . They're screaming . . .*

She looked at Justin: it was clear that he couldn't hear it.

They're screaming, she said again and again.

C'mon, Justin said, helping her up. *We're getting out of here.*

Back in the master bedroom, Mia rose on unsteady legs, moving toward the door.

Justin? She called out. *Justin?*

Someone appeared in the doorway: not Justin but Simon, eyes showing bloodshot white, flesh dangling in bloody streamers from his skull. The bloody knife hung dripping in his hand.

Mia screamed and fell back as Simon began to hack and slash and slice, his gruesome choreography reflected over and over in the mirrors that filled every wall. Blood and screams filled the air, spattered the glass, as the knife flashed up and down, back and forth. As his arm came up to deliver the killing blow, Justin ran in, howling in rage and hammering Simon with every ounce of strength he possessed. Simon spun, overwhelmed by the sheer brute force of the impact. The knife slashed, catching Justin in the face. The others appeared in the doorway, aghast and horrified.

In the tumult, Simon lost his grip on the girl. Mia wrenched away, off-balance, and pitched headlong into one of the mirrors . . .

. . . and they watched in horror as Mia fell toward the mirror, saw the glass ripple and go dark a split second before impact, saw dark hands come out to snatch her and pull her through.

Simon screamed and attempted to follow. But it was too late; the portal had already closed. The possessed boy went headlong into an unforgiving surface, impaling himself on a hundred jagged shattering shards. The Great Night fled, leaving Simon to die, choking on his own blood. Leaving the others as shaken witnesses to the impossible.

And leaving Justin, blinded by loss and pain, crawling through the wreckage, searching for his lost love.

14

They never convinced the authorities of what had happened. The Custis family clamped down hard on the burgeoning scandal, sparing no expense to spin it into a Just Say No cautionary tale for wayward youth. The manor was closed, and, after a suitable period of lying low, vast amounts of Custis money were quietly spent restoring and reclaiming it, and rewriting its history.

The mystery of Mia and what happened to her was central, and only deepened as their manic accounts strained all pretense of reality: pushed to the frayed edge of explanation, and despite the fevered protestations of her parents, Mia was officially labeled "missing," the case left open but unresolved. Rumors raged and alternate interpretations abounded: maybe a runaway, maybe brain-damaged and lost, maybe a secretly freaky little good-girl-gone-bad. A reward for information on her whereabouts was established, but never claimed. The story, lacking in a plausibly satisfying ending, eventually dried up, and the good intentions of the concerned community moved on to other things. And the machineries of reason set about to assigning blame.

Josh spent years bouncing in and out of private psychiatric care, kept drugged and off balance for so long that sometimes he almost believed he was crazy. And, of course, in certain respects he was; by then, the damage had taken its toll. But that still didn't change the facts. He knew what they'd seen.

For Josh, the veil had been parted forever. And he was determined to learn what it meant.

Amy too spent time in and out of psych wards and drug rehabs, as well as diving into every metaphysical study she could get her hands on. Like Josh, she was way beyond denial; she knew exactly what she'd seen . . . or, more specifically, heard.

Because she still heard them: the voices of the dead. That night had torn open her spirit somehow, left her unable to screen out their desperate cries or ignore the terrible desolation of their plight. She heard them as she walked down the street, stood in line at the grocery store, lay alone in her room at night. It was like a door had been pried open in the back of her mind, letting the voices come pouring in.

Seth took years to fully recover. The wounds he had suffered had punctured a lung and damaged his spleen beyond repair; surgery saved his life but effectively ended any thoughts of playing pro ball, and the agonizing struggle to regain control of his mind and body proved a constant reminder of what he had lost. And sometimes late at night, when all was quiet and he closed his eyes to sleep, he saw flames flitting into tormented neon sky, bodies writhing and crying out in voices seared by the unholy pyre, and heard the thunder of horses whipped by ghostly riders. He worked graveyard shifts and kept vampire hours, sleeping fitfully, and only when the sun was up. And he prayed to God one day it would stop.

Of them all, Caroline alone flat-out refused to admit she'd seen anything or remembered anything at all. Nine months later, she had a more indelible reminder: a baby girl. She told no one who the father was, not even Josh . . . especially not Josh. She spent the better part of the next twenty years drifting through bad relationships with even badder men, raising her daughter single-handedly and fiercely striving for some semblance of the normal life that she hoped could save her from what she'd seen, and what she could never hope to unsee.

And Justin . . .

As with all good cautionary tales for wayward youth, it was decided that someone had to pay . . . at least, someone still breathing. Justin took the rap in the manslaughter case of Simon Baxter, and for conspiring with him to provide the drugs. The charges put him squarely in the grip of a system whose job it was to grind him down to a nub, and he took it seemingly without a fight. The loss of Mia had completely pulled his plug, disconnecting him from his heart; it was as if his spark had gone out somehow. He took his punishment stoically, without complaint—it paled in the end to the infinitely greater damnation he visited upon himself.

But in the end, the question lingered: what actually happened? They had only fractured images and nightmares: of ghostly riders at war in a whirlwind, of the screams of lost and tortured souls. Of blood and suffering. All of their lives had been shattered, both inside and out.

And for twenty years, they had been unable to face the truth.

Until it was forced upon them.

15

The freshly reunited Underground was understandably upset when, in the midst of their grieving reminiscence, Josh informed them that Justin wasn't exactly dead.

"If he's not dead," Seth stepped in, "then who's in the goddamned box?"

Before Josh could answer, Seth stormed to the front of the church. He wrenched open the lid and stared, aghast. Caroline and Amy followed behind him, reached the coffin, and peered over the rim.

"Oh God," they gasped. The others followed and stared, stunned. Justin's severed hand lay on the satin lining. As they watched, the fingers clutched weakly.

"I'm sorry I had to do it this way," Josh said from behind them. "But you wouldn't have come if I told you the truth. You had to see it for yourselves."

"This is *bullshit!*" Seth roared, and whirled to confront him. Josh stood his ground, unwavering.

"I wish it was," Josh said. "But it's time to face what we know, what no one else has ever believed . . . what we haven't wanted to believe ourselves."

"Meaning what?" Seth demanded.

Suddenly the woman at Josh's side spoke. "Meaning, Justin is still alive. He's just crossed over."

Caroline looked at her skeptically. "And you are . . . ?"

"My name is Joya Hayes," she said, "and I'm here to help you."

"We don't need your help," Caroline said caustically.

"Yes, you do." Joya stepped up, her gaze pinning Caroline, piercing and sharp. "The place you all stumbled upon that night is a nightmare, but it's not a dream," she told them. "It exists in a realm between this world and the next. It has no name, but we call it Underworld. And your friend is there."

Silence reigned as the impossibility of it all sank in. "It's true," Josh added. "Justin went over, but something went wrong. And now we have to get them out."

It was Zoe who finally spoke, her eyes blazing with a light that suggested that, danger and strangeness and all, this was the most exciting thing she'd ever seen.

"You said 'them,'" she noted. "Who else is there?"

Josh looked at them all. And then began to explain.

part two
middle passage

16

Just south of Tidewater, Virginia—outside the tourist-ridden, overbuilt environs of Norfolk and Virginia Beach, and the smaller, cozier confines of Stillson Beach—lay some three hundred square miles of pine scrub and peat bog originally surveyed by the young George Washington and aptly christened the Great Dismal Swamp.

At the heart of the swamp, where the sea crept in to feed the dark waters of Lake Drummond, the terrain was particularly inhospitable, eerie and bleak. It was home to copperheads, mosquitoes, and countless creeping or buzzing things. The Indians who first hunted the tidal plains gave it a wide berth. Most who ventured into its depths never came back; those who did were invariably half-mad, babbling stories of dead souls blind and suffering in the still, black pools and quicksandlike bogs.

It was a brooding and powerful place, but for centuries it was kept in check by its relative isolation, sustaining itself by feeding upon the natural world or gobbling the occasional hunting party.

And then the white man came.

The settlers heard the legends, but for the most part they considered them ignorant native superstition. It was the New World, after all, and land was land. It was all up for grabs . . . and ultimately ripe for the likes of ruthless and greedy colonial hustlers like Silas Custis.

Custis was an instinctive opportunist. He began his career as a factor from London, who as a young man found himself employment on the Gold Coast at the main base at Cape Coast Castle, which operated under the charter of the governor, a nephew of the Duke of York. Their principal stock in trade was human flesh: African slaves, to build the New World.

Custis was long on ambition and short on scruples, but in marked contrast to the majority of his ilk, he was not uneducated or void of foresight, was not careless, prodigal, or addicted to strong drink and driven by an attraction to debauchery with native women. Rather, quite the opposite: Silas was sanctimonious, stern, and vain, coldly charming yet quietly desperate for status and tirelessly obsessive in pursuit of his goals. He studied well the workings of the factory on the cape: cosseting the wealthy caboceers and corpulent Governor's Council, currying the favor of the sundry merchants, scribes, artificers, and soldiers who manned the vast hive complex of iron and wood and stone. And though his salary of seventy-five pounds per annum sounded tolerable, even princely, for a young man by Leadenhall Street standards, the Cracka scrip issued by the General Office was worthless outside the domain of the Company, and the limitations to ambition filled him with a profound determination to rise above his station.

Silas thus resolved to become not merely proficient but expert in all facets of his chosen trade. He studied the optimum timing of a cargo, which depended as much on chance as good planning and heavily upon the various fanciful humors of the Negroes, whose survival would make great demands upon one voyage for a commodity—stewed yams for cargo taken from the Bight of Biafra, or plantains for the Congolese or Angolans—which might then be roundly rejected on the very next voyage. He learned the peculiarities of the flow of trade on voyages, and that the windward and leeward sides of the coast were as much opposite in their demands as in their distance—that iron bars not at all desired at the Leeward Coast were much in demand at Windward, along with crystals, corals, molasses, and brass-mounted cutlasses; that brass pans from Rio Sesthos fetched high mark in Apollonia, while Callabar seemed always to have need of cowrie shells, copper, and tobacco; and, of course, the near-universal appetite for arms, gunpowder, tallow, wool, and cotton of all denominations, and of course rum and good English spirits to lubricate the frayed nerves of empire.

Silas became skilled in the multitudinous corruptions that infused and infected every aspect of the circuit: shipping watered rum, faulty iron bars, and aged flintlocks that often as not blew up in the hands of the African traders who acquired them, while guarding against their own tendency to pay back in gold dust diluted with copper and brass filings in return. His skill and ruthless attention to the fattened purses of his betters eventually earned him favor in the eyes of the Governor General, who came to rely upon Custis and eventually appointed him chief administrator.

But Silas learned to profit from the facilitation of trade not merely for the sake of his masters: he paid bribes in silver and took kickbacks in gold, quietly amassing the means of his ascension. In time, his contacts spanned both sides of the Atlantic: on the Gold, Slave, Grain, and Ivory coasts, from Fort James at the Gambia River through Fernando Po and Old Calabar down to Cabinda at the mouth of the treacherous Congo; to the bustling docks of London, Bristol, and Liverpool; to the cane plantations of Jamaica and the Leeward Islands of the British West Indies; and, of course, to the burgeoning American colonies, where Silas's keen instinct told him his future invariably lay.

Business boomed. Too well, in fact. By the mid-seventeen hundreds, the colonial slave trade had burgeoned beyond all expectation, with over sixty thousand souls a year flooding into Virginia and the Carolinas alone, one hundred thousand or more to the colonies as a whole. But with this flood of commerce came problems: as demand outstripped supply, his associates were increasingly hard pressed to find adequate—much less suitable—stock. Silas was expert at the sorting—he knew that those of the Gold Coast, Gambia, and the Windward points were most highly prized, the Fanti, Ashanti, and Coromantees being cleanest of limb and judged more docible than others, the irony being that they were also more apt to revenge and murder the instruments of their slavery, given half a chance, and were more clever in their machinations.

Conversely, he knew that from the Leeward side and on into the interior the quality shifted steadily for the worse: the Ibibio and Efiks from eastern Nigeria being gentle but prone to melancholy, and hence to suicide when their fate became too much for them, and an Angolan Negro was considered a veritable proverb for worthlessness, except as compared perhaps to a Hottentot. He knew of the tendency of Whydah slaves toward smallpox and afflictions of the eye, whereas Windward cargo fell more heavily prey to influenza and venereal taint, most often courtesy of their European enslavers.

But as time passed, too many of the cargo were simply too proud, too wild, or too unwilling to submit. They were difficult and expensive to handle. They corrupted the others and gnawed relentlessly at profits. Indeed, apart from the inevitable spoilage of the Middle Passage, many of their captive cargo seemed to actually prefer death, even one lost in roiling waves and feasted on by seagoing scavengers, to the life of bondage and misery that awaited them. Worse yet was the ever-present threat of death wish and fixed melancholy suddenly exploding outward in mutiny or outright and violent revolt, the distinct possibility of which extended throughout the journey and long beyond the arrival of cargo to market, and never really went away.

As a matter of business, this quickly became intolerable. Prices ratcheted inexorably upward, until by 1756 a single African man of good limb and docile disposition fetched the bartered equivalent of one hundred and fifteen gallons of rum, with a woman of breedable age a comparative bargain at ninety-five.

Times were changing, and would change more still; Silas could see the inevitable depletion of good native stock, combined with the simple ability to breed more at home, would lead to an inevitable and irrevocable erosion of business. He heard increasing rumors of rumblings from the northern ports such as Boston and Manhattan about the moral and ethical dilemmas posed to good Christian folk by their trade; indeed, as far inland as Philadelphia, with its damnable concentrations of Quaker and Huguenot blood, the bleatings were reaching a fevered pitch, with cries to unduly levy or even ban the trade altogether.

But these circumstances also offered unprecedented opportunity for any man with the courage, the vision, and the conviction to exploit it. What was needed, Silas came to realize, was a way station between Middle Passage and market, and even within the market itself, where unruly cargo could be taken and broken.

And Silas Custis was just the man to do it.

He had learned and climbed, and, above all, he had lasted. The average life span of a white man on the Gold Coast was a little over two years. Silas had lasted ten. By the age of twenty-nine, Silas Custis was well-connected, well-known if not well-liked, and more than a little bit feared. It was time for him to make his move.

In 1768, Silas acquired a charter of three hundred and forty acres in the colony of Virginia, at the edge of the great swamp, where Lake Drummond met the inland waterway. It was here his dream became a reality etched in nightmare.

He had taken much from his years of service in the Gold Coast and knew well the infinite utility of lash and brand, of chain and barracoon, in the hand of one who knew how to wield them with cold and calculating deliberation.

And thus was born Custis Manor: the house of horrors, on the plantation of pain, where those already stripped of their freedom could be more purposefully raped of their will. Where torture was a given and ghastly death the ever-present wages of resistance. His overseers were men of low and ruthless repute, chosen for their capacity for unflinching brutality and unwavering loyalty.

Silas, being thorough, had heard the many foreboding legends surrounding his new domain, but they only seemed to bolster his design: the already inhospitable land came cheaply, and its remote and forbidding quality both terrified and dissuaded prying eyes.

Not that anyone was really looking: the general ignorance of the conditions of the trade, combined with the unshakable conviction that hot lands could not be properly cultivated without Negroes, and the convenient belief that slaves were but simple creatures of burden, altogether happier and healthier on the veritable paradise of the plantations as compared to their heathen African wilds.

Silas Custis became a well-connected shadow figure to the Founding Fathers. Though his reputation was unsavory, his stock was prized; even if they never invited him to the parties at Mt. Vernon and Monticello, his was the iron hand that broke their servants. The struggling new land turned a conveniently blind eye to the remote reaches of Custis Manor. Indeed, landholders throughout Virginia and the Carolinas would pay Custis for the privilege of sending their most impudent property to work for him for a time, savoring the grateful and obedient—albeit heavily scarred—chattel that would ultimately return.

Silas was wealthy, powerful, and arrogant. And the manor he built testified to that success, growing more and more self-contained and self-sufficient, virtually a kingdom unto itself. No authorities came to question or challenge his decisions. He answered to no one. There was no discipline so heinous, no cruelty so barbaric, that he couldn't practice it openly and with impunity at Custis Manor.

Of course, the more broken souls he fed to the place, the more terrible became the seething, concentrated darkness that dwelled there. And the more powerful it grew, the more successful and prosperous he became.

It was, literally and figuratively, a kingdom of the damned. And Silas Custis would be its sovereign lord.

17

By 1789, the wisdom of Silas Custis's plan had been borne out. The revolution had thrown off the shackles of English domination, and the violent birth of the American nation had left his services ever more in demand. Custis Manor burgeoned, maintaining a façade of gentility while incorporating the most efficient aspects of the factory systems from which his inspiration drew, and making even the most brutal statutes of the French West Indies' *Côde Noir* or the even more brutish Colonial slave codes, which descended from English law, seem positively quaint.

In near-perfect diametric opposition, however, was the growing and troublesome awareness of the innate discrepancy between his hellish practices and the stated ideals of the new land of liberty. Indeed, within scant years of the adoption of the Declaration of Independence in 1776, most of the newly christened states had officially prohibited importation of fresh slaves or had imposed punishing and exorbitant taxes on those who did; by 1788, New York had abolished import and export altogether, with penalties of up to one hundred pounds per offense. But still the need was there, to work sugar in Louisiana, tobacco in Virginia and Kentucky, or rice in the Carolinas. So, enterprising, erstwhile Colonials, unbound by ethics or scruples, simply smuggled them in. And again, Silas was there. His land made an excellent port for those wishing to escape detection, his coffers filled to overflowing, and at the age of forty he was flush with accomplishment.

It is said that when matters of survival are no longer paramount, one's attention turns to matters of legacy. As such, Silas reasoned it was time for him to produce an heir.

The woman he chose was one Priscilla Pierce, the handsome yet peculiar only daughter of a fine Richmond family. The marriage was more commercial contract than loving union, her father having depleted his fortune on bad speculations. Silas paid well for her hand and took her as his wife.

Priscilla promptly bore him six children in rapid succession. But the following years, though prosperous, were not without tragedy. Two of his children died mysteriously before the end of their second year. The cause of the first death—of his second child, James—was traced to a cook from Jamaica who, it was discovered, was proficient in vegetable poisons and *Obeah*, or murder by fetish; the second death, of his son Matthew, came at the hands of a wet nurse from Trinidad, who stabbed the babe through the base of the skull with a slim scarfpin. Silas, outraged at the betrayal and fearful of their audacity, had them both flayed alive and rolled in salt, their still-gasping carcasses hung in iron gibbets and left to rot before the assembled ranks of the other slaves.

Another son, Thomas—his favorite—was struck down by typhus in the winter of his fifth year. On top of all that, Silas came to despise Priscilla, whose frail temperament was ill-suited to the harshness of manor life. The cries of the slaves echoing through the night disturbed her, and as her own powerlessness became manifest, she lashed out at the very suffering that so aroused her, eventually beating to death a hapless house servant who spilled her afternoon tea. Her eccentricities tipped over into full-blown madness as the years progressed. Silas locked her away in the attic, ostensibly for her own protection, and there she languished.

This left him with two daughters, Anne and Isabel—whom he

promptly married off like cattle—and one bumbling son, Isaac. Poor Isaac was a tender man, taking as he did after his mother, and showed no aptitude whatsoever for the savagery inherent in the family business. His gentleness of spirit was further aggravated by a headstrong resistance to paternal authority. He ultimately fled the familial estate altogether and, against the violent objections of his father, married Angelica Stroudt, only daughter of Wilhelm Stroudt, a Philadelphia abolitionist.

At the age of fifty-six, Silas found his health deteriorating, his dynasty stalled, and his superstitious paranoia profound. And though his appetite for cruelty had not diminished, he was enjoying it less; it took more and more to arouse, much less satisfy, him. It was, as they say, the winter of his discontent.

Then two things happened to change all that. In 1820, there came word of the birth of his first grandson.

And the coming of the slave named Papa Josephus.

18

From the moment he arrived, the word spread quickly: a slave had come who filled the others with a terror even greater than that reserved for Silas. At first, Silas was perplexed: the old slave was nothing more than a shriveled raisin of a man, blind and ancient, thrown in almost as an afterthought with the last shipment from the West Indies. But very quickly he came to understand: this wizened old husk was no ordinary chattel.

Papa Josephus was *Tata Nkisi*, the Great Night, practitioner of a particularly vile and mysterious amalgam of African and Caribbean witchcraft. Silas was no stranger to the myth and folk magick of his property; it was impossible to spend decades in the trade without hearing the songs sung at night or the names of their gods uttered under the lash, or seeing the remains of makeshift altars furtively erected. Indeed, it was advantageous to understand what idols they were praying to, the better to more thoroughly topple them.

Nor was Silas a stranger to the larger threat implicit in the slave's presence: in a word, revolution. Slave uprisings and murderous insurrections were always an inherent risk, particularly from those who came from the estates of the British and French West Indies, as was readily attested to by the bloody coups of Barbados, Guadeloupe, Martinique, and virtually every other island; in San Domingo in 1793, the damnable Toussaint L'Ouverture had led his runaway Maroons so successfully against the French that they had ultimately decreed them a free nation, much to Bonaparte's dismay. No less a personage than the Governor of Martinique had proclaimed that the safety of the whites demanded that they keep the Negroes in the most profound and destitute ignorance, believing firmly that they should be treated as one would treat beasts.

But Silas knew all too well that beasts could not reason, or scheme, or dream. He could not allow such thoughts to take root and spread.

Silas resolved to break the old man.

But Papa Josephus would not flinch under the lash, no matter how often or how vigorously applied. And the slaves' fear of him grew all the greater as they witnessed both the old man's resistance and Silas's desperation. It was an intolerable imbalance of power. After a while, even killing the old man was out of the question; it would only make him invincible in their eyes, and Silas might lose his grip on them altogether.

There was but one thing left to do.

One night Silas came to the old slave's shack, escorted by his chief overseer, Luther, a pig-faced and powerful man of low bearing. The other slaves murmured fearfully as Luther took position outside the door and Silas went in.

Inside, Papa Josephus sat tending a small fire. He was shackled with a heavy iron collar, long spikes protruding outward; his back was covered with thick keloid scars, layer upon layer like fat tallow drippings, the latest still gleaming angry red. He looked up, blind eyes staring, as Silas entered. The old man did not flinch or grovel but simply regarded him with flat and unnerving detachment.

There was a small wooden table with rough-hewn stools; Silas bade him to sit. The old man rose on creaking limbs and obeyed, his unseeing gaze never leaving Silas's face. Silas reached into his coat, producing a pistol and a set of keys. As he laid them upon the table, the old man's head titled, hearing the sound.

I should have you killed, Silas told him. *As one would kill an infected animal to protect the herd.*

Silas waited for a reaction; Papa Josephus continued to stare, not so much at as seemingly through him.

Why do you not? the old man replied. His accent bore no trace of the pidgin English the other slaves spoke but was cultivated, tinted with a hint of French. *It is your right, n'est pas?*

Because I think you are more burden to me dead, Silas said, then looked at him, puzzling. *Who educated you?*

Papa Josephus shrugged withered shoulders. *My father was an African chieftain,* he explained. *He was educated by missionaries. In turn they taught me to read and write, anglais and français.* He paused. *My father taught me other things as well . . .*

Silas leaned forward. *What other things?* he asked.

Papa Josephus said nothing. Silas looked at the gun and the keys.

Teach me the secrets of your power, he told him, *and I will use mine to release you.*

Papa Josephus regarded the offer carefully. The old white man was crazy, of this there was no doubt. But Papa had lived in bondage his entire life, and he understood the difference between black and white man's magick. The black man's magick was powerful, true. But the white man's power was measured in gold and guns across thousands of hostile miles, and Silas held the proverbial keys to freedom.

I can teach you, the slave said. *But why should I trust you?*

Silas smiled. *What choice do you have?*

There was a moment of silence as Papa Josephus shrugged again. Luther peered inside, watching the impertinence, his right hand moving instinctively toward the whip at his belt. But Silas waved him off. No words were spoken, but the old man's blind eyes seemed to track the motion, as if he could sense the movement in the very air. Silas watched intently, trying to plumb each crag and fissure of the slave's face for some hint of exploitable emotion. But Papa Josephus merely fixed him with his flat, milky gaze.

You must know, he said, *there are things which once seen cannot be unseen . . . And there is no turning back.*

Silas smiled and extended his pale hand; Papa Josephus returned the gesture, thick manacles clanking.

The bargain was struck.

And slave and master became teacher and pupil.

That night Papa Josephus was taken from the slaves' quarters to the manor house. He was fed and bathed, his wounds tended. Clothing was procured of an altogether finer fit. And as he healed, Papa Josephus began to instruct Silas Custis in the ways of the Great Night.

Papa's way taught that human beings were made of two halves. One half was the external, the physical, "real" self. The other half dwelt in the spirit dimension. Papa Josephus taught Silas that magick was both the force that holds the parts together and that which wants to tear them apart, to hurl the bloody chunks into the stinking eternal abyss. Magick could heal, and magick could kill. But in the end, magick was but a tool to bend reality, shaping it to the will of the magician.

The soul was what the Great Night sought to possess, the prize in the eternal war between darkness and light. Those who became the Great Night had no soul, it having been systematically and ritually slaughtered, until all that was left was pure, unchecked *will*. The sorcerer had no conscience. What he saw, what he wanted, he *took*. Without compunction, without guilt, without an ounce of hesitation or remorse. That was the heart of his power and what made him so compelling: he was lust and greed and hunger, all rolled into one. There was nothing to hold him back.

Silas proved an apt pupil. He mastered the herbs and rituals of Papa's strange knowledge with a voracious lust that both frightened and fascinated the ancient *brujo*. And he always wanted more.

Power had its price, Papa warned. The conjurer of evil was always hungry for souls, always on the prowl. He must constantly feed on others to maintain his strength. That was why, once the *brujo* got inside a family, he would gnaw at the bloodline until no one was safe. At any sufficiently weak or vulnerable moment, the soul could be invaded and seized by the evil. Once possessed, it worked like an infection. One member of the tribe was possessed: from there the dark force could branch out, looking for other members to occupy, other souls to devour.

The ordinary human heart revolved around family, around home and tribe. It held dear the measured rhythms of life, the safe circle of the campfire that held back the night. Mortal man stayed happily within the fortress of ritual—doing things the right way, the good way, the way that kept the hunting bountiful and made the crops grow green.

The sorcerer was the enemy of all that. He was the bringer of darkness and death and despair, and he was most likely to prey on his own kin: because he was the absolute antithesis of family, and because they were most vulnerable to him. The Great Night was darkness incarnate, master of death and decay and madness, and his kingdom was made of rot and blood, unspeakable brutality and horror. The magick was rooted at the vital juncture of flesh and spirit. The body was both the battleground and the tool. Blood and meat, brains and body parts all played their roles; indeed, they comprised the supreme test, by deliberately and ritualistically propelling oneself into the most repellent experiences imaginable. By plunging into such horrors and mastering them, one achieved power.

There was nothing unreal or imaginary about such power. It was literally the ability to do anything. It was fearlessness and absolute single-mindedness, unfettered by guilt or doubt or shame. It was a power achieved by willingly becoming a monster.

And at its center was the *nganga.*

The *nganga* was the cauldron of souls, the heart of the Great Night's power. In the *nganga,* so terrible a vessel was created—filled with such ghastliness—that it was capable of capturing an entire universe of dead souls, all of whom became the slaves and agents of the sorcerer. When the *nganga* was properly prepared and taken to the proper place, it acted as a powerful magnet, sucking into itself the souls of the dead.

It was Papa Josephus who located the swamp's dark heart, the center for its terrible power. It was there—on a small and godforsaken island, approachable only by rowboat—that Papa ordered Silas to erect the shack where the *nganga* was to be kept.

And his darkest rituals would be conducted.

Papa Josephus had Silas take him to the slaves' graveyard on the far edge of the plantation. To build a proper *nganga*, the apprentice went with his mentor to a graveyard at night, under the waning moon. There they would seek out a *kiyumba*, a spirit of the dead.

The grave was selected. It was recent, a defiant young slave named Thomas who had been whipped to death a fortnight past. Sweating, heart thudding in anticipation, Silas did as he was told: soaking the ground of the chosen grave with rum, making the sign of the cross. Papa Josephus lit a cigar, puffing grandly, and ordered Silas to open the grave.

Silas dug in grunting silence until his spade thudded against the prize they sought. A cloud of rot wafted up in the humid air, and Silas doubled over, hacking and retching. Papa laughed, then told him with all seriousness that he must not shy away. The stench of human decay played a vital role in the making of the Great Night. It was a smell that mortal man recoils from violently and instinctively. It was something he must master, even learn to enjoy. When he had taught himself to savor the smell of human death, it was a powerful sign that he was well on his way to becoming himself master of the dead, a ruler of that dark province.

Nodding, eyes watering, Silas set to work, removing from the corpse the tibia, the phalanges of the fingers and toes, the penis and testicles, the ribs and the head. The brains were crucial, Papa told him. The best *kiyumbas* were those of people who died in torment—prized for the contribution their nature made. Once the key ingredients had been stolen from the grave, they rowed back to the shack for the ritual taming. Silas stripped naked and lay flat on his back on the floor, with ceremonial candles blazing around him. Papa Josephus circled him, drinking rum and smoking more cigars. The stolen body parts, wrapped in a black bag, were placed beside him. And, as Papa had bidden, Silas invited the Great Night to enter . . .

. . . and the dark force moved through him then, a tidal wave of vileness that consumed and subsumed him, oozing through the pores of his soul. The accumulated power at the heart of the *nganga* uncoiled inside him like a great serpent: Silas's body went rigid and spastic; foam flecked the corners of his mouth as he writhed and spat and vomited up the last dregs of his spirit . . .

By Silas's head were seven dishes filled with gunpowder. When they ignited in a flash of smoke and fire, Papa Josephus knew the time had come. He placed coins into the cauldron, to pay the price of the *kiyumba*'s soul. He put a scrap of paper with the slave's name on it in the vessel. The brains and other hacked-off parts followed. Then there was the matter of the blood. The *kiyumba* must be fed. Regularly, and always. Wielding a ceremonial knife, Papa Josephus killed a chicken, a snake, and a goat, feeding their blood and flesh into the pot. Then Silas stood, and Papa made ritual cuts in the white man's flesh, allowing human blood to drip into the thickening sludge. Other ingredients were added: seawater for power, mercury for quickness, candle wax, and a host of other things, each with its own muttered prayer. Herbs, peppers, cigar butts, bats, and frog guts. All went into the fetid soup.

Once the stew was mixed, Papa ordered Silas to dress, saying the contents must be spiritually cooked. To this end, the *nganga* was covered and loaded onto the boat, to be rowed back to the same graveyard from which the original ingredients had come. Once interred, the now-enslaved spirit of the *kiyumba* would call to the lost souls of the dead, drawing them to the lure of the rotten, fleshy stew, where they would become entrapped.

Three weeks passed. Silas recovered from the ordeal, feeling weak-ened yet empowered, as if something had simultaneously been taken from and given to him. When the moon waned again, Papa ordered the *nganga* exhumed and returned to the shack. It was by then in a condi-tion that defied sense and defiled sensation.

But it was nothing compared to what would follow: in the months to come, Papa Josephus instructed Silas in the use of the *nganga*. It was a small step from robbing graves to sacrificing living, breathing victims. Papa had instructed that the sorcerer must actually drink the blood of his victim: particularly the blood of the heart, the better to drink in the victim's soul.

Papa told him that if he did it fast enough, the victim would be able to watch.

Silas looked at the old black man and smiled. He was counting on it.

19

Month by month, the atrocities compounded. The cauldron had to be refreshed. New victims were taken: throats slit, bodies split like melons, hearts wrenched out and pressed to sucking mouths before their dying eyes so that the horror might be complete, the fear unending, the soul forever paralyzed.

There was no shortage of sacrifices, and absolutely no one to stop him. The slightest transgression was cause for the offending slave to disappear—bound and rowed out by Luther's torchlight to their doom in the black of the night. The screams that echoed back through the swamp did more to maintain an atmosphere of dread than all the torture in the world.

In the shack, body parts were hacked off and tossed into the bubbling pot, the madness underscored by the low and threatening Bantu curses and invocations that rumbled from the lips of Silas and Papa Josephus. As the brew simmered greasily over a low wood fire and the shack filled with the odor of rancid cooking decay, Silas stifled a gag; Papa Josephus looked at him sternly.

To stare into the nganga *is to gaze into the mouth of Hell,* he said. *Always waiting, always hungry for more. When you can do so unflinching, you will be* Tata Nkisi.

He urged Silas to breathe deeply. Silas grimaced and complied, foulness stinging his lungs and filling him with revulsion.

Breathe, Papa urged.

Silas looked at him with watering eyes and obeyed. A strange inversion had occurred in their perverse dynamic: by light of day, to the observance of others, Silas was master and Papa Josephus the servant. But in the dead of night, in the tiny hut, their roles reversed: Papa Josephus was the dark lord of their nightmare world, Silas his all-too-willing pupil. He had proven himself an able apprentice: rigorous and determined, wholly and unflinchingly committed. The loss of his soul was of little concern to him; so far as most people were concerned, he'd barely had one to begin with. And in truth, they weren't far off the mark: the years of cruelty had all but scraped him clean of conscience. Still, it was the reek of the *nganga* that was hardest for him to overcome; it tugged at the last hanging tatters of his humanity. When even that no longer fazed him, Silas knew that he would be ready.

Breathe, Papa commanded. Silas did, sucking in the vaporous scent of damnation. Suddenly the revulsion ebbed, and passed. His senses cleared. He looked at the old slave. Papa Josephus stared back blindly, and knew.

It was time for Silas to end his apprenticeship. And to claim his place as the Great Night.

The next night Luther rowed Papa Josephus out to the shack, alone. The light of a low fire flickered within the hut. As Papa entered, Silas was inside, waiting. A bottle of rum and two glasses sat before him in the dust. He smiled.

Come in, Papa, Silas said. *Sit with me.*

The old slave regarded him suspiciously, milky eyes searching; Silas rose and helped him to the floor. Then Silas took a seat across from him and poured from the bottle magnanimously, handing him a glass.

To your liberation, Silas said. He clinked his glass. Papa Josephus drank, not knowing what to make of Silas, his merry mood, the odd air of bonhomie.

We have much to celebrate, Silas explained. *You've kept your end of the bargain, old man. It is time for me to keep mine.*

Papa Josephus cocked his head quizzically; never had he truly expected this cunning *mundele* to keep his word, as white men's words were writ in ash and smoke. Silas lit a cigar, puffing grandly, and handed it to him.

Have you thought what you would do with freedom? Silas asked. *Surely you could not stay here, and I doubt the missionaries would take you back . . .*

Papa Josephus smoked and thought long and carefully before answering. *I would go home,* he said at last.

Ah, home. Silas smiled and poured another glass. *To home,* he said, toasting.

The old man drank quietly. As he did, Silas watched him, studying the dark fissures of his face. *And where is home?* he asked.

The old slave started to say something but stopped, hesitant. The shadow of dim memory flitted across his craggy features like the shadow of a bird taking flight. Papa's hand came up to stroke the thin gray strands of his whiskers. *Home,* he said again. *Home is . . .*

Papa stopped. Silas smiled, mercilessly amused, and added another faggot to the fire. The old man did not smile.

It is not time to speak of these things, Papa said. Silas disagreed.

You have taught me well, old man, he told him. *I will pay to send you wherever you wish. But first you must tell me, where will you go?*

Papa Josephus said nothing, gazing with blind eyes at the crackling fire. As he did, Silas saw the slave: his past in ashes, his present a nightmare, his power laid bare. For the first time, Papa Josephus looked, to Silas, fully human.

And that was his undoing.

Silas reached again: not for the bottle this time. For the knife. And in that last moment, as Papa Josephus felt Silas rise, he knew. An eerie calm came over him.

Where I go, Papa said, *you will follow.*

Silas smiled.

And the Great Night descended.

Silas celebrated by skinning Papa Josephus alive, sending the old man into the pot one piece at a time. Only at the end, when his severed heart rose, still pumping, to Silas's lips, did Papa Josephus allow his terror to penetrate his ethereal armor.

And then Silas swallowed his soul.

From that point on, Silas Custis was no longer concerned with raising an heir to replace him. He had no intention of being replaced. And he had no intention of letting his empire crumble. Silas was in for the long haul. On the occasion of Priscilla's unfortunate and not-so-mysterious demise, Silas invited his long-estranged son, Isaac, home: to put their past behind them, to reconcile and heal the rift in the family.

After much soul-searching, Isaac accepted and, accompanied by Angelica and their young son, Thomas, returned to Custis Manor. The reunion was heartfelt: after a lifetime of parental rejection, Silas was finally welcoming Isaac into his heart. A fortnight later, Silas took his son's heart in return. And fed the rest of him into the pot.

It was a logical move. Sometimes the *nganga* was in need of different qualities. The soul of a *mundele,* a white person, was much more docile, hence more easily controlled and directed than the soul of a nonwhite. Additionally, the spirit of a white person was more effective both in killing other white people and in giving the Great Night protection from them. If the *nganga* contained the souls of white people, then the

Great Night would be safe from the power of white people. Poor Isaac had done something to help along the family business, after all.

Isaac's widow, Angelica, was the second Custis bride to go irretrievably insane. That didn't, however, stop her from bearing four more children—for Silas, and much against what was left of her will—in the attic sanitarium.

And so things went, with Silas showing one more alarming tendency: not only was he refusing to die, he was no longer aging. His grandchildren grew up: tending to the estate and performing figurehead functions or diversifying into government and industry. Spreading the family's sphere of influence.

But there was never any question of who was running the show.

By 1857, Silas Custis was slightly over one hundred and thirty years old, though he didn't look a day over sixty. He wasn't entirely happy with the way the world was changing. Northern abolitionists were putting pressure on the Slave States, and the underground railroad was literally spiriting slaves right off the plantations. The manor was being mismanaged by his eldest grandson, Emmanuel, whose duties in the Virginia militia were growing increasingly cumbersome as the drums of secession thundered. And while all of these factors undoubtedly played a part, the force that finally brought disaster down on Silas's head was a fiery young slave named Celeste.

Celeste was breathtakingly lovely, intelligent and willful, and beloved of the whole slave population. She loved Lucas, a bright and articulate youth who was Emmanuel's prize house nigger, his manservant. Emmanuel Custis, now the titular head of the family and a colonel in the newly swelling ranks of the Army of Virginia, looked highly upon them, and in a moment of tender-hearted progressiveness had even gone so far as to give them permission to marry.

But Silas had a weakness for women like Celeste. Race was not an issue in this one regard. When Silas, in front of everyone, singled her out for use, Silas's overseer dragged her forth, and Celeste broke free just long enough to claw out one of his eyes. The murderously enraged Silas ordered her stripped and flayed until her flesh came away in bloody ribbons. But he was determined to devour more than just her body. Before the horrified gaze of Lucas and a thousand slaves, Celeste was bound and dragged to the dock, then tossed into the waiting boat. But as they began to row out to his chapel, the slaves at last could stand no more.

Lucas had held himself in check as long as he could. But he couldn't stand by and watch his love be fed to the pit. He cried out in rage and anguish, lunging at Luther. Luther raised his gun, ready to fire. In that moment, the other slaves revolted, throwing off their fear and lashing out at their tormentors. In the middle of the swamp, Celeste made her last desperate move, capsizing the boat and sending them both over the side.

Silas was the ruthless and all-powerful master of his domain, but his preternaturally preserved flesh wasn't up to the challenge of swimming to shore. He was the Great Night, but he couldn't breathe water, much less tread it for long; with no one to help him, he sank like a stone.

Emmanuel, horrified at the death of the father he feared, and even more terrified of the vengeful slaves, mounted a horse and galloped to town, wild-eyed and frantic with tales of murder and rebellion. He returned fortified by a company of militia, which caught and summarily executed some eight hundred men, women, and children; four hundred slaves were roasted alive, holed up in the barn. Lucas slipped away unnoticed in the chaos.

Silas's body was never found. It wound up entangled and lost, mummified in the muck. But his spirit, and the power of the Great Night, was deathless. And it still needed—*demanded*—to be fed.

20

Friday, August 29. Church of the Open Door.

The story was fantastic to the point of delusion, the implications sending tremors of dreadful memory through the assembled friends. Their anxiety radiated out to everyone in the room, charging the already tense atmosphere.

"This is crazy," Amy said. Her tone was defiantly skeptical, but her eyes said otherwise.

"Not all of it," Seth said, surprising her. His initial anger seemed to have quelled; the look on his face was now fiercely intense. "I've read about a slave uprising," he explained, "mostly obscure Civil War–era texts that sounded more like myth than history. But during the Great Depression, there was an adjunct of the Works Progress Administration called the Federal Writer's Project—the government sent writers around to interview former slaves before they all died off. They interviewed about two thousand of them between 1934 and 1941."

Kevin stepped up, his bureaucratic curiosity piqued. "Are you saying this is public record?"

"Some of it is," Seth replied. "The massacre part, anyway. The accounts never made it into any published work; you have to dig through the original transcripts. But one of them was from a woman who claimed to have survived." He looked at them all gravely. "Her name was Celeste."

"Celeste *Hayes*," Joya amended. "Our great-great-great-grandmother." She indicated Henri, who stepped forward. The sibling resemblance was undeniable. "She survived and handed down the secret of what happened there," Joya told them. "And with it, the secret of the magick."

"Whoa, hang on," Zoe suddenly said. "I thought the magick was bad . . ."

"Not necessarily," Amy said. "It depends on how it's used, and why. Right?" She looked at Joya, who nodded.

"Magick can be used for good or ill," Joya explained. "Silas used it to capture souls. We must use it to free them."

A collective ripple of shock ran through the tiny chapel. But as the concept took root in their imaginations, Caroline's head began shaking from side to side in a mantra of denial, going *no no no no* as if to physically eject the thoughts from her mind. She leaned against the dais upon which the casket lay, hands grasping the burnished brass railing until her knuckles blanched white. Kevin, who was feeling more than a little freaked out himself, moved in to comfort her.

"It's okay," he said.

"No, it's not," she said, angrily twisting away. "It's not even remotely fucking okay." She looked around, laughing caustically.

"Don't tell me you're all buying this!" she said indignantly. "This is all just some sick joke! Another Josh Custis custom head trip!" She looked at Josh. "But this is low, even for you!"

"No," Josh said, his manner radiating earnest urgency. "Caroline, I swear to you . . ."

"FUCK you, Josh!" she spat back. "You've lied to me my whole life! Everything you ever said or did is a lie!" She looked around at the men guarding the windows, at Joya and Henri. "You guys are actors, right? I mean, he paid you to mess with us, right?"

Caroline turned, her eyes wide and darting; their refusal to confess seemed to only inflame her outrage. "And this . . . ," she gestured to the hand lying in the coffin. "What is it, some special effect? Like something out of a cheesy horror movie?"

Everyone was staring at her with varying degrees of caution and compassion, as one might regard a potentially unstable mental case. Then to everyone's horror, Caroline reached into the coffin's interior, grabbing the severed hand by the wrist and hoisting it aloft.

"This isn't real!" she cried. "It's just some battery-powered rubber latex *thing*!"

She held up the hand for all to see.

And then it grabbed her back.

"GET IT OFF ME!" she cried. "GET IT OFF!"

Caroline flailed desperately, panicked and terrified. The hand disengaged, falling to the floor with a dull thud. In the ensuing pandemonium, Caroline grabbed Zoe, literally dragging her down the aisle to the high arched doors.

"Jesus, Mom!" Zoe cried. "Lemme go!"

"NO!" Caroline barked, eyes blazing with an almost feral maternal heat. "We're getting out of here, NOW!"

As they reached the doors, Zoe pulled away; Caroline released her and grabbed the handles. The doors were locked. Caroline whirled, enraged.

"Let us *out* of here!" she cried.

"To go where?" Joya said, her voice carrying over the din of the room. "Back to the world you thought you knew? It doesn't exist. You've been running for twenty years. It's time to stand and face it."

"Face what?" Caroline said, furious.

"The truth," Josh told her. "Ours. And theirs."

As he spoke, Josh moved toward her slowly, carefully; Caroline backed up like a trapped animal, eyes furtively searching for some means of escape. There was nowhere to go. And as suddenly as her rage had erupted, she seemed to wilt before them, as if some critical inner wall had turned to sand and crumbled against the press of an unforgiving tide. Caroline felt the entirety of her meticulously crafted normalcy collapse in the space of one fluttering heartbeat; she sagged and began to quietly sob, the raw pathos of unchained emotion welling up and out to touch them all.

They came to her then: Amy and Seth, Kevin and Josh forming a protective circle around her as Joya and the others watched. Zoe reached out to her mother; Caroline clung to her desperately.

"I'm so sorry," Caroline whispered, hugging her.

"It's okay," Zoe said, returning the embrace. "It's okay . . ."

But of course it wasn't, and they all knew it. As they helped Caroline to a seat in the pews, Josh nodded to Joya, who had retrieved Justin's hand and placed it carefully back in the casket. Caroline caught a glimpse of it and shuddered.

"Is that really him?" she began. "How is that even possible?"

"Justin used the magick to cross over," Josh explained. "But they tried to stop him, and something went wrong, and now here we are."

"Who tried to stop him?" Seth asked.

"My family," Josh replied bitterly, sounding both defiant and more than a little ashamed. "They're trying to use the power, and the magick, for their own sick fucking reasons. Justin volunteered to try and get a message through . . ." Josh paused, weighing his next words. "And he wanted to see Mia . . ."

"Say what?" Seth said. They looked at him, stunned.

"But Mia is dead," Caroline blurted. "She's been dead for twenty years . . ."

Josh looked at her and shook his head. And then proceeded to explain the tangled web fate had woven for them all.

21

Custis Manor. Underworld.

For Mia, it all happened in a heartbeat: one moment she was drugged and dying, falling backward into the mirror as Justin broke a chair over Simon's head. There was a jagged split second between, where her lover's face burned into her retinas like the image in an antique photograph. Then something grabbed her from behind, and she felt herself enveloped by cold, liquid dark. For one brief infinity's span, she existed in neither world. Then oblivion receded in a wash, leaving her afraid to move, afraid to even open her eyes. And she felt herself transported, carried bodily into a netherworld deep and dark, like a bad dream from which there was no awakening. Mia felt the last dregs of her strength drain away as the darkness swept over her.

And then, nothingness.

Mia groaned weakly.

Shhhhhh. A hand touched her forehead. She opened her eyes, saw that she was lying in a tiny shack on a small wooden bed, ropes strung in lattice to a pegged frame, with a bare straw mattress. A man was kneeling before her on the earthen floor. His skin was the color of polished onyx. His dark features were sharp and regal, his eyes ice blue, at once piercing and infinitely kind.

Be still, the black man said as he stood and moved toward a small, rough-hewn table. He was thin but powerfully built, all sinew and lean muscle, wearing a loose white shirt and black breeches. His skin glowed in the light of the low hearth fire.

Mia shivered and brought a hand up to cover her eyes. There was a great puckering gash in the palm. It gaped bloodlessly. The skin was pale and papyrus thin. She held her hand up in horror; she could actually see firelight sparkling through it, as though the molecular substructure were breaking apart.

What's happening to me? she asked, terrified. She tried to sit up, fell back, trembling and weak. The black man returned with a small metal cup.

Drink, he said urgently, placing the vessel to her lips. The liquid was warm, with a coppery taint; and though there was a moment of repulsion, it quickly gave way to appetite.

Mia drained the cup, the liquid sluicing through her and carrying with it a feeling of strength, of wholeness. Her savior took the cup from her hands.

Sleep, he said.

It was some infinite time later that Mia came back to consciousness. Her mind felt somewhat clearer, her thoughts less fragmented. She looked around. A low fire burned in the hearth of the shack, its wan light making the shadows seem to pulse and writhe.

Mia sat up on the bed. There was a small and curtainless window behind her. She could make out a glimpse of angry sky, black veined with blood red. Mustering all her strength, she stood on the cold dirt floor and cautiously peered outside.

Oh my God, she gasped.

Custis Manor sprawled before her like a Boschian nightmare come to hideous life. The mansion squatted, dark and foreboding, mist clinging to its columns and stretching across its surface like tumorous ganglia. More tendrils of mist rose up and twisted into the sky like a pus-colored spike pinning the house to the earth. In the distance, she could see phantom slaves stooping under the whips of demonic overseers. The moans of those who died under the lash were clearly audible, their suffering endless.

Mia heard a strange rumbling, mixed with the sounds of coarse, animal baying; as she watched, the spirits of those who had died trying to escape were run down by ghostly hounds that howled and savaged them. All seemed oblivious to anything outside their final, fatal patterns. Indeed, as she looked closer she saw deep, shadowy pits where their eyes should be.

A whirlwind howled in the distance, corkscrewing down from the roiling heavens. Coming closer.

Get back, a voice suddenly sounded behind her. Mia turned to see her benefactor emerging from the shadowed interior of the shack. As he pulled her back from the window, the storm blew past, bringing with it, and within it, the rumble of horses and the rattle of sabers, mixed with raging, inhuman cries. Mia watched in shock.

What are they? she asked.

Ghost riders, he replied. As they watched, phantoms of Confederate militia swirled and swarmed over rebelling slaves, murdering and being murdered in turn as the spirits fought their blind, eternal battle, locked in terrible, terminal embrace. The wind howled around and through them. And then, as quickly as it came, it was gone.

Mia trembled in the ensuing silence. *Oh God,* she whispered. *I have to wake up now . . . Please let me wake up . . .*

I cannot, the man said. His voice was soft, genteel and cultured. *It is a nightmare, but not a dream . . .* He looked at her, a terrible sadness in his eyes.

Mia wavered, feeling suddenly dizzy. The mysterious black man helped her to the little bed, pulled a rough and threadbare woolen blanket up to cover her. As she lay back, he regarded her curiously.

What is your name? he asked.

Mia, she replied.

I am Lucas, he said, a grim and strangely sad smile crossing his lips. *Welcome to Underworld* . . .

Mia visibly flinched. His words were shocking, but his every gesture was the soul of tenderness.

I don't understand, she confessed, trembling.

You will, he told her, then added: *Rest now. You will need your strength.*

Mia felt herself slipping away, back into the strange and heavy blackness. As her eyes fluttered, she saw him stand and gaze out the little window, and he murmured something else. She couldn't quite make it out.

But she thought it was, *And so will they* . . .

Time passed strangely there, not so much in a straight line as in whirls and eddies. It was as if the plantation were caught in some stagnant continuum, its inhabitants lost in the throes of a collective fever dream.

In the distance, the whirlwind would rage on its obscure course, revolving around its own vortex of death and despair. Mia saw the great barn burn in the distance, shrieks of agony filtering through the spectral roar as rebel slaves were roasted alive by marauding militia. The thin air would stink of scorched wood and blistered flesh. Then the maelstrom would sweep up and away again. And the vision would be gone.

They are trapped, Lucas explained. *Forever chained to their fear and suffering.*

Is that what we are? she asked, very much fearing the answer. *Are we trapped?* But Lucas shook his head.

Then why? Mia asked. *Why are we in this terrible place?* Anger and sadness flared in his eyes.

As long as they remain, he said, *I cannot go. They must be freed.*

But how? she asked.

Soon, he replied. *When you are stronger . . .*

Bit by bit, Lucas nursed her back to something like health. She was weak at first, lapsing into deep periods of unconsciousness in which she had terrifying visions of her family and friends: growing older, moving on, living lives without her . . . and of Justin, the look of terror on his face as he watched her disappear . . .

In the real world, her wounds would have been fatal. The deep slashes across her torso made breathing the thin and vaporous air difficult, the sensation only abating briefly after drinking from the cup Lucas always brought. Gradually, her strength returned.

The next time she awakened, her wounds had faded. The time after that, they were gone.

Your last moments in the manor, Lucas said as she drank. *What do you recall?*

Mia didn't know how to answer, or how to explain the drugs, the party, the chaos and carnage that ensued. So she answered in the most elemental way.

I remember pain, she said. She paused. *And I remember the mirror . . .*

Lucas nodded. *Every mirror is a doorway,* he explained. *This is what the bruja teaches . . . this is how the magick works.*

Bruja? she asked.

Sorceress, he explained. *I learned the way of power through her, and I used it to save you, stealing you through in the moment before Death could claim you.*

Mia thought of those last fearful moments. *Am I alive or dead?* she asked.

Both, he replied. *And neither. We are body and soul in the spirit realm.*

But just as spirits are unseen inhabitants of the material world, we are unseen to them. They can sense your presence, but they will not be able to find you . . . He paused gravely. *So long as you feed.*

Something in the way he said the last word chilled her. Mia looked at the cup and felt a burning desire for more of the potion that sustained her.

What is this? she asked.

Lucas looked at her and produced a razor-sharp blade, then lifted his shirtsleeve. Before her eyes, he sliced open his arm, black blood flowing out in gleaming rivulets. As the cup filled, the incision sparkled and closed. She looked at his arm.

There was no wound.

Lucas held out the cup to her. Mia looked at him and began to violently retch.

No, she gasped. *Oh no . . .* She was horrified both at what she had consumed and at the realization that, though her mind recoiled, her body craved more.

What have you done to me? she asked.

Lucas looked away and did not answer. But Mia saw the look in his eyes, and it frightened her.

It is a matter of survival, he explained. *You need blood to hold your physical self together in the spirit realm. To keep from becoming trapped like the others.*

Again he offered the cup to her. Mia took it, hands trembling, and drank. Repulsed at first. Then greedily.

As she finished, she threw the cup down in disgust and started to cry. Lucas picked it up.

I'm sorry, he told her.

If I feed on you, she asked bitterly, *what do you feed on?*

You don't want to know, he said.

Lucas looked at her gravely, then away. *When I first came here, I fed on the dark and slithering things in the swamp. Then I fed on . . . other things.* He paused and stared out the little window, a shadow of revulsion

139

passing over his dark features. *And after a time, I did not have to feed at all.*

He looked back. Mia met his gaze, her voice tremulous. *I'm scared,* she told him. *I want to go home . . .*

Lucas looked at her, his eyes deep and unnervingly clear.

So do they, he said.

22

Lucas led Mia through dark and murky woods to a spot on the far edge of the hellish grounds. Mia picked her way through the nightmare landscape carefully, her senses attenuated to the absolute strangeness of all she saw. The manor had receded to a distant and foreboding glow; the thickets of surrounding trees were spindly and ashen, their branches knitting together overhead like skeletal fingers. She dared not look for too long though, as when she did Lucas was quickly enfolded in shadow, making her feel entirely too alone. She moved faster, hastening to keep up.

Where are you taking me? she asked.

Shhhhh, he hushed her. *You will see . . .*

Lucas led her onward, then stopped and looked up. *We're here,* he said. Mia followed his gaze and gasped.

A body was hanged and dangling overhead: a pathetic, wasted stick figure twisting in the grip of rough hemp ropes. Its hands were gone, hacked off just above the wrists. Its skin was the color of leather and potash, covered in gray and crusted sores. Its limbs were shriveled and shrunken, the face sunken and grimacing. It looked dead, and in a just universe it would be.

But still it *moved:* weakly writhing, tormented. It was alive, if barely, and in pain beyond measure.

Oh God, Mia exclaimed. She stumbled backward and tripped, falling to the ground. As she got up, she turned and saw others, spaced every few yards in either direction, as far as the eye could see.

Mia shuddered violently. Then she noticed that not all the clothing was period, and indeed some of it was astonishingly contemporary. And she realized: she wasn't the first person Lucas had brought body and soul to this place, and the others hadn't fared so well.

This is why you brought me here? she cried. *To end up like them?*

Before she could cry out again, Lucas grabbed her, one hand covering her mouth, the other forcing her to the ground, his weight pressing her down into the loamy earth. She started to thrash . . .

. . . and then she heard the rabid, snarling growls coming from the stand of trees just off to the left. She froze, looking up at Lucas, and saw his eyes go slit thin, scanning the tree line. The snarling grew louder. And suddenly, they were not alone.

There were two of them: squat, hideous creatures with bandy legs and monstrous gravid bellies, lurching through the underbrush, led by their beasts. They were pop-eyed and porcine, pocked skin giving way to thin wisps of hair speckling their scalps and shoulders like grease-fire victims. Their arms were long and knobby, ending in large-knuckled hands with grotesquely long fingers. Each carried a coiled bullwhip and a long pike. One carried a lantern, its green glow sickly bobbing.

The beasts that strained before them complemented their masters completely: hides blotched, scarred from countless battles. Huge jaws gaped from tiny skulls, exposing tongues that dripped with foam. Sharp and uneven teeth glinted beneath their red and lidless eyes.

The guards grunted and muttered. One hound snarled and leapt as it passed a hanging wraith in a Gatsby-era dress, snatching a stray leg in its maw like a demonic chew-toy. There was a sickening snap as the of-fending limb came off; the beast worried it like a fetched stick.

Mia and Lucas stayed down as the guards passed, stayed down until their lamp was but a tiny bobbing green light receding into the distance. Lucas released her and they stood.

Guardians, he explained. *Servants of the Great Night, given wholly over to the darkness here.*

Uh-huh, Mia said, and nodded as if he had just said the most reasonable thing in the world; she kept nodding as her legs went suddenly rubbery beneath her. Lucas caught her as she started to fall, and gently eased her down. He kneeled before her.

You must understand, he implored her. *Had I not taken you when I did, you would have been lost, your spirit forever in the Great Night's grasp.*

What about them? she murmured, indicating the lost and writhing victims hanging from the trees. Lucas looked away shamefully.

I cannot, he said quietly, his voice melding with the rustle of trees and twisting hemp. *Not without revealing our presence. But every one of them knew the risks. And they went willingly.*

Why? she asked bitterly. *What could possibly be worth that?*

Come. Lucas held out his hand. *I'll show you.*

The ghost of the slave shambled down the path leading to the wharf when Lucas grabbed him. At his touch, the shade began to thrash blindly. The phantom was both horrid and tragic: its face gaunt and grimacing, its eyes sunken, withered pits. Mia watched as Lucas pressed it to the ground and ripped the shade's shirt open, exposing its scarred, scrawny chest. Extending one finger, he drew a line down the center of the slave's breastbone, like a surgeon wielding a scalpel. The shade went instantly rigid. The line began to pulse, then to glow a dull and angry red. Parting the luminous fissure, Lucas stuck his hand deep into the body cavity, working his way inside.

The shade took a great gasping breath as twin sparks of light went off in its shriveled eye sockets. Its entire body went limp as Lucas pulled his hand out. There was no wound. No scar. Lucas slumped back, visibly spent from the psychic surgery.

143

What is your name? he asked.

T-Thomas, the shade replied in a voice as faint as the rustle of dry, dead leaves. Thomas looked around, weak and confused. *Where'm ah?*

You're dead, Thomas, Lucas told him. *I'm sorry.*

The shade shivered; a teardrop the color of quicksilver trickled down its cheek. *Ah wanna leave dis place,* it whispered, terrified. *Please lemme go . . .*

Lucas took Thomas by the arm. *You will,* he said.

And though he spoke to the ghost, his gaze never left Mia's face.

And that was when she truly understood: it was an ethereal underground railroad, smuggling souls to freedom. Lucas looked at her. *Can you help?* he asked, then confessed: *I cannot do it alone . . .*

Mia met his gaze, her own terror matched by the feeling that, ghastly as this place was, and despite her own fear, she could not turn a blind eye to the suffering here. She nodded hesitantly.

Lucas smiled. *Thank you,* he said.

Lucas led them to a trap-door hideout beneath the smokehouse. Seven more souls were secreted there: four field hands worked to death one hot summer; a fourteen-year-old girl who'd been raped and strangled by Luther, the head overseer; a runaway who'd been ripped to pieces by hounds; and a nanny who'd been beaten to death with a fireplace poker by Emmanuel's wife simply for sleeping while the mistress's newborn baby cried.

The spark that glowed dimly in their eyes flared when the door opened. Silently, wordlessly, Lucas led them through the swampy woods that ringed the plantation. Mia brought up the rear, wading waist-deep through stygian waters, watching for the ghastly overseers. Wet things brushed against her skin and slithered between her legs; she said nothing and kept her mind fixed on the faint swish of water as they moved.

Eventually they came to the grisly boundary. Beyond them the woods lay thick with mist. The guards were dangerously thick too, as no sooner did one lantern disappear into the distance than another bobbed into sight.

How do we get past them? she asked.

Lucas opened his shirt in response, his fingers drawing down and penetrating his own chest to withdraw an ethereal gossamer thread that pulsed with the beat of his life force. He held it out to her.

Take this, he said.

Mia hesitated, then took it in hand . . .

. . . and instantly she felt a rush of energy pulse through her, and with it a sense of connectedness: pain and passion and sheer purpose swirling in and through her, infusing her and filling her with heat. Her eyes fluttered and she almost fainted; when she opened them again, he was gazing at her intently.

On my signal, he said, *send them one by one. Then follow . . .*

Mia nodded; Lucas crossed the boundary and was promptly swallowed by the swirling mist.

A moment later, a guard lumbered into view, leading another of the monstrous beasts; the creature paused, sniffing the air, and growled. The guard looked around suspiciously, wandering toward them. Thomas and the other shades trembled fearfully; Mia reached out and touched his thin and brittle shoulder, fiercely willing herself to remain calm.

The guard peered into the darkness, porcine nostrils flaring once, then again. Then, grunting, it yanked on the chain of the beast and pulled it onward.

Mia watched until it was safely out of range, then felt the ethereal thread in her hand pulse. It was time. She took Thomas's hand and placed it on the thread. As she did, the same rush seemed to pass through the wasted spirit; Thomas trembled under the force of it.

Go, she urged. *Now.*

She helped him up, and he followed the thread, picking his way through the enveloping mist until he too was gone from view. The thread pulsed in her hand as Mia turned to the next spirit, the girl.

145

What's your name? she asked.

M-Mary . . ., the spirit replied, the sparks in the shadowed pits of her eyes flaring.

Take this, Mary, Mia said. *Follow Thomas. You'll be all right.*

The girl nodded, terrified, and went. Mia watched intently, and then led the next shade, then the next, and the next, to the cord. One after another, she sent them over. And with each passing soul, she felt her own connection grow. To the lost souls. To Lucas. To his passion. And his mission.

The last shade stood, moving through the tree line and into mist that parted like a veil.

Another lantern suddenly appeared. Coming closer. Mia stared into the mist, watching the last slave disappear. It was her turn. The lantern came closer. It was now or never. Mia took a deep breath, and went . . .

. . . and there was a moment of threatened madness as Mia headed into the enfolding mist, trading the quantifiable horror of where she'd been for the absolute terror of the unknown. Time and space played tricks, distorting and stretching, disassembling and reassembling over and over. Mia clutched the cord and fought unconsciousness as nausea and vertigo swirled like a rising tide. She blacked out . . .

. . . then snapped back to find herself standing in the middle of a dirt road cutting through living green trees. The roiling sky was gone, and above them the heavens were clear and filled with countless billions of stars.

Lucas was there, steadying her. As she regained her bearings, he bid her watch as first one, then another, and another slave stood, staring at him. Lucas gestured to the stars and nodded.

Thomas was again first. He looked at the sky, and the others followed suit, gazing up into the heavens, then back to Lucas.

Ah kin go? Thomas asked, his voice trembling with wonder. *We kin all go?*

You're free, Lucas replied. *You're all free. Go home . . .*

The enslaved spirits nodded in thanks . . .

. . . and one by one, the pinpoints of light in their eyes glowed bright, until they rivaled the stars themselves. Then they flashed, nova white, as their souls flew up into the vaulted night.

And they were gone.

Their remains stood abandoned for a moment, then crumbled: useless husks turning to dust before their eyes. Lucas turned to Mia.

Now do you see? he asked.

There are thousands more. Too many for one or even two to save. Lucas pointed down the long, dark road. *Go,* he told her. *Bring someone who knows how to work the magick. Bring help . . .*

Mia nodded, still dazed and amazed by it all. She took several hesitant steps, turned to ask him. *But how . . . ?*

But Lucas was not there.

23

She walked for what felt like forever, utterly alone on a road that stretched into darkness as far as she could see. Framed on both sides by tall pine and fir, on a dirt ribbon extending into infinite black, the night was endless, brilliant with stars. Mia moved in what felt like a dream state, so smooth that it seemed she glided. She felt strangely at peace, euphoric and filled with a sense of purpose.

After a time, a glow appeared on the horizon, harsh against the velvet darkness. As she approached, it became clear, familiar, weirdly comforting. Suddenly Mia stopped.

Oh my God, she realized. *I'm home.*

The garish fluorescent flicker of a 7-Eleven sign shone before her. Unoccupied cars were parked outside, some with the motors still running. A police cruiser was pulled up before the open doors. Inside, the store was brightly lit, but no one was behind the counter, and no customers were visible in the aisles.

"Hello?" Mia called out nervously. "Is anyone here?"

There was no answer. Something moved just out of her field of vision, and she turned to see a solitary figure lingering near the beer case two aisles over, staring wistfully at the refrigerated contents. She moved toward him cautiously.

"Excuse me," she said. "Can you help me?"

The man at the beer cooler paid her no heed. Mia moved down the aisle, anxious and a little annoyed. "Hello?" she said.

The man continued to ignore her; he was young, grimy and disheveled, dressed in a rumpled flannel shirt and a baseball cap. She wondered if he was deaf, drunk, or just plain rude. He turned and stared blankly at her for a moment, and then looked over her shoulder and smiled as if in acknowledgment. Mia followed his gaze to the counter. Another man was there, this one older, middle-aged and balding, clad in what looked like a hospital gown. The man reached up to the racks of cigarettes hanging overhead. Then something caught her eye, and she looked up and past the counter to the concave security mirror mounted near the ceiling.

She gasped.

People, an entire store full of them, were cruising the aisles. The older man was not visible behind the counter; in his place a young Vietnamese employee rang up the register for a pair of black men buying Bud and munchies, as a gaggle of jocks and their dates joked and jostled by the Slurpee machine and a pair of cops scored capuccino and donuts. It was a store full of living people, leading ordinary mortal lives.

On the other *side of the glass.*

Mia felt her heart suddenly race in disoriented panic; she lunged toward the counter and the mirror. From behind her came the low and guttural sound of laughter.

Mia looked back to see the man at the cooler watching her. He leered and nodded, bobbling forward. As he rounded the end of the low aisle, she realized he had no legs below the knees, only wisps trailing off like an unfinished drawing. His body hovered impudently above the grimy tile.

Mia gasped and looked at the cigarette man behind the counter. As he turned, she saw that one entire side of his jaw was gone, a gaping, cancerous hole darkly beckoning. His eyes were red-rimmed and wet and looked very sad. He turned his back to her, flaccid ass cheeks drooping from the back of the smock, as he pawed impotently at the shiny glassine wrappings, unable to pick them up.

Two more lost souls, trapped by their attachments to the living world.

The world, it appeared, was full of them.

Mia fled, desperately heading for home, for family and friends, for something real and familiar. The only problem was, nothing was. The wide-open fields and pastures she remembered were now crowded with housing developments, shopping centers that had sprung up seemingly overnight, roads and schools where none had been before. She reached the edge of her neighborhood, a quaint suburban development named Fairfield. Her family had moved there when it first started, a smattering of plush homes plunked down in an old strawberry patch. Now it was vast, the formerly empty acres studded with baby mansions. She found her old house and made her way to the front door. She pounded on it; there was no response.

Mom, Dad! she called out plaintively. *Help me!*

No one answered. Light glowed from the dining-room window; Mia rushed to the edge of the porch and peered inside. A young family she'd never seen before was seated at the table. Mia screamed and pounded on the glass. No one could hear her. Her home, her family, was gone.

And she, it seemed, was trapped—on a plane somewhere between the hell of Custis Manor and the living world.

Mia backed up, completely freaking out. She felt utterly alone, fearful beyond measure. And that was when her thoughts turned to Justin.

By the time Mia reached Justin's place, a new feeling had arisen, matching and besting her dread: hunger. It was a boundless, gnawing need that coursed through her like liquid razor blades in her veins.

Mia made her way to Justin's, stood at the address. Justin's rundown house had been erased, every trace of it razed and replaced by a Mc-Donald's and a little strip mall with stores advertising tanning booths and real estate. It was as if it, and he, never were.

Oh God, she thought. *What's happened? Where is he? How long have I been gone?* There was a vending machine in front of the McDonald's, selling brightly colored editions of *USA Today.* She scanned for the date and felt herself go cold.

Eighteen years? Mia was aghast. Eighteen years, a span of time as long as her entire life up until that last fateful night, had gone by in what seemed one long, never-ending nightmare.

Mia desperately needed to find somebody who knew what had happened to her. And who might be able to do something about it.

And she could only think of one.

The beach house still said CUSTIS on the mailbox, and for that Mia was glad. The house was the same, yet subtly changed. There was an enormous television set, the likes of which she'd never seen before, three inches thick and hung from the wall like a painting.

A sleek Bang & Olufsen stereo system stood in one corner of the room. Just then a gaunt, intense man entered the room, a glass of scotch in hand. He crossed to a rack of small, boxed discs, touched a button on the stereo and fed a shiny disc into the extended slot. The room suddenly filled with music: lush, lovely, familiar. The Police. *Ghost in the Machine.*

Mia drew close to the window, heart pounding, afraid to say something, afraid not to. The man grabbed his glass, turned toward the windows facing the sea. He looked up, and his jaw promptly dropped. Followed immediately by his drink.

What happened to his hair? was Mia's first, absurd thought. His long locks were gone, replaced by a cropped coif receding into a widow's peak. But the face, and the eyes . . .

No doubt about it. It was Josh. Decades older but still Josh. It was amazing.

Even more amazing was the simple dawning fact that he apparently saw her too.

Josh stood before the window, unable to believe his eyes. He had been feeling weird for days: like something was scratching at a door in the back of his mind, wanting to crawl in. Everything had been going so well; he had long since gotten his life together, come to a state of balance that allowed him to function. His writing had taken off: a string of successful supernatural thrillers with subsequent movie sales that brought him fiscal independence from his family. His health was good. Even his bitter relationship with his father had softened somewhat, at least on the surface, as Josh's own star rose.

And then, in the middle of it all, the thoughts of Mia began coming. Vivid, recurring, they nagged at him: invading his sleep, filling his waking moments. He began drinking, trying to dull the feeling. He knew it was dangerous to get back into drugs or alcohol; the long years spent clawing his way back to sanity had taught him how precious his precarious mental balance was, how desperately he needed its mooring if he wanted to survive. Had they not taken that acid years ago—had Simon not spiked them, committing that unspeakably stupid act that had led to all this suffering—God only knew how much easier his life could have been. Justin might not have wasted his life away in prison. And Mia might still be alive.

He shook his head, feeling indulgent and stupid. Feeling like the crazy they had always accused him of being.

And then the vision appeared.

At first it was but a flicker of light and shadow, a momentary trick of the eyes. Then the form emerged: shimmering, ethereal.

"Mia . . ." he murmured. He felt like he was tripping again. He blinked, blinked again. "Mia, is that you?"

The vision looked at him and nodded, her mouth silently moving.

And in that moment all the years of fighting—his father, his brother, his shrinks, anyone and everyone who'd ever sought to tell him that what happened wasn't real, had never really happened at all—all those years of struggle came slamming home.

She hadn't aged. Her skin was translucent, as if lit from within, and almost transparent in places. She looked like an angel, or a hallucination. Then she smiled, and he knew: this was no dream. He moved toward her image, brought his hand up to touch it. She did likewise. As their fingertips met, there was a loud crack as the two opposing fields of energy united. Blue-white sparks skittered inside its surface, the atomic substructure of the glass rippling.

The glass shattered. Josh recoiled, half expecting a razored rain to fall. But it held, a thousand glittering shards kept in place as if by some obscure loophole in the laws of physics. A smear of blood graced the jagged, spiderwebbed striations.

Mia saw it and her eyes flared; she reached up from her side to touch the surface of the glass. The blood sucked through the cracks and came away on her fingertips. She brought it to her lips, and two things happened. Mia became instantly more substantial. And the cracks in the glass begin to mend.

Josh watched, stunned, as the cracks simply *withdrew*, drawing back to the impact point. Mia looked at him, her form more stabilized. But the hunger still burned in her eyes.

And as he watched, she seemed to phase in and then out of focus. As if she were slipping away . . .

"Noooo!" Josh cried, placing his still-bleeding hand to the freshly re-formed glass. She reached out in kind, and as her fingers touched the glass the blood sucked right through. With every new drop she seemed to solidify, become that much more stable. Josh opened his hand and smeared gore all over the window, watched in fascination as Mia fed.

She tried to speak; but though her lips moved, Josh could hear no words, only a high-pitched ringing deep in his inner ear.

"I can't hear you . . .," he cried. "I don't understand . . ."

Mia paused, then raised one delicate finger and began to write on the glass: her movements languid and surreal, as if she were moving underwater. The first word appeared as a glowing cryptograph.

Justin? it said.

Josh looked away uncomfortably.

"Prison," he said. "I haven't seen him in years."

Her expression filled with immense sadness and pain. His name faded, disappeared. She wrote again.

Need help . . .

Josh nodded, feeling enervated and more than a little mad. "What can I do?" he asked. Mia wrote again.

Magick.

They conversed for as long as they could; it took too much effort, not to mention blood, to maintain contact. Josh felt tapped: his mind reeling, his flesh bled to the danger point. Her image was fading, going two-dimensional and diffuse, like a badly lit hologram. She wrote again with great difficulty.

Back soon.

Josh's blood ran cold. "No, don't go!" he cried.

But Mia merely smiled and then flickered and faded away, leaving Josh to the task of finding someone who knew the secret of the magick. And how to use it.

part three
underground

24

Friday, August 29. Church of the Open Door.

For a moment there was silence, as Josh's captive audience allowed the ramifications of the story to sink in.

"I know this all sounds crazy," he told them. "I didn't want to believe it myself. But she came again about six months later, and I couldn't deny it anymore."

Amy looked at him. "Six months?" she said. "Josh, how long have you known about this?"

"Two years," Josh replied. "She first came to me two years ago tonight."

A collective gasp sounded amongst his friends. "After I accepted it, I started digging into my family's history," he continued, "and suddenly all kinds of things started to make a perverse kind of sense."

"Like what?" Zoe asked.

"Like why my mother—and all the women who married into the family, for that matter—ended up crazy, or dead, or both," he replied. "And why the house was sanitized and turned into a historical site."

"Why is that?" Seth asked.

It was then that Joya Hayes stepped in. "To protect it," she said. The look on her face was deadly calm and all the more frightening for it.

"You may not want to believe any of this. But deep down, you all know it's true."

Neither Caroline nor Amy nor Seth could argue the point. Josh stepped in, immediately trying to solidify their fragile resolve.

"When I first told Justin, he didn't believe me either," he said. "Until I introduced him to Joya and Henri, and they showed him how to work the magick. Then he understood. And he knew what he had to do. Justin went back to let them know that we were coming. Unfortunately, he got intercepted. But he's over there, and he's still alive. They're waiting for us."

"To do what?" Zoe asked.

"End it," he said. "Once and for all."

His friends looked around at the men guarding the windows, at Josh and Joya, at Henri and Louis. They all nodded.

"What do you mean?" Seth asked incredulously. The others echoed the sentiment to varying degrees. Josh smiled, an odd light sparkling in his eyes.

"Tonight we're going back to Custis Manor," he told his old friends, "and we're burning the fucker to the ground from the inside out. And because it's quite possible that we won't see each other again, I needed to explain to you what was happening. I feel like you all deserved to know. I'm sorry for misleading you. I hope you can forgive me."

He paused. And for the first time, the others noticed his hands were shaking.

"So you brought us all here just to tell us this," Seth said, as though sensing that somewhere another shoe was waiting to drop.

"Yes," Josh replied. "And to invite you to help."

Amy blanched; Caroline looked like she might just faint. Seth just rolled his eyes.

"I knew it," he said bitterly. "You're playing us."

At that point Louis looked at Seth. "You of all people should understand, brother."

"Understand what?" Seth replied. "That you lunatics want to get us all killed? I'm sorry for what happened there. Not a day of my life goes by when I don't try very hard to deal with that. But what can we possibly do about it?"

"More than you know," Josh replied. Joya backed him up.

"What happened there has been going on for generations," she said. "Others have tried and failed. But you," and with that she indicated the members of the erstwhile Underground, "you experienced the wrath of the Great Night and *survived.* That's never happened before. We don't know what it means. But it's a chance, one we've never had before. And the more of you that are there, the better."

"Maybe the drugs pried open some chemical door that somehow allowed us to survive," Josh added. "Maybe it was something else about us. I don't know. I just know this: if we try to stop it, we might lose, but if we don't, it will win. And then God help us all."

And there it was—a chance, however slim, to actually do something about human suffering, to help rectify a centuries-old injustice. And to repay an old debt to a friend who needed them, now more than ever.

At this point, Kevin was way more than ready to gather up his family and beat it back to Baltimore. As far as he was concerned, every weird thing he ever heard about Josh Custis had proven true: the man was a certifiable lunatic. Unfortunately, Kevin's family did not share this view.

Caroline was not only stunned but seemed suddenly hooked by the notion that Mia and Justin could still be alive. What's worse, Zoe was totally caught up in Josh: his story, his persona, everything about him. She was not about to miss out on it.

There was a similar conflict between Amy—who came knowingly into danger, though she didn't know its form—and Seth, who had no intention of leaving behind a widow at this stage in his life. Fascinated though he was, he was all for leaving now. Before it was too late.

Unfortunately for them, it already was.

25

It was about this time that Louis Hillyard decided he had just about had it with whiny white people.

Bad enough that they had relied upon a burnout like Justin Van Slyke to be point man on their operation; worse still that both Joya and Henri seemed hell-bent on trusting Josh Custis to not only fund their efforts but to get them into the manor. As far as Louis was concerned, Josh's name alone not only disqualified him from any position of trust but rendered him a figure of instant suspicion, to be summarily dealt with at the first sign of betrayal. But then to further stake the outcome of their efforts on the willing participation of a yuppie, a junkie, and a goddamned Oreo . . .

It was beyond stupid. It was a recipe for disaster.

Not that Louis trusted the rest of the team all that much more, and his misgivings were more than skin deep. Louis had a vast and bitter skepticism to go with his innate solidarity for his kind. Born to the bad avenues of Oakland, California, on February 21, 1965, Louis grew up in a time when giants walked the earth, as the clarion calls of Malcolm and Martin stirred the passions of a people long denied and for a fleeting moment it seemed that revolution and deliverance were not only possible but inevitable. From earliest memory his mother reminded him that his first proud cry of life came at 3:10 p.m., the exact minute that Malcolm fell at the Audubon Ballroom stage in Harlem. To her this was a sign of near-cosmic significance; to Louis, it was a ten-ton weight levied upon his young soul.

He grew up fed by Black Panther free breakfasts and had learned their Ten-Point Program practically before his ABC's, as Huey and Bobby duked it out with everyone from the local cops to Governor Reagan to Hoover's COINTELPRO thugs. But by the time he reached manhood, the movement had withered, eroded from within by infighting, stress, and conflict, and from without by indifference and the simple attrition of life. Revolution, it seemed, made for great theory but poor practice: it took too long and cost too hard, and even the most glorious of goals—full employment and guaranteed income, an end to oppression and all wars of capitalist aggression, demands for land, bread, housing, education, clothing, justice, and peace—seemed more like a wish list of crypto-Marxist fantasy than any kind of workable plan; nice gig if you could get it, but don't hold your breath waiting. And as long as the "or else" part of the bargain was measured in white men's guns and money, the dream seemed destined for failure.

One day he realized that even Momma's prophesies of his own importance had failed to account for the simple difference between East Coast and West Coast time. But Louis never had the heart to point that out.

After Momma died, Louis drifted away, his anger burrowing ever deeper. He hated the white culture he grew up under the yoke of but had come to loathe his own culture as well, replete as it was with con men, charlatans, gangsters, and fools. Even his admiration for the Panthers withered in the face of the split into warring camps, with Cleaver's hard-edged black nationalism on the one side and Newton's social-reformist idealism on the other, coupled with rumors of an opportunistic and increasing reign of terror inflicted on even the lowliest rank-and-file believers: turning girls out to do tricks for the most meager of "infractions" against the revolutionary order, running extortion rackets against Oakland's pimps, dealers, clubs, and bars, and even flat-out murders—a troublesome Berkeley nightclub owner found dead in his car at the San Francisco airport, straying members shot, stabbed, or OD'd into oblivion, or Betty Van Patter, the Panther's white bookkeeper, turning up dead after being summoned to a meeting at the Lamp Post bar, where Huey used to like to hang.

Little was proven; no one seemed to care about the sundry extinguishments of lesser lights. But Louis found himself put off by it all, increasingly alone and at odds with the world, making his way through the belly of the great white beast, assiduously avoiding anything that could result in arrest and imprisonment, even joining the army in a perverse bout of personal, youthful rebellion. He learned weapons. He learned discipline in the face of an omnipresent enemy. But above all, he learned to trust no one.

And then he met Joya and Henri. And they explained to him the secret of Custis Manor, and the magick.

The very notion of it stirred a profound sense of calling in Louis's soul. Most of the problems that plagued his people he could do little to nothing about, short of sacrificing himself to some unforeseen and bitter end. But this . . . impossible as it seemed, he had resolved to do something about it. Or die trying.

As for the others—Louis knew Henri was a brother to be trusted; Henri's two young homes, Khalil and Russell, rode in on Henri's say-so and had performed admirably both in their first foray to the manor and in their subsequent arrest and interrogation at the police station. That was comforting, but he still wondered how they would fare when the spraying they were called upon to do turned from acrylic to lead.

Which left him with Mohammed and Rajim: a pair of wannabe badass knuckleheads if ever there were. Louis had seen more than his fair share in the army and on the streets: young bloods all pumped up on anger and testosterone, looking for someone or something at which to aim all that displaced rage. He trusted them about as much as he believed in their Muslim trappings, regardless of how many *Asalaam*

Alaikums they mumbled; he bought it about as much as he believed in the militant Stars of David they wore, along with Mohammed's half-baked rap about how blacks were the true Chosen people and the real tribe of Israel, or Yisrael, or Shabaaz, or some such conveniently righteous crap. He had plumbed the arcane convolutions of the Nation of Islam, which shored up racial pride by invoking tales of how whites were a race of devils genetically engineered some six thousand years ago by a black demigod named Yakub for the express purpose of torturing everyone with their ungodliness; of course, the teachings also prophesied a cosmic mothership manned by African supermen that would lob nukes from outer space in fulfillment of some bastardized prophecy, but that was just a little too L. Ron Hubbard for his tastes. Louis never failed to marvel at the lengths to which people would go to find something worth believing in. Himself included.

For him, the real wild card in all of this was Joya, and her power to work the magick. He had no doubt she had power, but the closer they got to their mission the more he worried how it would weather a stand-up fight. At this point, Louis was half inclined to say fuck the magick and rely upon his own abilities to rectify history. Like say with twenty kilos of C-4.

Louis looked across the room, taking in the small and pitifully inexperienced gathering. As his attention turned to Rajim, his hackles went up. Rajim was supposed to be guarding the rectory door.

But he was not there.

"Motherfucker," he muttered. Louis crossed from his post by the front door to the entrance to the rectory. He opened the door and gazed down the hallway. To the left was a small, cramped office, to the right the door to the bathroom, which was closed. At the end of the hall a set of stairs turned and led down to the basement. Rajim was nowhere in sight.

Louis reached into his jacket and pulled a fat black Glock, held it down by the side of his leg as he advanced. As he got to the end of the hall, he heard the creak of the stairs . . .

. . . and suddenly Rajim appeared. He saw Louis and looked vaguely surprised. "S'up?" he said.

Louis looked at him, both relieved and annoyed. "You a'ight?" he said.

"I'm a'ight," Rajim replied. "Just checking security." His eyes were hidden behind dark sunglasses; even so, he would not meet Louis's gaze.

"You're supposed to be on the door," Louis told him.

"I'm on the motherfuckin' door!" Rajim protested. "I went to take a leak, a'ight?"

"I thought you were checking security," Louis said.

"Yeah, dawg," said Rajim. "I took a piss, and *then* I checked the back."

Louis looked at him skeptically. He noticed Rajim was sweating. He looked high, or ill, or both.

"Lemme see your eyes," Louis demanded.

"Wanna see my dick too?" Rajim snapped indignantly. He tried to push past; Louis blocked his path.

"Lemme see your motherfucking eyes," Louis warned.

Rajim hesitated; Louis stood poised, the Glock still in hand, looking altogether not a man to be fucked with. Rajim pulled off the shades and glared defiantly. Louis scowled; Rajim looked wired and pissed, but not under the influence of anything obvious.

"Happy now?" Rajim said.

"Sorry," Louis said, backing off. "My bad . . ."

"Damn right, yo motherfuckin' bad," Rajim grumbled and headed for the door. Louis watched him exit, then lingered at the head of the stairs. Something was wrong. The cellar light was on. Suddenly the bathroom door creaked open; Louis turned, his gun rising.

Amy emerged, her eyes going wide. "Jesus!" she squeaked, hands going up.

"What the fuck are you doing?" Louis snapped, lowering the gun, looking hugely annoyed.

"What?" Amy said defensively. "I was in the can!"

"You were in there by yourself?" he asked.

"Duh, yeah," Amy said. "Who else would I be in there with?"

Suddenly Louis shushed her. There was a light switch at the top of the steps. Louis clicked it off. Darkness enveloped the basement below. Amy came closer.

"What's wrong?" she said. He ignored her.

"Louis?"

Suddenly Louis saw it: a thin slice of light bisecting the shadows below. As he watched, it widened, other shadows crossing it. He heard the shuffle of footsteps and hushed voices downstairs. He turned to Amy.

"Get back!" he growled, pushing her hard. Amy fell ass backward into the bathroom as Louis slammed the door shut.

And the first shots rang out.

Back in the chapel, everyone froze as the volley of gunfire sounded. Seth looked around and saw the brothers spring into action, weapons brandished. In the space of a heartbeat, he did a mental headcount, came up one critical member short.

"Amy!" he cried, turning toward the rectory door. But as the door creaked open, it was not Amy but Louis who tumbled out, clutching a spreading red wet stain on his shirt. As he fell, the Glock slipped from his grasp and skidded to Seth's feet. Just then Seth looked up and saw a thin-lipped, bony-faced white man appear in the doorway holding an AR-15 assault rifle.

"Get down!" Seth cried.

The white man fired a deafening burst, high-velocity lead spraying the room, dinging chunks out of the pews, the coffin, pinging divots out of the walls, as the others scrambled for cover or position.

Seth howled with rage and grabbed the gun, firing wildly into the doorway. The fourth and fifth shots hit with a sound like a hammer smacking a ham, knocking the man back into the hallway until only his shoes protruded, twitching. From behind the door, unseen hands dragged him back.

"Fuck," Seth gasped. Just then more gunfire emanated from the hall-way, the muzzle flashes of a half-dozen weapons violently strobing death.

Seth dove behind one of the pews a microsecond before the slugs chewed it to pieces; acrid smoke filled the air as the brothers fanned out. Mohammed looked up to see Rajim moving toward the front door, flinging it wide.

What the fuck you doin', man?!" he called out,

Rajim turned to Mohammed. His eyes were rolled back deep into his skull, showing bloodshot white. He grinned a mad rictus. And shot Mohammed five times in the chest.

Mohammed did a spastic jig and flopped back, dead. The other brothers turned in shock and opened fire on Rajim, killing him instantly as the fire from the rectory entrance redoubled.

Josh and his friends huddled, terrified, caught in the withering cross-fire. The door to the rectory hall splintered under the impact; a moment later, a small metallic cylinder clattered into the aisle.

Kevin had grabbed Zoe and covered her in the narrow space be-tween the pews: in a dizzying split-second of terror and adrenaline his brain processed what he saw. He barely had time to scream.

"GRENADE!"

Then, boom.

Silence: eerie, deafening. As abruptly as it had started, the assault stopped. The pews were a shambles of torn and ragged kindling. The air was thick with smoke and the scent of fire. Outside they heard gun-ning engines and screeching tires as the marauders roared away. Kahlil, Russell, and Henri rushed out, cursing and popping futile rounds at the retreating attackers.

Josh scrambled to the dais, found it upended, the casket a pocked and shredded ruin. And Justin's hand was gone once again.

"Fuck!" he hissed, then looked around frantically. "Is everyone okay?" he called out. The group emerged from the wreckage, dazed and dirty, bleeding and shell-shocked. Just then they heard a scream coming from the rectory hall. Josh ran back to find Amy standing horror-stricken. At her feet lay one of the wasted assailants. His fingers had been chopped off, his face a shotgunned crater.

"What the fuck," Josh gasped. Amy trembled as if she might unglue at the seams. Josh hugged her protectively. "Don't look," he told her.

"L-Louis," she murmured. "He s-saved my life . . ."

Josh helped her back into the chapel, where the others stood in witness to a grim tableau. Louis lay in Joya's arms, blood soaking his shirt, in a great amount of pain. Amy fell to her knees before him, tears streaming down her cheeks.

"I'm s-sorry," she said.

Louis shook his head. "Not your fault," he said, adding: "It ain't that bad."

Just then Henri came in, winded and wired. Louis looked at him. "Rajim," he hissed. "He let 'em in . . ."

Henri nodded frantically. "He capped Mohammed too," he said bitterly. "Motherfucker sold us out."

Louis nodded, wincing. Amy looked around at the panic-stricken group. "Are you guys crazy? He's hurt. We gotta get him to a hospital!" she insisted.

"No," Louis protested through gritted teeth. "Doctors mean cops. We still gotta get it done."

"You're hurt, Louis," she blurted. "You could die!"

"If we don't stop 'em, we *all* die," he told her. He looked from Amy to Caroline and Kevin, Seth and Zoe. "They know who you are now. They'll go to your house and kill you in your sleep. Is that what you want?"

They all looked dumbstruck, horrified. Louis turned his focus back to Amy, a fierce determination writ in his features. "Noninvolvement just became a nonissue," he told her. "You in it now. For real."

Amy looked at him and nodded. In the distance came the wail of approaching sirens. They helped Louis to his feet. Then quickly, wordlessly, they made their way out the back.

26

Doris Tabb was elbow deep in bubble wrap, happily packing a purchase as the convoy of vehicles wheeled into her driveway. Shortly after Caroline and her family had left for the service, the shit had hit the online shinola, pardon her French, as she scored major in auctionland: some faceless bozo with the screenname *rebelyell* clicking the *View Seller's Other Items* button and proceeding to hit *BUY IT NOW!* over and over on dozens of her listings. At first she was nonplussed; Doris had seen this before, orgiastic consumers going off like Skinner rats on crack over some obscure object of virtual desire, and she was no stranger herself to the curiously addictive nature of skimming sites, checking prices on things she wanted, thought she wanted, or even had already bought, just in case she had paid too much. But this guy was serious, using online payment services and dogpiling her e-mail box within minutes, requesting expedited shipping.

Doris was not inclined to argue—the tab came to just under two grand, plus handling charges. Not bad for an afternoon's work. The pantry door was flung wide and her kitchen counters, table, and chairs were festooned with all manner of African Americana destined for a P.O. box in Richmond. A cardboard box sat on the table next to a scissors and a roll of packing tape. She heard the sound of car doors slamming; a moment later the kitchen door burst open.

"What the hell . . . ?" Doris gasped as Caroline and Zoe piled in, looking disheveled and distraught, followed quickly by Amy, Seth, and Kevin helping the wounded Louis, next by Joya and Henri and the heavily armed remainder of their party. Doris's eyes went wide at the sight of so many black men with guns standing in her kitchen.

"Don't ask," Caroline said. "You don't wanna know. . . ."

Doris stood, mouth gaping like a guppy on a radiator as Seth and Kevin helped Louis into one of the chairs; he sat back wincing, then peered down at the table. A Sambo ashtray stared back at him, little ceramic face beaming, tiny hands holding a sign that read PARK YER BUTT HERE! Louis looked at Caroline.

"You gotta be kidding," he murmured.

Kevin stood back, quietly freaking, his hands smeared red with Louis's blood. He made for the kitchen sink, turned the water on and scrubbed furiously, trying to clean them. Just then Josh entered, peering over his shoulder as he closed the door. "It's okay," he said, "I don't think we were followed." He turned, saw Doris.

"Mrs. Tabb," he said, smiling uneasily. "Long time no see."

"Aw, jeez," Doris muttered, rolling her eyes.

In the space of a heartbeat the house had gone from suburban placid to paramilitary panic: men moving into the other rooms, setting up perimeter watch as Caroline morphed into control mode. She grasped her mother's shoulders, peering into her eyes and nodding as if trying to hypnotize her. "Mom, it's too much to explain right now, but we need your help. Okay?"

"W-what do you want me to do?" Doris asked.

"First, we need bandages, first-aid stuff," Caroline said.

"In the bathroom," Doris replied. "Why?"

She looked over and saw Amy helping to unzip Louis's jacket, saw the bloody shirt. Doris looked pale, a little wobbly. "I think I need a drink," she murmured.

Caroline turned to her daughter. "Zoe, go see what you can find," she said. Zoe nodded nervously and headed for the hall.

Joya surveyed the cramped, kitschy kitchen as Henri came back from the interior. "S'cool," he said to her. "You got what you need?"

"No," she replied, "but we gotta do it anyway. We don't have much time."

Josh checked his watch. "She's right," he said. "Sun sets in less than an hour."

Neither Caroline, Kevin, nor Doris had any idea what they were talking about. Caroline looked at Joya. "What do you need?" she asked.

"Someplace private," Joya replied. "Where no one can disturb us."

Caroline thought about it for a second. "Basement," she said. She looked at her mom. "Is that okay?"

"Now you ask?" Doris said, then waved her off. Josh and the two women exited; Henri turned to Louis.

"You all right?" he asked.

"Naw, man, I'm fucked up," Louis answered, "but we gotta stick to the plan. We need weapons check and prep, now." Henri hesitated; Louis glared at him. "Move!" he barked.

Henri nodded and looked at Seth. "My man," he said. "Wanna help?"

Seth nodded, and together they headed out the door to the vehicles parked outside. From downstairs came the sound of boxes thumping and shifting, a muted reshuffling. Just then Zoe came back in from the hall, bearing bottles of rubbing alcohol and hydrogen peroxide, and some rolls of gauze.

"I found these," she said, handing over the meager supplies. Amy took them, smiling wanly.

"Thanks, sweetie," she said. She grabbed the pair of scissors from the table and cut Louis's bloodied shirt away, laying bare a small oozing hole in the fleshy part of his side. She gently leaned him forward and looked at his back. Louis winced and said nothing, but it was clear it hurt like hell. "Sorry," she murmured, then: "It's through and through. I don't think it hit anything major." She felt around the wound gingerly. "I think you broke a rib. You need a doctor."

"No," he hissed. "I told you . . ."

"Asshole," she muttered, then eased him back. She wadded some gauze and soaked it in the alcohol and peroxide. "This is gonna hurt like hell," she said; Louis nodded, bracing himself, and she placed it on the wounds.

It audibly fizzed on contact; Louis sucked wind and bit his lip as Amy unreeled more gauze and began wrapping it around his waist. "Where'd you learn to do this?" he asked.

"Paramedic on Avenue A," she replied. "Used to trade tricks for meds." She looked at Doris. "Do you have any painkillers, anything?"

"Tylenol?" Doris ventured.

"Shit," Amy hissed. She sat Louis back in the chair and reached into her bag, withdrew a small pouch containing her works and laid it on the table. Her hands were shaking. Louis looked at the gear askance.

"Tell me you ain't gonna fix now," he said.

"Not me. You," Amy said, pulling out one of the glassine packets he had supplied her with. "For the pain."

Louis looked at her for a moment, then nodded. Amy looked at Doris, Kevin, and Zoe.

"Y'all might want to go into the other room."

Doris nodded, more than willing to cooperate. But Zoe stood her ground. "No," she said defiantly. "I wanna help . . ."

Kevin turned. He had been staring at his freshly rinsed hands, head shaking in a quiet mantra of denial. But Zoe's words snapped something in him.

"No way," he said to Zoe. "No freakin' way."

Kevin looked at them all, feeling like the only sane inmate in the asylum. "Oh, come on people, enough is enough!" he cried. "Bad enough we're caught up in some whacked-out terrorist tug-of-war and we only broke about fifteen billion laws today; I won't have my family sucked into this too!"

"Speak for yourself, Kevin!" Zoe snapped. She spat his name with such unvarnished contempt that it took him aback. Just then Caroline entered; Kevin looked to her imploringly, as if she might inject some sanity back into the proceedings. "Caroline, please," he began. "Tell her we've got to go, now!"

But to his immense surprise, Caroline did not. "I'm sorry, Kevin," she said. "I can't. I have to do this . . ." She paused, looked at her daughter. "We both do."

Caroline looked at Zoe; there was a fire alight in her eyes, one that immediately struck him for its apparent absence in their entire time together. She looked scared and wired and worried. But also, strangely excited. It was a fire now burning in her daughter's eyes as well.

Kevin didn't know what to say. And as if the moment could not possibly become any more awkward, it was at that instant that Josh came back in. He sensed the massive tension radiating in the air and stopped short.

"Joya says she's ready," he said.

Caroline looked from Josh to Kevin, a bright sheen of tears welling. It was as if this entire insane drama had sparked something deep within her, brought the long-banished wildass girl screaming back into the world. She held out her hand to her husband.

"Please," she said.

"This is nuts," Kevin sighed. He took her hand in his own, their fingers intertwining. He looked at Zoe, and she suddenly looked down, feeling sheepish, exposed. Kevin kissed her on the forehead, then turned to face Josh.

"All right," he said. "What now?"

The interior of the basement was dark and smelled of mold, old cardboard, and newsprint, now laced with the sweet scent of burning incense and tallow. As they descended the stairs, they saw the boxes and detritus pushed back to form an open space in the center of the room;

a circle had been drawn on the floor in a fine red powder, a number of candles lit and placed around its circumference. Joya stood in the center of the circle, clutching something to her breast, murmuring in a soft, hypnotic cadence.

Josh led them to positions surrounding her; as they completed the circle, Joya looked up, her blue eyes bright and fiercely focused.

"This is ritual magick," she said, her voice soft and preternaturally calm. "Its purpose is to prepare us for what is to come. To invoke *Ghana*, the spirit of the living earth, and enlist her support in our cause. To bestow her blessings on us and make us spirit warriors equipped to enter the underworld. Do you understand?"

One by one they nodded, their expressions a mixture of determination laced with dread.

"Good," Joya said. "Is everyone here HIV negative?"

They looked at each other, nodding nervously. "Why?" Caroline asked.

Joya then revealed what she held in her hands: a ceremonial dagger with a short, sharp blade. She stepped up to Josh and held the dagger out. Josh took it in one hand, held the other palm facing upward, and drew the blade across. A bright line of blood welled up. Joya took back the dagger, then moved to Caroline and held it forth.

Caroline hesitated, then took it in hand. And did the same.

One by one they were initiated: cutting themselves, the commingling of warrior blood bonding them together in their quest. This was the level at which the *bruja* must step to the edge of the abyss in order to combat the darkness.

By the end of the ritual, it was obvious that something had happened. There was an incredible feeling of power that surrounded them, permeating the air through which they moved and breathed.

"Crossing over will open your inner eyes," Joya told them, "and will allow you to see, for better or worse, the true inner nature of all you meet.

"But you must beware of the Great Night's tricks," she continued.

"The house is full of fearful memories, and he will use your deepest fears against you.

"Your inner sight will guide you," she said. "You must trust each other. And trust your heart."

Joya blessed them and wished them all luck. They may not have been as ready as they would have liked. But they were as ready as they would ever be.

27

The sun was just starting to set as Chief Jackson stood at the edge of the boardwalk and stared at the disembodied heads of the black man and woman. The heads were canted at forty-five-degree angles within a circle and stared inland with lifeless eyes, with the eternally surging tide as a backdrop. Their expressions were frozen in something that was part stoic resolve, part infinite sadness, as if contemplating a vast and merciless unknown. He did not know their names; no one did. That was kind of the point.

The heads were large, over nine feet tall from base to crown, sculpted from thick cast bronze and mounted on marble pedestals. A word was emblazoned at the base of the monument: DIASPORA. And beneath it, in smaller letters: MIDDLE PASSAGE, 1619–1865. It was a local landmark erected in far more liberal times, when notions of social justice were more than just cable news pundit bait and the memorial was intended to both remind and inspire, perhaps to provoke thoughtful reflection to sun-baked visitor and local alike. But Chief Jackson knew the more unctuous locals simply called it *Big Niggerheads.*

Jackson popped a cherry-flavored TUMS, quietly crunching. It was his second roll of the day, and its chalky sweetness did nothing to alleviate the sour rumbling in his gut. Labor Day weekend was upon them;

as Jackson psyched himself to go on camera for an upbeat law-'n'-order local news spot, his anxiety level was already a palpable thing—five arrests on drunk-and-disorderlies, three fights, a trash fire of suspicious origin, and one assault with a deadly weapon. All before seven o'clock. All with the promise of more to come once the sun went down.

Jackson stared out at the sea, where pinkish light glinted off the cresting surf, and took a deep breath of warm, salty air. Behind him were an assortment of news crews and stringers from the cable channels. Scruffy techs toyed with cables and mikes as buff and salon-tanned reporters mumbled their lead-in lines with salacious solemnity, gimlet-eyed with anticipation of camera-friendly chaos.

Jackson sighed; he was still distraught over the loss of Elizabeth Bergen. Her death had deprived him of a trusted colleague and friend, and despite the trashing of the lab, her own autopsy had revealed cardiac arrest as the cause. The nagging mystery only served to deepen his unease. That, and the missing hand of Justin Van Slyke.

Vexing him further was this afternoon's assault at the Church of the Open Door, where arriving officers discovered a bullet-ridden interior containing the bodies of two black males and the mutilated—and as yet unidentified and unidentifiable—remains of a white male. The absence of paraphernalia indicated that this was not about drugs.

No, it couldn't be that easy, he thought. *A nice simple drug deal gone bad would be a cakewalk in comparison.* Because this appeared to be racial and, as such, political. The mystery firefight meant that at best there were some heavily armed insurrectionists running around and duking it out with some equally armed opponents.

And at worst?

Jackson didn't want to think about it. This was not good news: for him personally or the town in general. His available man- and woman-power was already stretched along the whole strip on the oceanfront, with additional mobile units doing DUI spot checks between Atlantic and Pacific avenues and a search chopper doing laps up and down the length of the boardwalk. On the main drag, tricked-out cars bunched and crawled along at a snail's pace: late-model low-riders, plush Beemers and hulking SUVs, all packed with rowdy collegiate youth hailing from black fraternities and sororities across the country, from Alpha Phi Alpha and Zeta Phi Beta, as well as those whose grades, ambitions, or resources precluded higher education but who didn't want to miss the party. They gridlocked every intersection, blasting vintage Wu Tang and Tupac from thunderous stereo systems and daring somebody, *anybody*, to give them a hard time.

It was *American Graffiti* in a gulag, with absolutely everyone wearing a chip on their shoulder. And Jackson was in charge of keeping the lid on. So when the call had come not fifteen minutes ago, Jackson was thrilled to learn that his higher-ups had been reminded by *their* higher-ups to remind him of the incident at Custis Manor. And though there had been nothing directly correlating the incident at the manor to the one at the church, they wanted to caution that it could happen again, with far worse than spray paint.

And so, with the whole town poised for confrontation, Jackson was put on alert to have his people babysit a landmark bastion of good old-fashioned Southern racism. He told them flat out that it was out of the question; he'd give his officers a head's up, and if anything happened they would respond as quickly as possible, but beyond that he simply couldn't spare them. But somehow he knew that wouldn't be the end of it.

Jackson looked at the memorial: the setting sun graced the sculpted features with a burnished glow and also illuminated the inlaid brass lettering of the circle, which commemorated the myriad contributors who had made the monument possible, sorted according to donation level and christened with portentously noble titles: *Trail Blazers, Torch Bearers, Heroes*. Their ranks included everyone from *B'nai B'rith* and *Kiwanis* to the *Stillson Beach Black Municipal Employees Association* and the *African Holocaust Committee*. And one name he had never really noticed before, that shone fiery with reflected light.

Custis.

Jackson frowned. He couldn't believe he had never noticed that before, but indeed it would seem that the Custis Historical Preservation Society had made a hefty contribution to the cause, enough to rank it as a Torch Bearer at any rate, though Jackson wondered exactly what kind of torch a Custis would likely wish to bear. *Probably one that came with a rope,* he mused.

It was perverse, especially given the recent uproar over Governor Langley's proposed National Museum of Slavery. It was an idea that had first been advanced as a "Negro Memorial" by a group of aging black Civil War vets in 1915, some fifty years after Lincoln's skull had been reduced to patriotic pulp by John Wilkes Booth. Congress had authorized an edifice to be built in the nation's capital in 1929 and had envisioned it as a neoclassical structure to rival the Supreme Court. Several months later came Black Monday; the stock market cratered, and the ensuing Depression washed away any practical hope of the project's fruition in a tidal wave of bleeding red ink.

The idea lingered, however, and was picked up in the last decade of the twentieth century by then Democratic Governor Doug Wilder, whose personal beliefs, no less his racial heritage, held that the nation, if not simply the state, still needed such a place to finally and fully address the complexities of what was chastely christened the "peculiar institution." When he left office, Wilder continued to champion the cause from his post as a professor of public policy at the University of Virginia, eventually garnering a parcel of forty acres of land from a sympathetic developer in Fredericksburg. The site perched, pristine and perfect, in the green hills on the banks of the Rappahannock River near I-95, less than an hour from both Richmond and Washington.

Two years ago, Langley had thrown his weight behind the project. Promising more than a grim repository of culturally embarrassing artifacts, Langley promoted the memorial as a living, interactive educational and healing tool . . . not to mention a great way of siphoning millions in tourist dollars from the DC metro area.

Political and neocon opponents descended quickly, decrying it as a four-hundred-million-plus liberal boondoggle. They made much of Langley's financial ties to the proposed site . . . especially since it was conveniently located near a larger, twenty-four-hundred-acre parcel owned by the same sympathetic developer, in which Langley was purportedly invested, and which was destined to sprout golf courses, resort hotels, stores, and corporate office complexes like mushrooms. They asserted that Langley stood to gain a very large slice of what could be a very rich pie.

Senator Custis had remained visibly outside the fray, though Jackson was sure his public persona of mannered elder statesman was countered by his backdoor benificence with groups like the Sons of Confederate Veterans, which was to Jackson's eyes merely a gussied-up front for more malign organizations. When President George W. Bush had signed legislation in 2001 to appropriate several million dollars to commission a study on building a National Museum of African American History and Culture in Washington, and the report came back in 2003 recommending that a museum be built next to the Reflecting Pool, Custis had applauded along with the rest of the august body of the Senate. And then he sent his son Duke to do his dirty work for him.

Duke, while not commenting directly on either the Washington plan or the Langley/Wilder project, quietly moved the board of the Custis Society to align with the hugely underfunded Museum of the Confederacy, located in a smallish 1970s-era building situated in Richmond between Jefferson Davis's Confederate White House and the Medical College of Virginia. Originally founded in 1890 by a group of genteel society ladies who longed to preserve the fading greatness of their Southern heritage, the museum had fallen on hard times, and stalwart protectors of the Old South feared that it would disappear altogether in the swelling tide of race-mixed liberal indifference. Indeed, the encroaching effects of cultural betrayal had been felt as recently as 1991, when Museum curators, armed with a grant from the National Endowment for the Humanities, had presented an immense show, "Before Freedom Came," which examined the legacy of slave and slaveholder alike through the prism of artifacts and documents culled from dozens of private collections. The exhibit featured bullwhips, cat-o'-nine-tails, leg irons, and writs of sale. The board was not pleased.

And then Duke Custis came along. Duke met with them and suggested that they go public with an alternate plan: to expand the existing museum and keep it—and the hoped-for influx of jobs and dollars—in Richmond. The Sons of Confederate Veterans jumped at the idea—anything that screamed "jobs" was a smart play in an election year, especially in the more ethnically concentrated urban centers where votes could swing easily into Langley's camp. But more—and, to Duke Custis, most importantly: it would keep the ability to define the past—and, hence, the future—in the hands of those to whom it rightfully belonged.

As the competing plans were bandied back and forth, Duke backed his words with action: installing a museum exhibit at Custis Manor called "To Old Virginny," which presented the radical but not entirely historically inaccurate notion that some slaves not only supported but actually fought for—and in some cases side by side with—their masters. The exhibit drew fire from all the usual suspects, but it also drew cash: checks written quietly and given without fanfare to Custis Manor, the Museum of the Confederacy project . . . and to Duke's burgeoning soft-money campaign coffers.

With spirits buoyed, they subsequently staged a rally at the historic Tredegar Iron Works in Richmond, which had once forged cannons for the rebel cause. But the event quickly went awry, as members of the KKK showed up in full hooded regalia and draped the statue of Lincoln and his son Tad in Confederate flags and sang "Dixie," and members of assorted neo-Nazi groups trucked in squads of shaven-headed hoods to scream "White Power" at anything with a lens. Counterprotestors from the ACLU tore down the offending banners, and members of the ACH—the African Holocaust Society—set them ablaze. A full-scale melee erupted; twelve people were injured, two critically. The resulting footage was regurgitated twice per news cycle for a fortnight on Fox and

MSNBC, the "fair and balanced" tilt of the former landing squarely on the shoulders of the counterprotestors; the passionate umbrage against flag burning, it seemed, extended even to the Stars and Bars.

That was a scant six months ago—long enough to be gone but not nearly long enough to be forgotten. As Jackson stared down at the name emblazoned at his feet, he realized that this whole situation made him profoundly uncomfortable, even more so because he was now stuck squarely in the middle of it.

And he was, after all, a black man himself.

Just then his little Nokia cellular phone chirruped; Jackson turned and saw the Channel 3 reporter, a thirty-something sandy-haired stud muffin named Wink or Dink or Chip or something, signaling frantically to his watch: five minutes to live on air. Jackson waved him off and hit the answer key.

"Jackson," he said, then gritted his teeth. "Yes, Senator Custis . . ."

28

The chopper sliced through the dusk sky like some primordial insect, banking east over the mouth of the Chesapeake Bay at a tad over three thousand feet, dying sunlight gleaming off its sleek metal hide. It was a top-of-the-line Augusta 109C, generally regarded as the Rolls Royce of copter aviation, and went for a tad over $1.25 million, used. It boasted twin Allison 250-C14 turbine engines with a multiblade rotor system for all-weather safety, an endurance range of two and a half hours or just under five hundred miles, whichever came first, and a top speed of one hundred and ninety-four miles per hour, which meant that it could cover the distance from Annapolis to Tidewater in a little less than thirty minutes without breaking one forty. The VIP interior was done in early executive spartan, with cushy if rather stiff-backed leather seats, deluxe wool carpet, silent soundproofing, and an onboard-refreshment center, should refreshment be desired. It could carry six passengers in a pinch, but at the moment it held only one.

Senator Eli Custis sat, bull-like frame pressed into a window jumpseat, and gazed out at the view, a cellphone in one hand, a drink in the other. The phone was a GSM with 128-bit encryption for added security, but the reception still sucked. The drink, by contrast, was yummy: single malt, expensive, in a crystal tumbler. He sipped it, ice quietly clinking, and spoke over the muted hum of the rotors.

"Chief Jackson," he said pleasantly, "I understand you have your hands full tonight. . . ."

Jackson's voice came back, tinny and remote, mumbling stiffed-necked apologies about resources and manpower. Eli nodded, knowing that that was what he would say. "I understand completely," he said, then added: "I just want you to know that I'm behind you one thousand percent, and I'm sure you'll do your best. Don't worry about a thing."

Jackson thanked him, his tone a mix of relief and vague suspicion. Eli nodded, knowing also that that was how Jackson would react. He exchanged a few random pleasantries and hung up without saying good-bye.

The copter banked inland, heading for the airport. Eli sighed and finished his drink. One downside of a lifetime spent playing power games was that after a while one knew the moves of the players almost before they were made. The call to Jackson was an exercise of random ass-covering born of habit: if things went well tonight, Eli would be covered; if not, the brunt of the blowback would be borne by expendable underlings. Whatever happened, Eli would be elsewhere. And soon enough, he would be free.

The pilot's voice squawked over the com: ten minutes to ETA at Norfolk International Airport. Eli fumbled for the buckle on his seatbelt and snugged himself in. His hands trembled ever so slightly: not enough to be noticed by the casual observer—at least not yet—but enough to worry him. It was another sign of the steady attrition of the power that coiled within him, a sign of the ultimate betrayal of flesh to spirit. The power sat in his broad chest like a serpent, slithered through his veins and clutched at the corroded meat of his heart. And as he gazed out at the coming night, Eli beat back the dawning realization that the very thing that had suckled and succored him all these years was feeding off him, leeching his strength as surely as the electrolysis of ground water would eat a steel pipe thrust deep into the earth. He felt hollowed and brittle, as though his body had been reduced to a mere vessel to contain and transport a naked appetite not wholly his own. Eli caught a glimpse of his reflection in the thick glass of the window and realized: where others saw a smooth and practiced confidence, he saw a depleted husk. It scared him more deeply than he dared admit.

Tonight was an auspicious occasion, one that he had both longed for and dreaded for nearly forty years. The ceremonial changing of the guard, with all its attendant loss of power, was also a welcome relief—because with it came the lifting of the burden. Eli was old, and tired, and his efforts of late had lacked a certain . . . enthusiasm . . . that the paterfamilias considered essential. He had known for some time that it was time to cede the mantle, and Lord knew his firstborn was champing at the proverbial bit to get his clammy hands on real power. As for the other . . .

Eli winced at the thought. The news he had received today was distressing in the extreme, particularly so close to such a momentous and delicate event. From this night forward, the Custis mantle of power would be borne by Duke. Duke would call the shots. Duke would sit at the head of all manners of Custis family business, in this world and . . . elsewhere. And, perhaps most important of all, Duke would have to feed the *nganga.*

But if there was always a devil in the details, this one's name was *Joshua.* Eli knew too well that his sons had always been a study in contrasts, as if God Himself had deigned to mock the Custis gene pool by splitting it neatly down the middle, granting each brother that which the other was denied in almost equal measure and thus rendering them equally, if inversely, vulnerable. Duke's natural appetite for cruelty was matched by Josh's all-too-tender sensibilities; Josh's natural intelligence was countered by Duke's evident and obvious intellectual shortcomings. Duke had mastered the art of sublimating himself to power; Josh resisted any such assertions, even to end up outcast . . . but in the end,

Eli wondered if it were not Josh rather than Duke who was the true leader of the two. And the more dangerous.

Eli had not spoken to his youngest son in over twenty years. Joshua had always been a problem child—soft yet strangely willful, defiant even under the sternest strap, and seemingly determined to go his own way. But now it would appear that Josh's way was on a direct collision course not just with Duke, or even Eli, but with the *Custis* way. And lest he think otherwise, the power reminded him: that could not be allowed. Under any circumstances.

Eli shuddered and steeled himself for what was to come.

A black limo was waiting on the tarmac, lights off, motor running. The driver stood outside the passenger door, one of the clean-cut, lantern-jawed, pig-eyed thugs comprising the bulk of his son's political machine. He lowered his head and opened the door as Eli approached. Duke was seated comfortably inside. He smiled as Eli entered.

"Hi, Pop. How was your flight?"

Eli glared and smacked him across the face. The blow resounded sharp and harsh in the luxurious confines. Duke's eyes watered, but his placid expression did not change.

"That's for screwing up today," Eli hissed. "You said you had this under control."

"Relax, Pop. It's gonna be fine." Duke was still smiling, but his eyes showed no mirth. As the car pulled away, Duke reached for the minibar, poured two fingers of Old Granddad into a tumbler with some cracked ice, and handed it to Eli. Eli hesitated a moment, then accepted.

"It better be," he muttered.

"It will," Duke assured him, then added: "The bundle's already on board."

Eli's blood went cold. The "bundle" was six years old, still alive, trussed and thrust into the deeply carpeted interior of Jimmy Joe's Town Car's trunk. Eli flashed back to his own rite of passage, back in

'53, and realized anew the sickly pallor his own father had shown. It was part of it: the shift in personal strength, Duke waxing tough as Eli waned into frail contemplation of his ever-more-perilous mortality. The drink was cold comfort in his hands. But he could always have another.

The car thrummed along I-64, the hum of the tires neatly masking the whimpers from the trunk as they headed for the manor.

They arrived at the gates as darkness fell, the sky quickly deepening from blue to indigo. The grounds sprawled before them, a faint breeze rustling through the trees. Armed security manned the gates, eyes glinting from headlight glare as the limo glided past. They nodded.

As the limo rolled down the long, winding drive, Eli felt his nerves tingle and the heaviness in his chest seem to shift, as if awakening and taking a little stretch. Duke seemed to feel something too, judging from his expression, which subtly shifted from smug serenity to a barest hint of unease.

Then they were at the house, and the sight of Jimmy Joe and his posse standing by the town car made Duke happy again. Father and son exited the limo and strode to the waiting servants. Jimmy Joe nodded to Duke, then thumbed a remote, and the trunk of the town car clicked open. They peered inside. Nestled within the carpeted interior was a drugged and trussed girl named Ally Marsh, plucked from the street so neatly that the wheels of her bike were still spinning when they left. And tossed at her sneakered feet, an extra prize, wrapped in a Hefty bag. Duke opened the bag, revealing Justin's hand, dirty and somewhat the worse for wear, but theirs again.

Duke turned to his father. "Like I said, Pop. Gonna be fine."

Eli looked from the severed appendage to the darkened house. Duke watched his old man carefully. "You wanna go in?" he asked.

"No." Eli replied, a little too quickly. "Let's just do this already."

"Whatever you say," Duke smiled. "You're the boss."

Eli looked at him, and for a brief moment their eyes met: and though Duke was smiling, Eli could feel the contempt his heir's expression masked, and the unspoken coda implied in the look. *But not for much longer* . . .

Taking the stolen limb, and the bundle, they trundled down to the little skiff that would ferry them out to the island. And the final stage of Transition.

29

Custis Manor. Underworld.

Justin lay, head swimming with visions. He did not know how long he had been there, his consciousness ebbing and flowing in strange swirls and eddies, the obscene and disorienting hellscape leaving him feverish and disoriented. He lay back, trying to arrange his random fragments of thought like a skittering rosary of liquid mercury.

He remembered a man with skin like polished ebony hovering over him, speaking soothing words in a tongue he did not understand. He remembered the taste of hot copper on his tongue, followed by an ethereal warmth in his chill and aching flesh. He remembered entering the glistening aperture of the mirror, cold hands pulling him inexorably into its depths. He remembered the faces of the guards, warped and distorted. He remembered hot hands wrenching him back, gripping his arm . . .

Justin opened his eyes with a start. He was on a creaking rope bed in a small hut. A low fire burned in the hearth, casting deep and flickering shadows. He looked down. His right hand was gone.

Justin tried to sit up, only to sag back, weakened and depleted. He closed his eyes and wiggled his fingers, felt a strange and tingling sensation where his right hand had been, as if it were responding from some vast and indefinable distance. Yet when he took a deep breath and forced his eyes open, he beheld the stump. The edge of the wound sparkled faintly, as if his life force were made visible and slowly seeping away. But this was more than some bad acid phantom-limb twitch; if he lay very still, he could make out faint *sensation*: a jumble of random nerve messages his brain struggled to interpret. They told him his hand was moving, being transported. And like mindless nerves transmitting not merely synaptic information but emotion, his transposed flesh seemed to radiate something else back to him.

Fear.

Justin sat up fully this time, eyes focusing on the dim-lit interior of the shack. A figure knelt by the small hearth fire, draped in a long, hooded cloak. As he moved, the rickety bed frame creaked; the hooded figure turned toward him, eyes flashing from within the shadowed folds. It stood, almost gliding across the hard-packed earthen floor; as the figure neared, its arms raised, pale hands reaching up to throw back the hood . . .

. . . and Justin gasped as he realized there was *another* fear that had gnawed at him, quite apart from the horrors of this place or the sensed dread of his missing hand, and altogether deeper. The terror of seeing Mia again. And being judged not worthy.

And yet there she was, suddenly revealed before him after so many years. There were no words to describe it, no thought that his intellect could possess, just a pure and fierce rush of love and longing and ripped-raw naked emotion. He trembled as he said her name, part whisper, part prayer.

Mia?

Mia came to him, her arms enfolding him as she buried her head in the nape of his neck. Justin felt transfused by the warmth of her, felt her heart beating steady against the wild cacophony of his own; as they breathed together, their two hearts came into sync, beating in tandem.

It's you, he murmured. *It's really you . . .*

Is it? she whispered back, and gently disengaged.

And it was then that Justin could see her clearly. She was the same age as he remembered her but had been subtly transformed, as if her suffering had deepened and ennobled her. Her eyes flashed silvery tears, like war paint dredged up from the core of her being to lace the minute striations of her face.

I can't believe you're here, she said. *I missed you so much.*

I missed you too, he told her. He leaned back, feeling suddenly light-headed. Mia opened his shirt, then leaned forward and placed her lips upon his chest, right over his wildly beating heart. As she did, he felt a rush of warmth and strength infuse him. The wooziness passed; Justin sat up.

Mia unfastened the cloak, letting it fall away. She stood backlit and radiant, her naked skin glistening in the strange light of the room, shadows and fire glow dancing off the subtle curve of her hips, the gracious plane of her belly, the small, soft swell of her breasts. It was as though she had been refined and purified by this hellish place, becoming the primal embodiment of a feminine warrior principle, at once fertile and fierce. Justin wanted her more than he wanted one more breath; decades of savaged desire coursed through him like liquid fire, awakening every nerve ending with ravenous need. She slid into the small bed beside him. Her nipples were dark and ripe; Justin reached up with his one good hand to touch her.

And then stopped.

What is it? she said. *What's wrong?*

Justin looked at his calloused hand, the corded veins and sinew of his forearm. He could feel the fissures that time and pain had etched upon him. Twenty years ago his world had crashed and burned and the best of him had perished in the flames; now she was here, phoenixlike, a goddess suddenly risen. They were together again. And he had never been more afraid.

This is wrong, Justin said. *You haven't changed, and I'm* ... He paused, embarrassed and ashamed. Mia took his face tenderly in her hands and kissed him deeply. Then she whispered in his ear.

Yes, I have, she said. She looked at him, green eyes lit with an inner fire. *And no, you're not.* ...

All this time, she told him, *the thought of you was what kept me going. When I close my eyes, it's still you that I see.*

Josh told me he would find you, she added. *I knew you would come.*

I didn't come here to fight Josh's war, Justin confessed. *I said I'd help him, and I will. But I came here for you.*

Mia smiled her crooked smile again and climbed astride him.

Yeah? she said. *Prove it.*

They made love then with the abandon of the damned. In the distance the hellhounds bayed; their passion was a blood scent on the wind. Love was an aberrant blasphemy in this place, and it wreaked havoc on the bestial instinct of the hands.

When the baying drew nearer, Justin and Mia huddled, holding themselves in check. Until the beasts passed.

This isn't Josh's war, Mia whispered. *In a world of hate, love is the only weapon we have.*

After a while, the howling died out. Leaving them to each other. And the next stage of the plan.

30

Friday, August 29. Custis Manor. 7:47 p.m.

To put it bluntly, Clayton Pierce was bored out of his tits. He stood his post by the heavily padlocked outer gate, sucking Marlboro reds and taking in the empty swath of the parking lot, the flat black ribbon of road that extended, dark and unlit, in both directions as far as he could see. The woods on the other side of the road rustled thick with crickets, frogs, and fireflies. The sun was down now but it was still bitch-kicking hot. His cheap suit chafed and made him sweat. The bulge of the Colt Python snugged into his armpit pinched, shoulder holster binding. Mosquitoes tried to fly up his nose with annoying regularity; he blew plumes of smoke out his nostrils to ward them off. It made the filter bitter and soggy. He wanted a beer. He wanted something to eat.

But mainly, he wanted to kick some ass.

Clayton glanced over at Ellis DePugh, who seemed significantly less unthrilled. Ellis was amusing himself by hocking loogies into the night air. Like Clayton, Ellis was in his twenties, though Clayton guessed he had a good five years on the boy, judging from Ellis's sunburnt baby face and relative maturity level; Ellis had been plucked by Jimmy Joe Baker from a do-nothing Klavern in Red Lion, Pennsylvania, just over the

Maryland line, much as Clayton had been hand-picked from his own local streetside chapter of the Aryan Brotherhood. The AB's motto—which was the jail tat stenciled across his solar plexus, by the way—was *"Kill To Get In. Die To Get Out."* Clayton had gotten in seven years ago, but at the moment he was considering renewing his vow on Ellis DePugh.

Ellis hocked another one and let fly, a thick, ropy stringer that arced and twirled on its way down to smack the pavement. Ellis seemed inordinately pleased, but Clayton had more than once considered the pink-faced Yankee boy's brain a single-celled organism, smooth and unblemished by serious thought.

"Knock it off," Clayton growled. Ellis looked at him and grinned, showing poor dental hygiene. Brotherhood be damned, one of these days Clayton was apt to pop him good. It vexed him greatly that they were considered on the same tier, organizationally speaking, which was to say that they were the shit-shoveling grunts manning the Custis trenches, risking life, limb, and liberty on behalf of their presumably shared cause, only to be left out of the loop when the real fun started. Which at the moment was set to happen down the road and around the bend at the big house. Jimmy Joe had promised advancement pursuant to effort, but hell, what was *enough*?

It was unclear. While others were having at it in a full-on firefight at that church, wasting jigs, Jews, and race traitors with righteous fury, Clayton had been assigned to idiot Ellis, who at best was a hopeless retard whose sole redeeming quality was loyalty born of witlessness, and then sent to do some grade-B scut work, namely snatching some little black bitch from a trailer park on Route 17, all the way across the friggin' river in Portsmouth. Taking the kid was no big deal, logistically speaking: she was maybe six and none too bright, so all he had to do was roll up, make like a nice man asking for directions, and then spike her with a high octane cocktail of Seconal and Pavulon. Down she went, paralyzed and mute, but still aware. Jimmy Joe had been explicit: it was important she remain aware. But he never said why.

Even with Ellis driving, they were gone in less than sixty seconds, down the road and heading home, and they delivered their bundle in a little over an hour simply because the eastbound Hampton Roads Bridge-Tunnel traffic had been a bitch.

Clayton felt no remorse for the girl. He had been raised in the sweltering flatlands of St. Augustine and steeped in the fiery oratory of Christian Identity, the old-school edge of Charles Conley "Connie" Lynch—and the Klan there was noteworthy for its tough-minded unwillingness to suffer the weak of spirit. When Clayton was eight, his daddy had played him scratchy tapes of a rally back in '63, after some notable church bombings in Birmingham had claimed some collateral casualties in the form of four little girls. Lynch had exhorted the crowd with unflinching logic, demanding to know why people should be forced to feel sorry for them: *"They weren't children,"* Lynch had insisted. *"Children are little people, little human beings, and that means white people . . . There's little dogs and cats and apes and baboons and skunks and there's also little niggers. But they ain't children. They're just little niggers . . ."*

Pretty much said it all: one more coon on a milk carton, as far as Clayton was concerned, and to hell with her. But Clayton had been born to fight white and do right, in the spirit of his elders and betters—men like Gerald L. K. Smith, founder of the Christian Nationalist Crusade and later Christian Identity—and he wanted to make his mark. Clayton had grown up knowing that the ten lost tribes of Israel were actually the predecessors of Nordic, British, and American Whites; as an American, he was part of the *Manasseh,* the mystical thirteenth tribe, excised from common knowledge by nefarious Jews, who weren't true Israelites at all—as indeed, the so-called state of Israel itself was a hoax—but rather the outcast seed of a historically separate kingdom (and fathered by guess who? Clayton seldom failed to remind himself). He knew in his blood and bones that the nonwhite races were pre-Adamic mutations, fashioned by God to live outside the Garden before the Fall (and engineered again by guess Jew/who?), and when God gave Adam and Eve the boot, Eve was implanted with *two* seeds—one of Adam's, and one of the wily Serpent's. From Adam's seed sprang the strong and noble Abel and the whole white race; from the Other came the wicked and conniving Cain and his hooknosed, kosher kin. God then, in His infinite wisdom, decreed eternal racial conflict, leaving it to the sons of Abel to fight and earn their way back to Paradise.

With that much behind him, and dreams of Valhalla ahead, Clayton was impatient with politics and pecking orders, and itching to prove himself. So he was sorely pissed that his contributions seemed ill-noted of late and while perhaps not as glamorous as going in guns blazing at the Church of the Open Door, they were no less risky, especially in an era of Amber alerts and ZOG-inspired public surveillance and all. But he did his duty like a good white warrior.

And his big reward? Guard duty. With Ellis DePugh.

It truly sucked.

So when Clayton spied the figure shambling through the shadows down the road, precisely the right chemical combination of boredom, hate, heat, resentment, adrenaline, and ambition crystallized into focus. Something sparked deep in his brainpan: the kind of stray, fleeting impulse that, if seized upon by appropriate force of will, might be transformed into something more than a devil's workshop in hot and idle hands . . . and which might even be seen by those whose opinion mattered as something inspired.

"Ellis," he muttered. "Check it out."

Ellis paused in his nasal revelries long enough to follow Clayton's gaze. The man was stumbling and mumbling down the edge of the road. As he came within range of the gate lights, they saw more clearly: he was a black man, in dark, baggy cargo pants and a hooded sweatshirt. He looked wasted, drunk or high or both. A bum.

"What the fuck?" Ellis snickered.

" 'Boo's too fuckin' *dumb* to live," Clayton said. But what he was thinking of was the length of heavy chain stowed in the trunk of his car, a mint green El Dorado parked just inside the gate, and of other dark country roads, in other states and times. He was thinking *Jasper, Texas time.*

Just then a minivan appeared in the distance, headlights glaring, moving toward them at near-highway speed. As it approached, the bum weaved perilously, almost tumbling into a narrow grassy ditch by the side of the road, then weaving back into the oncoming lane. Clayton and Ellis grinned, anticipating high-impact splat.

But at the last instant, the driver swerved, leaning on the horn as the minivan passed within inches of the teetering drunk. Clayton got a glimpse of a panicked soccer mom–type at the wheel, her mouth a perfect O of shock as the minivan sped by then laid on the brakes, screeching past the gate to stop some two hundred yards to the other side.

The minivan sat in the middle of the road, engine running. Clayton looked at Ellis. "Goddam it, go see if they're all right," he told him. "I'll deal with him."

Ellis nodded like a bobble-head doll and took off, unslinging his gun as he headed for the minivan. Clayton turned his attention to the back-woods homeboy who now stood like a scraggle-assed scarecrow squarely in front of the fresh-painted sign that announced WELCOME TO CUSTIS MANOR, and apparently oblivious to how he had just cheated a richly de-served death. It pissed Clayton off. He moved away from his post and closed the distance, walking, not running, toward the bum.

"Hey!" he called out. "Hey, boy!"

But as if to add insult to narrowly averted injury, the bum ignored—or was too fucked up to hear—him, and instead turned toward the sign, legs spread, head tilted back. And before Clayton's disbelieving eyes, the bum unzipped his fly, whipped it out, and started to pee.

"Mother*fucker*," Clayton hissed, picking up his pace. He called back to Ellis, who was at the minivan now. "Get them OUTTA HERE!" Ellis nodded and knocked on the driver's side window.

Back at the sign, the bum laughed, a golden stream arcing up to tag the neat, cursive script. It sparkled in the glare of the floodlights and made Clayton's blood boil. He felt the heavy Colt slap against his ribcage as he moved closer, thought about unleashing it. But no, this buck he wanted to take apart the old-fashioned way.

"Hey BOY!" he spat, almost upon the bum now, a stream of invective coursing through his mind. "Boy, you fuckin' *deaf*?"

Clayton glanced back. Ellis was gone. The minivan's reverse lights winked on, gears whining as it backed up.

Clayton turned back to the bum, who had whirled to face him. A primordial part of Clayton's intellect kicked in, screaming *Not drunk! Not a bum!*

Not good.

Clayton had time to reach for his gun and pull it free. Then something small and sharp flashed in the black man's hand as it arced up, caught Clayton in mid-solar plexus and punched through. The impact stopped Clayton dead in his tracks; his knees buckled like a cheap card table and he went down, the blade staying in to saw a red divot across his AB motto, bisecting it neatly between the *"IN"* and the *"DIE"* before it popped out with a wet, puckering sound.

Clayton collapsed to his knees. The mysterious black man stood over him, his eyes sharp, focused, and clear, and pulled back the hood of his sweatshirt. "Name's Henri, douche bag," he said.

Clayton tried to speak, but all that came out was froth and bile. Henri gave him a little nudge with one knee, and Clayton Pierce fell over to suck wind and die, a few steps short of Valhalla.

Henri wasted no time, searching the carcass for keys and then dragging it into the weeds. As he emerged, the minivan pulled up. Caroline was at the wheel, Josh riding shotgun, the others waiting in the back with the no-less surprised and rapidly cooling remains of Ellis DePugh. Josh looked at Henri nervously.

"Are you okay?" he asked.

Henri held up the keys, jingling.

And they were in.

31

Custis Manor. Underworld.

Silas Custis emerged from the manor house cloaked in swirling, milky mist. He was concentrated evil, compressed into form, and everything about him conjured impressions of death and decay: a sinister figure descending the manor steps and heading for the wharf. His charnel kingdom sprawled before him, hellhounds baying in the distance, punctuated by the piteous shrieks of slaves dying in abject terror again and again.

Justin watched from his hiding place on the banks of the murky water as Silas boarded a small skiff on the distant side and pushed off, heading into the heart of the swamp. Justin's strength was returning, his missing hand now bandaged at the wrist, less as a therapeutic measure than simply to blunt the bloody distraction of it. With Mia's assistance—and the macabre feedings she had expertly administered—Justin had practiced moving, first around the shack, then eventually venturing out into the strange nocturnal landscape, acclimating himself to the odd physics of the place. The air itself was thin and strangely scented, and seemed to move and crawl within his lungs; the ground too seemed alive, like some great beast lost in a deep and impermeable slumber. The sky overhead churned and roiled continuously, a dense gunmetal gray. Everything was tinged with an eerie electric glow. It reminded Justin of bad trips gone by; worse yet, it reminded him of their last night at the manor.

Justin looked at his watch, saw the hands spinning and twirling madly, counting nothing. He took it off and tossed it into the black water, where slithering things chased it to an unseen bottom. Time meant nothing here.

But elsewhere, oh yes . . . Back in the world, their friends awaited and plotted their turn. They were coming soon, but when and how he would know, Justin could not say.

Fortunately, Lucas did, or said he did, and they were not in much of a position to argue. Justin did not like it; he felt uncharacteristically helpless, a babe abandoned on the doorstep of an obscure and unforgiving Hell. But as his strength grew, he felt more of a sense of, if not impatience, then certainly urgency. And after Lucas showed him the ways of Underworld, much as he had originally initiated Mia, Justin knew: this place must end. And somehow, they must help.

Justin watched Silas depart, hating him. Suddenly Lucas sounded behind them. *Do not stare too long,* he admonished. *It is not safe.*

Justin nodded, hunkering down. But he couldn't stop watching the hideous figure. Sure enough, Silas turned just as his boat was swallowed by the trees, his gaze seeming to seek them out in their hiding place. Justin shrank back involuntarily.

Come, Lucas said. *We must go.*

Justin nodded.

No shit, he thought.

32

Friday, August 29. Custis Manor. 7:56 p.m.

The plan, such as it was, was as simple as it was unforgiving: Get in. Free the spirits. Destroy the manor. And get out. Taken as a whole, it was also either breathtakingly bold or stark raving stupid. It was a toss-up as to how any of the former Underground members would have cast their vote, had they been given one, which they weren't.

The first part was comparatively easy, if "easy" included rapid lethal force. After breaching the gate, Henri and Russell commandeered Clayton's El Dorado and drove down the winding road to the manor. The rest of the team hung back in the minivan with the headlights off, watching.

The Custis vehicles were parked in front of the manor and guarded by two drivers, who stood idly smoking and chatting. They looked up, perplexed, as Clayton's car glided up; as the drivers approached, the passenger-side window rolled down, revealing Russell. On his face was a toothy grin; in his hands was a Heckler & Koch MP5SD, a short, light-weight assault weapon with a telescoping buttstock and extracapacity clip. An integrated aluminum silencer/flash suppressor wrapped around its stumpy muzzle and protruded from the window like a fat black cigar.

"Evenin', gents," Russell said and popped off four quick 9mm rounds in two-round bursts. The silencer coughed—*phut-phut, phut-phut.* The drivers dropped, stone dead.

Henri and Russell parked and bailed from the car, signaling to the others. The minivan rolled up and everyone piled out. As Kahlil strode over to Russell and high-fived him, and Joya embraced Henri, Caroline, Seth and Josh exchanged immensely worried looks. They were afraid— of their increasingly irrevocable roles in multiple homicides, of the fact that any remaining illusive shreds of normalcy had now fled them for- ever. But even more, they were afraid of the house itself. It had been a lifetime since any of them had seen it, nightmares notwithstanding. The manor did not disappoint: at once placid and sinister, it towered imperiously over them, as if daring them to enter.

For his part, Henri didn't much care who they killed at this point; if you were white and on the grounds, you were fair game. Only Josh and his party were exempt from this, and not by much; Josh's authority was rapidly waning among the brothers, who clearly had their own agenda, and Henri had no problem putting a laser-dotted cap in Josh's ass should it come to that. Henri considered the simple existence of Custis Manor an abomination, Dachau as Disneyland. That alone warranted its destruction, in his eyes. The rest was just grease on the collective wheel of karma. There was not a thing they could do to quell the vio- lence that was to come. It had its own velocity, its own momentum, and it would not stop until Custis Manor burned. Fortunately, that was part of the plan.

Unfortunately, there were a few decidedly unplanned aspects: namely, the firefight at the church had not only revealed the betrayal of Rajim but had further cost them the now-dead Mohammad and the wounded Louis, whom they had no choice but to leave back at the house, along with Kevin, Amy, and Zoe. And while the latter were of little conse- quence in Henri's estimation, the former comprised the entirety of their munitions team. Which left no one truly experienced enough to set off the bombs.

Henri smiled grimly as Kahlil opened the back door of the minivan. They'd just have to fake it.

The men moved quickly, off-loading gear. Caroline and Seth watched as the first items emerged: oddly enough, they were speakers, cased in black PVC enclosures, and a road case containing a small rack-mounted powered audio mixer and MP3 player—a full-on DJ rig. Then came a pair of tall wooden African drums, beaded and painted, decidedly unmodern and exotic. Caroline looked on skeptically as Henri inspected them.

"We having a party?" she asked sarcastically.

"Sort of," Henri replied.

Next came a series of aluminum flight cases containing a veritable treasure trove of high-end firepower. Josh had spared no expense: it was like a Christmas wish list, if Santa were a Mossad agent. There were more HKs—MP5As with laser sights and MPK5s, a dual-grip, close-quarter weapon of choice, highly favored by SWAT teams and discriminating drug lords alike—along with what looked like several thousand rounds of ammo in Gortex-sheathed bandolier rigs. There were Night Owl night-vision goggles with integrated infrared illuminators and precision optics that offered a focus range of roughly nine inches to infinity. Two other cases contained the heavy ordnance: no Tim McVeigh–style jerry-rigged manure bombs, but C-4, military grade, packed in tidy two-kilo bricks, with digitally synched detonators. In all, it was sufficient to blast the mansion to toothpicks.

Henri and his crew suited up, locking and loading, as Caroline and Seth warily watched. Josh peered into the distance, toward the wharf. "We gotta hurry," he said.

"Relax," Henri told him. "This is our gig now. You just along for the ride." Though weapons were in abundance, none were offered to Caroline.

She took offense. "What, am I supposed to be defenseless?" she demanded.

"Nope," Henri replied. "You supposed to be *bait*." Henri looked at

Seth. "How 'bout it?" he said, holding up an HK. "Know how to use one?"

"Not really," Seth said. He detested guns and always had, all the more so after today's debacle. Henri put the machine gun down, then reached into his waistband and withdrew a fat revolver: the former Clayton Pierce's freshly liberated Colt Python.

"Here," he said. "Six-shot, point 'n' shoot." Henri demonstrated, thumbing the hammer back and forth so the cylinder clicked and rotated. "Gun so dumb even a white boy couldn't fuck it up. Got a kick, though." He held it out to Seth.

"Don't want it." Seth shook his head. "Don't need it." Henri regarded him gravely and shoved the gun in his hands anyway.

"Yet," he said.

33

Inside the house, they unloaded the gear and quickly fanned out: Kahlil and Russell moving up the massive stairs as the others paused to survey the great hall. The recently defaced portraits had been removed, leaving faint outlines on the walls. For Josh and company, the absence of the glowering visage of Silas Custis was a minor blessing at best, but they took it where they could find it. Caroline looked around, doing a nervous headcount.

"Where's Joya?" she asked the others. Suddenly Joya appeared framed in the doorway to the grand ballroom, clad in flowing, many-colored ceremonial robes shot through with fine iridescent threads. She looked at once out of place and ethereally magisterial, like something from another world. She gestured inside.

"Here. This is the nexus. This is where it began."

The others shivered instinctively, wondering how exactly she knew. Joya explained it was a natural power point and the site of the original rift that Josh and his friends had unwittingly opened so long ago. As Henri stood guard, she called Caroline to assist her, while instructing Josh and Seth to set up the sound equipment.

"What are we doing this for?" Seth asked as he busily snaked cable across the floor, connecting speakers to the main rig.

"Sound is part of the ritual," Josh explained. "It will establish the primary anchor point for entry into Underworld."

"Oh," Seth grumbled. "Right."

Joya gave Caroline a small bag containing the same red powder they had seen on the floor of Doris's basement. "Make a circle," she told her. "Large enough for us all." They nodded and began working in opposite directions from where they stood, describing an arcing circumference across the polished wood floors.

They were just finishing as Kahlil and Russell returned, bearing a large, standing mirror from elsewhere in the house; this they placed in the center of the circle as Henri finished rigging wires to charges to detonator, hot-wiring ordnance. He nodded, and the men stripped off their weapons and took positions in the center of the room, beside the circle, and with the drums. Josh fired up the sound system; power lights winked on. He went to the MP3 player and pressed a button.

Suddenly the room filled with sound: soft at first, voices like wind riffling through distant trees, set against a low, slow beat, deep as the pulse of the earth. Joya nodded to Kahlil and Russell; they began to play, synching themselves with the beat. The ethereal voices grew syncopated, weaving through the rhythms in what to the uninitiated seemed a strange and exotic tongue; as it grew, Kahlil and Russell joined in with the equivalent of primal shout-outs, punctuating the message, underscoring its urgency. The mixture of live and recorded audio, reverberating through the cavernous room, created a hypnotic soundscape that surrounded and infused everyone in the room.

The rhythm mounted in urgency, the chanting growing both focused and slightly frenzied, a visceral pagan pulse pulling them inexorably into its spell. As the intensity grew, Joya began chanting to herself, her voice fusing with and riding over the wall of sound.

Joya held out her hand and bade each of them enter the circle. This they did: first Caroline, then Seth, and then Josh. One by one, she reached up and opened their shirts; one by one they bared their chests to Joya's ceremonial blade, riding the crest of the words even as she pierced the first veil of flesh: tentatively at first, then faster, as the pain became familiar. And the blood began to flow . . .

. . . and then Joya began drawing the symbols on the glass, writ in the blood of the Underground. The mirror responded, rippling blackly before them, spidery veins spreading across the flat silvered surface, which suddenly metamorphosed, becoming somehow deeper, darker, the reflection suffused with a strange, otherworldly glow. Their flesh prickled, tiny hairs goosing up like dermal radar, hackles rising. The air itself felt suddenly alive; outside the windows, they could see first dozens, then hundreds of fireflies swirling and banging against the glass, their winking insectoid light flaring and glowing entirely too brightly, their random patterns of flight suddenly synchronizing into a discernible pattern: a spiraling vortex, corkscrewing upward. Inside the drum circle the sound crescendoed like waves crashing against a rocky tidal break, and beneath it they heard, riptide quick, an ominous crackling sound, as if time and space itself were rending at the core.

And as they watched, the mirror irised open to allow them entry.

Joya turned to Caroline, Josh, and Seth.

"Now," she said.

One by one they stepped through: Josh first, followed by Seth, each absorbed into the surface and disappearing. Then it was Caroline's turn. She took a deep, halting breath and stepped through, and as she disappeared within, the surface of the glass went placid and still.

Suddenly Henri flipped a switch on the timer. A beep sounded and little LEDs registered *60:00,* then started clocking back in one-second increments: *59:59, 59:58, 59:57* . . . Joya looked at Henri, aghast.

"What are you doing? What if they don't get back in time?"

"Not my problem," he said flatly. "This place goes with or without them."

"Turn it off," Joya said, stepping out of the circle.

"I'm sorry, sister," Henri replied. "There's no stopping it now."

It was 8:20 p.m.

34

Custis Manor. Underworld.

Deep in the swamp, Silas felt power in the air. The sky twisted above him as fetid water lapped at the worm-eaten edges of the skiff upon which he stood, glimmering blackly in the moonlight. Silas dipped a long, gnarled pole into the muddy depths and pushed the skiff along with white-knuckled hands. As he did, a shudder passed through him and Silas looked down. Somewhere below lay the bony husk of his mortal remains. Silas remembered his last tortured moments of life, redolent with outrage and betrayal, the vile and pungent waters filling his throat and searing his lungs as he sank thrashing below the surface. He remembered his last glimpse of sunlight, the vision blurring into swirling murk. He remembered his wildly beating heart seizing up in his chest, going cold as the waters that enfolded him, as the spark of withered mortal life passed rudely from his flesh. And he remembered the dawning dreadful realization as he rose into the forever night of his unearthly domain: that he was a slave to the power coiled in this place, even as those he had dominated were enslaved to his designs. In his own way, he was trapped as truly they were.

Behind him, Silas heard the distant yet urgent pulse of tribal chanting. He drew his cloak of shadows around him, thrusting his pole into
the dark waters to propel himself forward. The intruders were out
there, seeking entry. They would be coming soon.

His ear turned toward another low and urgent chanting coming from
a tiny islet before him, upon which stood the small and ragged hut. The
faint glow of firelight pulsed in the windows. His progeny were there,
making offerings to invoke him. The stench of the *nganga* beckoned,
soon to fill the air with the scent of fresh young blood. Silas felt the
hunger uncoil within him. The moment of Transition was at hand.

In the grand ballroom, the mirror stood shrouded in dust and reflecting emptiness. Suddenly its surface crackled and rippled, and they
emerged.

Josh came first, gasping and shivering and crumpling to the floor. He
was followed next by Seth, who bore the passage somewhat better but
stood on unsteady legs. He shook it off and looked around, his eyes ad-
justing to the ethereal light.

Too fucking weird, he muttered, then helped Josh to his feet. The two
men looked at the vast room, now emptied but for the mirror, which
pulsed within its massive gilt frame. From within they could hear
sounds, muffled and distorted. They sounded like cries for help.

Shit, Josh hissed. Seth watched as Josh thrust his arms elbow deep
into the oily surface of the mirror. The spidery veins striating the glass
spread into his skin, worming their way up his arm. *I can't reach . . .* , he
gasped.

Seth shuddered and joined in, one hand gripping the edge of the
frame as the other pushed in, first to the elbow, then to the shoulder. A
moment later the men pulled back, bringing Caroline out, gasping. She
promptly retched, shaking from the passage; Josh held her steady as her
head cleared and she looked around.

Oh my God, she said. Even her voice sounded strange, the words reverberating and trailing in little inverted whispers, skittering like rats in the corners. *Where the hell are we?*

Not Hell, a voice sounded behind them. *Certainly not Heaven. This is a place in between.* They turned and saw Lucas standing by the door. He strode toward them purposefully, extending his hand. Josh shook it, then turned to Seth and Caroline.

This is Lucas, he said. *He's with us.*

Seth and Caroline shook Lucas's hand, nodding uneasily. As they did, they noticed, in the odd light of this place, that their skin looked the same—translucently dark, like flesh under a black light, and lit as with an inner fire.

Seth looked back at the mirror. Outside, an infernal gale howled, carrying with it the sound of distant screams. The massive house creaked and groaned like a beast emerging from a deep slumber, as though their very presence had disrupted its repose. Lucas gestured to the doorway.

Please, he admonished. *Your friends are waiting. We don't have much time . . .*

Lucas turned and headed for the door. Josh and Seth and Caroline looked at him and quickly followed.

In the main hall they ascended the great staircase, which turned and twisted at funhouse angles. Like the rest of the house, it seemed both moldering and frozen in time; the very walls seemed to ooze corruption. As they reached the landing, they saw two figures standing in the long hall, their backs turned toward them as they stared into one of the bedrooms. Caroline gasped.

My God. Mia . . .

The couple turned then, and their hearts fluttered as one. After twenty years of guilt and nightmare recrimination, Josh, Caroline, and Seth could scarcely believe their eyes. Both Mia and Justin had been transformed, their features chiseled and intense, their flesh supple yet weirdly enhanced, as if their likenesses were carved by the hand of a furtive god. They had become spirit warriors, fearsome and elegant, somehow more than themselves: not of this strange world, yet no longer of the mortal realm.

At first, the others were disoriented and frightened. And then Mia and Justin embraced them, and they realized that these ethereal creatures were indeed their friends. Once, and always.

I missed you so much, Caroline murmured, tears flowing down her cheeks like silvered streams. Mia held her, her warmth infusing her friend's chill flesh. Mia reached out to touch Seth's cheek. He was crying too. Josh looked at Justin, and the two men hugged like long-lost brothers. Josh saw the stump where Justin's missing hand belonged. *Are you okay?* he asked.

Yeah, Justin replied. *No pain. Just strange.*

It was then that Lucas interrupted the reunion, told them what they must do to awaken the trapped souls. As they listened, he directed their attention to the room they faced. It was one of the bedrooms, moldering and uninhabited. A large four-poster bed swathed in curtained muslin dominated the interior. It took the newcomers a moment to recognize it.

Oh my God, Caroline whispered and looked at Mia. She met her gaze with one of infinite sadness and understanding. Lucas commanded their attention.

Watch, he instructed.

As they did, they saw a blur of frenetic motion appear, bringing with it a swirl of choking sound. It careened across the room like a dervish, a bizarre Tasmanian Devilish hallucination, shifting in and out of focus. And the members of the Underground looked on in horror as the phantom stopped, glitched, and came into focus.

Simon, Seth muttered. Justin and Mia nodded. It was the spirit of their old friend, eternally locked in his moment of madness and mayhem, the moment he had attacked Mia. The bloody knife was clasped in one spattered hand, his fingers knotted and gnarled, as if he and the weapon had become one. His face was a ragged meat collage of mutilated rage and pain. They watched as he screamed and lunged at the empty bed, the knife coming up and down again and again, slashing at the diaphanous curtains, killing no one and nothing, forever. They could see Justin tense, reflexes coiling instinctively. It was then that Lucas whispered.

You must do this, he said. Justin steeled himself and stepped into the room.

SIMON! he cried.

The spirit whirled, gasping the thin air. His eyes were black and sunken pits, his expression crazed and savage. In the space of a heartbeat, he was off the bed, lunging and whirling toward Justin, knife raised as he howled in inchoate agony. And as before, Justin met him with greater force, slamming into the ravaged ghost, the two merging into one twisting and gyrating mass. The room shook with the impact, great timbers creaking and groaning from the psychic onslaught. Plaster cracked and fell in ragged chunks from the walls, the ceiling.

It was then that Lucas entered, followed quickly by Seth, Caroline, and Mia. They fanned out, forming a wary perimeter around the warring duo. Suddenly the frenzied motion halted and they saw Justin straddled across Simon's scrawny torso, his knees pinning the dead boy's thrashing arms to the floor. Simon's head thrashed like a rabid dog on meth, mangled features contorted, spittle flecking from the corners of a jack-o'-lantern maw.

And as the others watched, Mia came to him then, descending like an avenging angel of infinite power and grace. She knelt beside Simon and reached out, gently but firmly cupping the ruined contours of his face.

Shhhhhh, she whispered. *Shhhhhhhh . . .*

And just like that, Simon stopped, momentarily transfixed. His sunken chest heaved, breath quivering raggedly. Mia leaned close.

Shhhhhhhhh . . .

And as Simon's soul hung abated, Justin reached out with his one good hand and opened the lost boy's shirt. The others gasped as Justin's hand pushed through gray and pitted flesh, working its way toward his heart. Simon mewled, tiny and piteous, as twin sparks lit in blackened eyeless sockets. And Simon's flayed brow furrowed. Dauntlessly, Justin touched Simon's soul. As the sparks glowed where his eyes had been, he crumpled, sobbing.

I'm sorry, he murmured. *I'm so sorry . . .*

The others watched, amazed, as Mia and Justin helped the boy up, embracing him. When Simon rose, the huge divots in his face had partially healed. He looked at his old friends, smiling uneasily. Then his features grew pensive. Gone was the madness and manic energy; he looked like a lost and frightened child.

I wanna go home, he said in a tiny voice. *Can I please go home?*

Mia and Justin looked at Lucas. He nodded.

And as they hugged and released Simon, the sparks in his eyes grew bright. Mia placed a tender, almost maternal kiss on his now-healed brow. Simon looked up as if seeing something beyond them, beyond the room, beyond time and space and comprehension. The dead boy's spirit cast one glance back at his old friends. The sparks grew so bright they had to look away, celestial illumination filling the room. Then they faded.

And when they looked back again, Simon was no more.

Mia and Justin looked at their friends, at Lucas. For one perfect moment, they were all swept up in the conviction that somehow everything would work out.

And that was when Justin began to scream.

35

Back in the *nganga* shack, Duke looked ready to hurl. It was one thing to benefit from the trappings and privileges of dark familial power, quite another to have to roll up his sleeves and do the dirty work himself.

Which he was now, in no uncertain terms, obliged to do.

"Gurk," he belched, gorge suddenly buoyant and rising. The *nganga* squatted before him, black and ghastly. Its lid was off as tongues of fire roasted its contents to a fetid and simmering boil. The stench was thick and vivid, its vapors compounded in the claustrophobic confines of the little shack. Duke looked green as he stared into it, saw squirming things bubble and pop in the tumescent goo. He started to get up, and Eli's bony hand clamped down on his shoulder, hard and surprisingly strong.

You wanted it, boy," he hissed. "You got it. Now *pay* for it!"

Duke looked back, eyes brimming with acrid tears, mucus streaming from his nostrils. The old man was stripped to the waist and smeared with ash, as was Duke, in preparation for the ritual. A fat stogie was clenched in his yellowed teeth, its end glowing amber. Eli's pale and flaccid flesh quivered with anticipation, and for a moment Duke thought he could see something slither under the old man's skin.

"Pop, I cah . . . I can't," Duke pleaded.

"You *can*," Eli intoned. "And you *will!*"

Behind them lay the drugged and captive child. As the ritual had commenced, Eli had explained that every scrap of skin or knuckle joint that was sacrificed offered that much more power to the Great Night. In theory it had seemed doable; Duke had spent a lifetime relishing petty tortures. But now, confronted with the source of his power and the price to be paid, he had quavered. And so before the main course was served, Eli had opted for an appetizer.

"He is coming!" Eli commanded. "Do it!!"

Duke looked down: in one trembling hand he held a pair of rusted shears; in the other, Justin's severed hand. The pinkie finger was missing. Duke looked into the *nganga* and watched the sheared phalange slip below the surface. He promptly vomited. Eli smacked him in the back of the head.

"Fool!" Eli bellowed. *"Do it!"*

Hands shaking, Duke made another snip.

36

Custis Manor. Underworld.

Justin screamed and held up his stump as they all witnessed the flesh begin to curdle and wither. Mia grabbed onto him as Justin collapsed, writhing in agony.

Do something! she cried.

Where is the hand? Lucas asked. Josh blurted out the story of the hit squad, the assault on the church. As he listened, Lucas stared out into the swamp, in the direction of the islet. He looked at them gravely.

Keep going, he said to Caroline and Seth. *Find who you can, and free them.* With that, he turned and made for the door.

You can't leave us! Caroline called out. *Where are you going?*

Somewhere you cannot, he replied, eyes flashing. Then Lucas took off, leaving Mia, Josh, Seth, and Caroline behind with the suffering Justin and their own mounting terror. Josh looked at his friends; Caroline was horrified but adamant, tears of fear and anger welling. Their fragile reunion, so long in coming, was unraveling before them. She reached out for Mia and hugged her desperately.

Fuck this, she said. *I won't leave you! I can't . . .*

You have to, Mia told her. *We'll be all right.* Her voice was soothing, but her eyes said otherwise. She looked at Josh, who nodded grimly.

Caroline held onto Mia like a drowning woman in a ocean of despair. She stifled a sob as Josh pulled her away, sobbed again as Seth enfolded her in a protective embrace. Mia cradled Justin's head; Justin moaned, tremors wracking his flesh.

Go, Mia told them. *We'll see you soon . . .*

She smiled bravely. They all smiled back.

But no one really believed it.

Josh led Seth and Caroline through shadowed fields; by the time they had exited the manor, Caroline's tears had all but dried. Her expression was now one of steely resolve: the world she had known, the nonstop parade of work and bills and pressure and obligation to all things real and rational had evaporated, as if it had never existed. They moved furtively through the strange and fevered dreamscape until they came to a series of wretched hovels stretching out into the blackness. They could see the souls of the lost cowering in shadowed doorways, could hear the sound of many voices murmuring uncertainly.

The slaves' quarters, Josh whispered. *The highest spirit concentration is here.*

So how do we do it? Seth asked.

Like this, Josh replied. One by one, Josh seized upon the spirits, repeating the ritual he had been taught; one by one, the spirits were freed. Caroline and Seth joined in; warily at first, as each lost soul struggled weakly, only to succumb, then more urgently as the growing ranks of the saved awakened and stood trembling and disoriented. The spirits milled uncertainly, not knowing what to do with their sudden liberation.

Each of you has the power to free another! Josh called out. *Help them!*

Slowly, the tide began to turn. Once awakened, few of them refused the opportunity. Their collective energy came visible as a beacon swirling into the heavens, a spiraling tower rising up, drawing the liberated souls toward it like moths to a spirit flame. As their spirits intertwined, glowing golden threads extended from their hearts, joining the growing weave of light.

Release your pain! Josh called out. Those who did were themselves released, souls disembarking from spent spirit bodies that instantly cindered and burned in the supercharged air. Their soulfire stoked the mounting flame, which grew brighter with every passing second. Beckoning to the legions of the lost. Calling them to freedom.

As bit by bit, the beacon grew . . .

37

Back at *casa* Tabb, Amy chain-smoked, thoroughly wired. Kevin leaned against the counter, eyeballing the cordless phone hanging in its cradle on the wall. Zoe paced and stewed, full of righteous rage. Doris watched Louis, who sat, feverish and high, at the cluttered table. His pain, alleviated only by Amy's dwindling stash, was palpable to all. A thin sheen of sweat beaded his brow. His head occasionally nodded, his fingers twitching ever so slightly. But his hand never strayed far from the gun laying next to the Little Black Sambo ashtray.

The gun that had been there ever since the others had left.

Kevin watched Louis's head bob and inched ever so carefully toward the phone. "Don't even think about it," Louis said.

Kevin held his hands up in supplication. "I don't understand you!" he said. "They're out there doing God knows what, and you need help!"

"I'm fine," Louis said.

"You're not fine," Kevin said. "You're hurt and you're high! How is that okay??"

"It is what it is," Louis replied.

"Tell me about it," Zoe muttered back, for different reasons altogether.

219

It had come as a rude shock, having gone through the madness of the day, when Josh and the others had emerged from the basement and readied themselves to go. He had conferred with Amy at the last moment and then announced to Zoe, Kevin, and Doris that they were not to come along. He had explained that Louis would be a liability in his condition, Amy needed to stay behind to tend to his wounds and help keep the others under control, and the rest of them . . . well, it was just too dangerous. Doris had nodded and heartily agreed; Kevin had seemed agitated but weirdly relieved, though he remained deeply concerned about Caroline.

But Zoe . . .

Zoe was seething. She felt cheated and dissed: dragged into a bizarre familial drama that had morphed into an even more bizarre unfolding unreality, only to be reduced to mere *child* status in the end.

"This sucks," she said bitterly, for roughly the ten billionth time. "This is so fucked . . ."

"Zoe, please," Kevin said. "Josh was right." He could scarcely believe the words as they came from his mouth, had never believed that he would say such a thing. It was further evidence of their total departure from reality. Zoe huffed and glared at him, brimming with fury; Kevin looked at Amy and Doris imploringly.

"Josh was right, Zoe. It's too dangerous," Amy said. "You don't know what you'd be dealing with . . ."

"And you did?" Zoe spat back. "I'm older than you were when this all first happened!"

"And I've spent the last twenty years dealing with it!" Amy countered. "Is that what you want? Do you want to wake up screaming every night? If you get to wake up at all?"

"I just want to end what you started," Zoe said.

Amy winced, visibly stung. "We didn't start this, Zoe."

"No, you didn't." Louis looked up, his eyes hooded yet strangely clear. His fingers touched the smooth porcelain of the little black caricature. "None of us did," he amended. "But we gonna finish it."

And with that, Louis picked up the gun and stood, bracing himself against the wall.

"Everybody up," he said. They stood, suddenly fearful; their hands all raised warily. "Over there," Louis said, gesturing toward the pantry with the gun. Everyone moved toward the door; Kevin first, followed by Doris. They stood in the cramped confines of the pantry, flanked on all sides by mammies and sambos, toms and picaninnies, coons and brutes and golliwogs, all smiling as if in on a very secret joke.

Which left Amy and Zoe, hovering at the entrance uncertainly. Louis looked at them.

"What's it gonna be?" he said. "In or out?"

Zoe looked at him, then at Amy, Kevin, and Doris. She pulled the door closed, the lock clicking shut.

Louis tossed his keys to Zoe.

"You drive," he said.

38

Friday, August 29. Custis Manor.

The black Bronco rolled through the gate like a shark through murky current, headlights off as it glided down the drive. As Zoe pulled up to the house and keyed off the ignition, Louis reached down between the seat and the console and withdrew a fat black maglight. His condition had visibly worsened, his eyes red-rimmed and puffy, his pain dulled but evident through the narcotic haze. Zoe looked suddenly worried as adrenaline and attitude gave way to growing anxiety.

"Are you sure you're okay?"

"Never mind me," he said. "Worry about yourself."

"I'm ready," Zoe said.

"No, you're not," Amy's voice sounded from the rear seat. She was looking at the vast and implacable façade of the house. Even in the dim dashboard glow she looked ashen, uneasy. She looked at Zoe. "I think you should stay out here."

"What?!" Zoe blurted flatly. "What the fuck are you talking about? I've got as much right to be here as you do!"

"This isn't a contest, Zoe," Amy said. She looked at Louis imploringly.

"You don't understand the power of this place. It feeds on what's inside you. Pain. Anger. Secrets . . ."

"I don't *have* any secrets," Zoe said. "My mother is the one with the secrets, and she's already in there!"

"It's not just your mother, goddammit! It's about your father too . . ."

"I don't *have* a father!" Zoe hissed, her eyes narrowing to wounded slits. "My stepfather is locked in a fucking closet, and my real father is—"

"Josh," Amy said, cutting her off. Zoe stopped, stunned. "Your father is Josh!"

Zoe said nothing at first, her silence oppressive in the Bronco's close confines. It all clicked shockingly into place. The way Josh looked at her. The simple math of it all. Which, when followed to its inevitable origin given her age and their history, equaled an even more appalling epiphany. "Oh God," she gasped, feeling ill. "Oh God. You're telling me I was *conceived* in this fucking place?"

"Worse," Amy told her. "It's like Joya said: this place isn't just a part of you, it's *in* you. *His* blood. *His* history. And he'll use it against you if he can."

"Fuck you," Zoe hissed. "*Fuck* you." Her voice was steely but her eyes were bright with tears. Amy reached out for her.

"NO!" Zoe said, and threw the door wide. And before they could stop her, she was gone. Running from the brutal truth of it all. Running into the fields.

"Shit," Amy muttered and started to follow. Louis shook his head and took a bitter breath.

"Let her go," he said.

Inside, Amy and Louis moved cautiously, peering warily into every shadow, every nook. As they approached the great hall, Louis suddenly stiffened, nostrils flaring.

"What's wrong?" Amy asked.

Louis drew his gun and motioned for her to shut up. The great hall was dark and dreadfully silent as they entered; a thin pall of acrid haze hung over the vast expanse like an alien atmosphere. A trail of bullet holes pocked the plaster walls in wild connect-the-dot chains. Suddenly Amy gasped.

"Louis . . ."

Louis turned, and the maglight beam swept the darkened interior. Then he gasped too.

And they beheld an abattoir.

Just past the long table, the bodies of Kahlil, Russell, and Henri slumped grotesquely over the ritual drums, splayed and gutted. Long ropes of entrails coiled and snaked through their pooled blood, obliterating the circle and conjoining in a tangled mass at the center. Worse yet, the mirror had been shattered into a thousand ragged shards; glittering fragments littering the floor like islands in a rapidly congealing charnel sea. Joya's ceremonial dagger stood abandoned in the carnage, its tip stuck deep into the hardwood floor. But Joya was nowhere to be found.

"What does it mean?" Amy asked, terrified.

"Off the toppa my head, I'd say it means y'all are fucked."

They turned in shock as a small red dot of glowing light appeared dead center on Amy's chest and Jimmy Joe Baker emerged from the shadows, holding an AR-15 assault rifle with nightscope and laser sight. He grinned imperiously.

"Drop the iron," he said flatly, "or I drop the bitch."

Louis hesitated a moment, fingers clenching the weapon. "Don't do it," Amy whispered. "Louis, please . . ."

The dot moved from Amy's chest to a point between her eyes. Louis released the gun, and it fell clattering to the floor.

"Good boy," Jimmy Joe said. "Now kick it on over."

Louis obeyed; the gun skittered and slid through the muck. Jimmy Joe gestured skyward with the muzzle of the rifle for them to raise their hands. As they did, Jimmy Joe circled them, a toying predator. "Very good," he said. "Now get down."

Louis did not move. "I said, *down!*" Jimmy Joe barked and jabbed the butt of the rifle viciously into his side. Louis buckled and collapsed in agony.

"Bastard!" Amy hissed and turned toward him; Jimmy Joe smashed the butt of the gun into her solar plexus. Amy sucked wind and went down on all fours on the gore-soaked floor. She fought the urge to pass out, her ears ringing madly, the pain overwhelming.

"Y'all been a royal pain in my ass," he said. "But it's over now. Your little pals ain't coming back. And you ain't ever leavin' here. Question is, which one do I do first?" He pointed the muzzle first at Amy, then at Louis.

"Eenie, meenie, miney, moe. Catch a . . ." he chuckled, ". . . by the toe." The gun moved back and forth as the sick sing-song continued.

"If he hollers, let 'im go . . ."

Amy's fingers grazed against a gleaming shard, and for a heartbeat she thought she saw something spark across its surface, a faint blue-white filigree of light.

"Eenie, meenie, miney . . . aw, fuck it," he said. And turned the gun on Louis.

"NO!" Amy wailed, grasping the shard and whirling. Amy thrust forward with every ounce of strength she had, sinking it deep into the juncture of hip and thigh. Jimmy Joe screamed and fell back, the stub of the glass protruding from his crotch, blood jetting blackly.

"Bitch!" he roared. "You fucking bitch!" He reeled, off balance; it was a fleeting window of desperate opportunity. Amy grabbed Joya's dagger and stood, bringing it down between his shoulders, blade crunching through meat and bone and embedding to the hilt. Jimmy Joe howled and began to thrash wildly . . .

. . . and then before their eyes he began to *change*, his visage rippling and distorting as electric tendrils of energy arced from blade to glass and back, pulsing across his flesh then seeming to burn inward, pallid skin bubbling and charring and dropping away in molten chunks, revealing something bestial and putrid. Jimmy Joe Baker gnashed and howled in inchoate rage, transforming into something grotesque and inhuman, monstrous and deformed, less a man than a thing.

But it was still alive. And it was pissed.

The Jimmy Joe–thing whirled, its mouth distending into a raw and gaping hole, its eyes black and sunken. It snarled and lurched toward her . . .

. . . and that was when the shots rang out, round after round after round pumping into the creature. It stumbled forward, puppeteered by leaden death, then crumpled and collapsed to the floor at Amy's feet. She looked up to see Zoe standing at the door, Louis's gun in her hands, the magazine emptied. She sneered defiantly.

"Fuck this," she said. "Let's kick some cracker ass."

Amy nodded, shivering. Louis looked at her.

"You're bleeding," he said.

Amy looked at him, then down at her hand. In the adrenaline-fueled shock of the moment, she had not noticed that a shard of mirror had lacerated her badly, an angry wound now gaped across her palm, blood dripping off her fingertips to spatter the floor. She hissed in shock and anticipation of pain. But as they watched, the edges of the laceration seemed to glow: dimly at first, then brighter.

Amy held her hand out, as if afraid of it. The glow peaked and faded. Amy wiped the blood away. The wound was gone, leaving only a faint mark, like an alternate lifeline, crisscrossing her palm.

"Whoa," she murmured.

Back at the Tabb house, something slammed against the pantry door, then again, then again. Wood cracked and splintered, finally giving way as Kevin came tumbling out, flushed and royally pissed. Doris emerged a moment later as Kevin grabbed the phone.

"What are you doing?" she asked.

"What I should have done a long time ago," he told her. Kevin punched three digits and listened.

"Operator," he said. "I need to report an emergency . . ."

39

Chief Jackson had his hands full when the call came. The circuit had been getting rowdier by the hour, as nightfall combined with alcohol and attitude to ratchet up the evening's festivities. Up and down the boardwalk came reports of crowd control growing edgier, with an increasing emphasis on "crowd" and a decreasing grip on "control." Kids were swarming the bars, sidewalks, and boardwalk; Jackson's nightly tally thus far featured some twenty-three drunk-and-disorderlies, four more fights, and a record twelve indecent exposures, which ranged from errant beer-sodden youth peeing off the pier to kids mooning from cars on the strip to a bit of freelance Mardi Gras flashing by a gaggle of Sigma Delta sisters on the seaward balcony of the Riptides Inn. And whereas most of the kids present were there to have a good time, the problem was that some people's ideas of fun left much to be desired.

Case in point, one Clifton Webb.

The young black man stood cuffed and fuming, leaning against Jackson's patrol car as Jackson finished running his name for priors and outstanding warrants. It came back clean. His age was twenty-one, but Jackson pegged his emotional maturity level at half that, and astonishingly enough he really was a junior at Washington Carver. Webb's frolic of choice featured cruising Atlantic Avenue with a pack of his fratboy homies, setting off car alarms by smashing the windows of a stray half-dozen vehicles parked along the strip. When the cops arrived, Webb's pals bolted in all directions, though Webb, being full of large quantities of both alcohol and attitude, had paused to relieve himself on a store-front window.

"This is police brutality!" Webb bitched loudly to anyone who cared. "This is inhumanity!"

"Shut the fuck up," Jackson muttered. Just then his cellphone rang. Jackson picked up.

"Jackson," he said, then stopped. "What?! When?"

Clifton Webb watched as Chief Jackson began to pace, cellphone plastered to his ear. Then Jackson hung up and fished out his keys.

"Your lucky night, asshole," Jackson muttered, uncuffing him. "Get the hell out of here."

Clifton Webb looked at him warily, suspicious at his strange good fortune. "I'm pressing charges," he began. Jackson glared at him.

"NOW!" he growled.

Webb thought better of it and scrambled off into the night. Just then, Jackson spotted a patrolwoman named Penny Milton. She was young, some two years out of the Tidewater Police Training Academy and recently reassigned to his command. He waved her over.

"Who do we have available?"

"No one, sir," Marsh replied. "It's pretty crazy out there. Is there a problem?"

"Dispatch just got a call about a possible incident at Custis Manor," he said, trying to downplay his unease. Officer Marsh whistled, low. Just what the evening needed.

"Do you want me to go check it out?"

"No." Jackson shook his head. "I'll go. Could be a crank call." He smiled gamely. And desperately hoped he was right.

40

Friday, August 29. Custis Manor. 8:50 p.m.

In the grand ballroom, any sense of relief was fleeting and quickly subsumed by despair. Half of their team was dead or missing, the other half was on the other side—the side now shut off by the destruction of the portal. Then Louis checked the timer on the detonator and things went from very bad to incredibly worse.

"Fuck," he muttered. Amy and Zoe came over in time to see the little LED display on the detonator click from *30:00* to *29:59*, and counting. "It's not supposed to be on yet," he said. Amy looked at him incredulously.

"Can't you turn it off?"

"Not without blowing everything up," he said flatly. He looked at Zoe. "I'm sorry . . ."

"Sorry?" Zoe exclaimed. "You're fucking sorry? My *family* is in there!" She gestured to the broken mirror. "What are we supposed to do now?"

And that was when Amy hushed them. She was staring at the ragged fragments of glass littering the floor as the tiny hairs on the back of her neck prickled. Zoe looked at her.

"What is it?"

Amy ignored her and moved to the center of the room. As she watched the scattered shards, they faintly glowed like fireflies, first one, then another, and another. "Do you see that?"

Zoe and Louis looked at her, perplexed. "See what?" Zoe asked.

Another fragment flashed. "That!" Amy said. She scooped it up and gazed into it.

And for a fleeting moment, something within gazed back.

"What is it?" Zoe asked.

"The mirror," Amy murmured. "Something's in there!" She shuddered, remembering dark figures writing on tenement walls. From the corner of her eye she saw another shard flash and fade.

"There!" Amy cried. "Pick it up!"

Zoe did so. Amy took it in hand. The two pieces fit together perfectly . . . and as they peered into them, the reflection went dark and they saw a glimpse of a hand beckoning.

Across the room, another piece sparked and glowed. They rushed to scoop it up; it too fit perfectly. Another flashed, and another. Amy knelt and began to assemble them on the floor like pieces of an arcane puzzle, calling out each next sparking fragment as Zoe ran to grab them.

And the timer counted: *28:00 . . . 27:59 . . . 27:58 . . .*

"Hurry!" Louis called out as they madly scrambled.

"Last one!" Zoe answered, handing Amy the shard. She fit it into place, and they could see Joya floating in the darkness as if beneath the surface of an icy pond. She pressed against the other side of the glass; it moved but would not yield.

"There's still a piece missing!" Amy hissed, and then realized where it was. She scuttled over to the bestial remains of the former Jimmy Joe Baker, Joya's blade still wedged in his lumpen back. She pulled it out and rolled the body over. Then, taking a deep breath, she took the dagger and dug out the missing shard. As they fit it into place, the cracked surface rippled and went liquid and dark, then bright with ethereal light.

And from deep within, Joya's hand emerged.

Just as quickly as it had appeared, the hand faltered, began to slip beneath the surface. Amy grasped it and pulled with all her might. It wasn't enough. Zoe joined in, and then Louis, reaching elbow deep into the glimmering pool of light . . .

. . . until at last Joya emerged, shivering and shaken but alive.

They hugged her fiercely and helped her to her feet. Joya stood on unsteady legs and explained in halting tones of Henri starting the timer and the resulting argument in which they failed to notice the stealthy appearance of Jimmy Joe Baker. She recounted the attack, of diving into the portal as the first shots rang out. As her head cleared, she saw the remnants of the slaughter . . . and the body of her brother.

"Henri," she murmured. Joya's eyes glistened with tears for a moment as she touched his prone, still form; then she shook it off. "How much time do we have?" she asked. Louis checked the timer.

"Not much. Twenty-five minutes."

Joya nodded and turned to the fragile outline of the re-formed mirror. Its placid surface trembled ominously, a psychic seismic shudder.

"The magick will not hold much longer," she warned them. "We have to go back through."

The others traded uneasy glances; their apprehension, which was legion, was dispelled by the look in her eyes. It was now or never.

So in they went. While behind them, the timer ticked away.

41

Custis Manor. Underworld.

And this is how all Hell at long last broke loose.

In the grand ballroom, they emerged from the mirror one after another: Louis first, then Joya, Amy, and Zoe. The house seemed to shudder at their presence, beams creaking behind the pallid walls as the floors groaned beneath their feet. A strange light glowed beyond the windows, radiating out from the distant slaves' quarters.

Come, Joya urged. *We must hurry.*

As they moved into the great hall and toward the entrance, they looked back and saw that Amy had stopped at the base of the staircase, staring upward as if hearing something else entirely. Her skin was pale and clammy, her eyes wide to drink in the darkness.

What is it? Zoe said. Amy looked at them, incredulous.

Don't you hear it?

They all listened, and there it was: a high, keening moan, distant and piteous, soon joined by another, and another. The cries conjoined like a doomed chorus of madness and lament, each voice melding together yet utterly alone. It was the sound that had burned itself into Amy's neurons decades ago. The sound of the imprisoned Custis women. She had never really stopped hearing it.

But they could all hear it now.

Amy started moving up the stairs. *No!* Louis said, gripping her arm. *We're not here for them!*

They're suffering too! Amy twisted in his grasp, her eyes blazing. *He uses their pain too! We have to free them!*

Louis tried to pull her back, and Amy suddenly pulled Joya's dagger and held it up, not so much a threat as a warning. Louis let go, and Amy fled up the stairs, heading for the attic. Zoe watched her for a moment, and then she too was running up the stairs.

There was nothing else to do. They followed.

By the time they caught up, Amy and Zoe had used Joya's dagger to pry open the attic door, revealing the blind and long-tormented souls of their enemy's own doomed family tree: the tortured wives and mistresses, the abused children, the unfortunate in-laws dragged into Silas's hellish domain. The spirits milled and clawed at the walls, oblivious to all but their own suffering.

Amy turned to Joya and Louis. *We have to help them,* she said imploringly, her own eyes wet with tears. *Please . . .*

Joya looked at Louis, and he nodded; and like Lucas and Josh had instructed the others, she showed them the way. Zoe and Louis watched for a moment. Then they too joined in. Working together.

Working to free them all.

Seth, Caroline, and Josh ran through the fields. Behind them lay the slaves' quarters and the growing beacon of light, now visible in the distance as a spiraling ethereal pyre reaching up into the demented heavens. They had watched in awe as dozens became hundreds, became thousands: each freed slave spirit, thus empowered to free yet another, fed into the whole, their numbers swelling like some grand cosmic display. It was altogether glorious. But it could not help but attract attention.

Indeed, as they had retreated, Caroline heard a distant snarl behind her and the clank of heavy chain; she turned to see a line of spirits being driven forward by ghastly guards bearing sickly glowing lanterns, hellhounds snapping in tow. The spirits were bound together in a coffle, each one manacled to the next, wrist to ankle, in double file: hundreds chained together as they had once been in life as they were driven to market. As they were now being driven mercilessly forward by the lash.

The guards saw the rising beacon, their faces twisting grotesquely as they barked orders in guttural tongues and drove their prisoners relentlessly into the heart of the camp, their hounds savaging those who fell, ravaged limbs dragged on by the sheer momentum of the march, as the guards tried to comprehend the wrongness of the light in their dark realm. But as they did, the freed spirits set upon their brethren, the liberating spark traveling down the chained line like lightning, the manacled slaves rising up into the air and swirling around the beacon, then swinging down like a vast bullwhip of bodies and iron, cutting a swath through their tormentors. Guards and hounds scrambled and were pounced upon by their former captives, who tore and sundered them as the great spirit chain rose and fell and arced up again, glowing in the beacon's light.

A light that began to take on not merely the color of liberation but of righteous fury. And vengeance.

It was at that moment that Seth, Caroline, and Josh had fled, like children who had played with fire and accidentally burned down the world. And in a sense they had, for it seemed that for every spirit who released and flew up into the light, another ten descended to lay waste to their captors.

Caroline, Seth, and Josh watched in horror. What they had started, they could not stop.

They could only run.

And run they did, hearts pounding as they crossed the open field, Seth in the lead, followed by Caroline, then Josh. But they weren't heading for the house.

They were heading for the barn.

Where are we going? Caroline called out desperately, trying to keep up. *Seth!*

But Seth just kept going, legs pumping furiously as he covered the distance. Seth was big but fast, and as they tried to keep up, Caroline suddenly stumbled, ploughing into the wild and uneven earth. Josh caught up to her, wired and winded.

Are you all right? he asked.

Yeah, she said. *But where the hell is he going?*

But before he could answer, a strange breeze stirred the air around them, leaves and twigs and tiny stones tumbling past as if pulled by some unseen force. They watched in horror as a dark cloud began to form on the far side of the barn, looming like a thunderhead, threatening to engulf the structure.

And Seth right along with it.

Oh no, Caroline gasped. *Please God, no . . .*

But God was far from this forsaken place. Josh helped Caroline up, and together they ran, frantically calling out the name of their friend.

For Seth's part, it was not that he could not hear them or did not care. He was a man in the grip of a flashback in reverse, the terrifying memories cascading through his brain and filling him with cold dread. He had seen this before and knew how it would end. He had seen it replayed in ten thousand nightmares since. But this time he wasn't having a dream—the dream was having him. And he was determined to end it.

As Seth ran to the doors of the barn, he heard the swell of galloping hooves, the clank of bit and bridle. The storm swept over the roof and around the sides, swirling around him. He pounded on the doors. *I won't let you burn,* he cried. *I won't let you burn again!* Seth placed his massive hands on the heavy wooden beam that held the doors shut.

And the barn burst into flames.

NO! he screamed, as tendrils of fire crept up and he heard the cries of the spirits trapped inside. *NO!* he wailed and pressed harder as behind him the ghostly militia swirled, red-eyed phantoms on horseback caught in the grip of their fevered apocalypse. Torches glared in bony hands as the riders circled through blinding smoke. At first they could not see him, lost as they were in their grim machinations. But as he strained against the beam, the spectral mounts snorted and bucked, suddenly aware of his presence. A rider in tattered Confederate battle garb spied him and snarled, drawing its rusted saber and raising it high.

NO MORE! Seth roared.

And threw the beam free.

The doors blew open and out they poured, the wretched, flaming souls of those who had perished a million times over, released from their damnation. They spun past Seth like dervishes, throwing him back with the force of their exodus. Seth landed hard in the dust as the rush of freed souls roared forth from the burning barn . . .

. . . and straight into the path of the ghostly riders.

The impact was an earthquake avalanche of rupture and chaos. The whirlwind howled up, taking slaves and riders alike into the vortex, which spread across the sky. Within the boiling clouds, lightning clashed, and Seth could hear horses, and sabers, and screams.

The whirlwind moved away on its own dread course. But unlike his nightmares of flashbacks past, the barn was still burning . . . and emptied. Bruised and exhausted, Seth struggled away from the flaming wreckage.

And into the arms of Caroline and Josh.

Zoe's hand was deep in the dead woman's chest when the first tremor hit. The house lurched like a living thing, plaster cracking and raining in ragged chunks around them as the foundation groaned and rumbled.

They did not know what had happened, did not have time to find out. There were too many spirits still needing to be freed.

The dead woman was a *mundele,* and obviously of high caste—a former Custis wife or mistress, the social privilege of her life now corroded in death. Her elegant dress was moldering and decrepit, her once-neat hair disheveled and stringy. The dead woman trembled from Zoe's touch as Zoe steeled herself against her own mounting terror and pressed deeper, probing.

Please, Zoe murmured, desperately searching. *What is your name?*

The spirit shook her head and mewled, as if fighting the memories. Zoe closed her eyes and pushed deeper . . .

. . . and when she opened them again, she saw herself in the dead woman's place, clad in her ragged finery, her own features ashen and withered, eyes empty and clouded, mouth flung open in an asylum scream . . .

No! Zoe gasped, fighting the illusion. *I'm not you! Tell me your name!* She pressed deeper still . . .

. . . and the dead woman's spirit suddenly took a great heaving gasp, as the light went off in her eyes. She shuddered and collapsed at Zoe's feet, weeping wretchedly.

I am Priscilla Custiss, it whispered. *And I want to leave this dreadful place. . . .*

You can, Zoe told her, and helped her up.

The spirit stood, tears rimming its hollow eyes. Its pale fingers reached out to caress her cheek. *Thank you,* it murmured. *Thank you . . .*

Louis, Amy, and Joya came to Zoe then and gently pulled her away. *We gotta go, little girl,* Louis said. *We've done what we can. . . .*

She's the last one, Amy told her. *We did it.*

Zoe turned to see that the attic packed with mad and tormented souls was now empty but for herself and her companions. Just then, another tremor wracked the building. As they moved away, Zoe cast a glance back at the ghost of Priscilla Custis. It smiled at her wanly as it began to glow, dimly at first, then brighter.

Then it crumbled to dust.

They were on their way back down when they heard the soft cries coming from the bedroom. Amy peered in and saw Mia cradling Justin's head in her lap, stroking his sweat-matted hair.

Oh my God, she gasped and rushed to her friends. She embraced Mia tightly, then looked at Justin. Any joy of their reunion was bleakened by his condition, which had deteriorated massively. He could not stand, much less walk, and could barely talk. Justin looked up at her, shivering through his fever.

Hey, kiddo, he said weakly. *Long time no see.*

Amy started to cry. Louis knelt at Justin's side. Justin looked at him; even through his delirium, he could see that Louis was hurting too. Justin took hold of his hand, squeezing it.

Look like shit, bro, Justin said.

Look who's talking, white boy, Louis replied. They smiled grimly, brothers in suffering.

The glow from the windows was growing more intense, casting undulating shadows across the walls. Zoe peered outside and saw the fires, which were spreading, coming closer to the house. She didn't know Mia or Justin, and she was starting to freak. *My mom,* she said. *Where is she?*

Mia looked from her to Joya. *They're out there,* she replied. In the heartbeat it took for that to register, all pretense evaporated; Zoe looked completely, utterly wired. And for the first time, deeply scared.

Fuck! she cried. *We have to get them!*

Louis looked at Justin and Mia, then to Amy.

Take her, he said. *Meet us downstairs.*

That was all Zoe needed to hear. As Louis and Joya helped Mia get Justin to his feet, the two women took off. Running out the door.

And into the now raging Underworld.

Amy and Zoe moved through the fields, desperately calling out. Underworld was literally coming apart at the seams as the death force that had sustained it gave way to full-on uprising and spirit war. Below them the firmament convulsed; above them the spreading storm, thunderous and wide, churned and boiled toward the spiraling beacon at the slaves' quarters, which were now burning as well. They could see tiny figures silhouetted against flame, slave spirits taking down guards like enraged swarms of ants as others capered insanely in the shadow of the conflagration.

But just as it seemed all hope was lost, they heard the sound of rapid footfalls crunching through the underbrush and turned to see Josh and Caroline and Seth emerging, ragged and exhausted, from the darkness.

Mom! Zoe cried, and rushed to her. Mother and daughter embraced as Caroline felt the years of pain and alienation dissipate like mist.

Omigod, baby, Caroline said. *What are you doing here?*

But this was not the place for speeches, or hugs, or explanations. Josh looked at his friends nervously. *I think it's time to get the hell outta Hell, kids,* he said.

They couldn't have agreed more. They took one last look at Underworld, and the warring souls they must now leave behind, then raced madly back to the manor. While behind them the beacon grew towering into the sky, its colors threading through a furious blood red.

Growing deeper, as the storm wormed closer to the light. And impact.

In the grand ballroom, the mirror was cracking: a single glowing fissure spreading serpentine from the uppermost corner. Joya looked at it anxiously as the others huddled behind her uncertainly. Outside, the sounds of chaos and tumult grew louder, the conflict growing ever closer to them.

We must hurry, she told them. *The magick can't hold much longer!*

But when Joya pressed her hand to the surface, it did not yield. She looked at Amy.

The dagger, she said. *Give it to me!*

Amy nodded and complied, trembling as she held it forth. Joya looked at the assembled group and bared her wrist, ready to slice, when suddenly Mia stopped her.

Your blood won't feed it here, she told her. *Mine will.*

And with that, Mia took the blade and sliced her hand open. The others gasped as she painted the surface of the spreading rift and two things happened. The blood sucked through the crack, mending it. And the surface of the mirror rippled and went dark.

Go, she told Joya and Louis. *They'll need you on the other side!*

Joya looked at Mia, and a hidden understanding seemed to pass between them. Then she nodded and stepped through: the mirror opening to receive her, then rippling dark again. Louis followed quickly behind her, and as he passed through, the crack began to grow once more, now joined by another in the other corner. They spidered forth, working their way toward the center. Mia cut, and cut again, sealing the rifts with her essence, then turned to her friends.

Now you, she told them. *All of you. Quickly!*

But her friends hesitated, looking from her to Justin and back. In that moment, a dread passed between them, born of fear and guilt and years of bitter recrimination.

But what about you? Zoe asked.

Mia looked at the girl, at her lifelong friends. She smiled bravely.

You first, Mia said. *We'll follow.* . . .

There was no use arguing. One by one, each of them hugged her and stepped through: Zoe first, then Caroline, Amy, Seth, and finally Josh. He paused at the brink and looked at them.

No words were exchanged, but as Justin struggled to his feet and joined Mia, they looked at Josh and nodded.

Then Josh stepped through.

Leaving only two.

42

Silas stared at the angry sky, cursing the reverberations now shaking his domain. In a land of unending nightmares, this was his. The enslaved were rising up to cast off their enslavers, the power of their terror now wild and unchained. The beacon of light rose defiantly in the distance, taunting him.

In the little shack, the moment of Transition was upon him, the doorway between worlds opening. And Silas resolved that upon its completion he would exact retribution that would shudder the legions of the damned.

Inside the shack, the ritual had reached a fevered pitch. Duke knelt, the stench of the smoking pot and their fetid offerings clouding the room as Eli hovered over the bound and helpless child, wildly chanting. Both men were hideous to behold, sweat dripping off their contorted flesh as they manifested the true nature of their spiritual corruption. And as he breathed in the desecrated vapors, Duke felt imbued with foul power, felt the revulsion and mortal dread slip away, replaced by a hunger the likes of which he had never known. Duke was gaining strength even as it leeched from Eli, leaving the older man more and more sunken and decrepit. The pitted iron opening of the *nganga* itself had become a mouth: a greedy, meaty, dripping hole that offered a glimpse of an even deeper darkness as it yawned wide to accept their offerings. Within was the bottomless darkness of an even deeper hell: that primal bedrock of evil upon which Silas's power ultimately rested.

Suddenly the many blazing candles and bottles of rum began to shimmer and rattle on their coarse wooden shelves.

"Tata Nkisi!" Eli urged. "The Great Night! He is here!"

Duke looked up as the smoke from the fire rose and uncoiled, solidifying into form. And from within the gathering mass: eyes, gazing out with feral intensity. Duke blinked back sweat and saw the smoke coalesce into the face of his forebear. Silas spread his cloak wide to reveal a hideous scarred opening in his chest, a puckering ovoid slit that dilated to reveal his shriveled, putrid soul. He descended, ready to take his tiny, shivering victim . . .

. . . and it was then that Lucas appeared behind him, following Silas through the breach and aborting the ritual as he attacked. Silas reeled and screamed, as much stunned as enraged. The two spirits came through the smoke and careened across the interior of the *nganga* shack locked in a brutal death-dance, their piercing blue eyes ablaze with primal, irreducible hatred. They were the eyes of sworn enemies. Of oppressor versus oppressed. Of father versus son . . .

Meanwhile, on the physical plane, Eli and Duke were losing their collective minds. Eli clutched his chest and fell back, cardiac arresting, as Duke scuttled and scrabbled for safety, in the process knocking over the sacrificial altar, the bottles of rum, and dozens of blazing candles. In seconds, the first licks of flame appeared as the dry, weathered wood of the shack caught and began to burn. The *nganga* gaped hungrily as Silas and Lucas hovered over it.

For one terrible second, they wavered in stalemate.

And that was when the storm reached the beacon.

It was a collision of blistering magnitude, a tectonic tsunami hemorrhage of incandescent karmic force. The power of the massive spirit release ripped a hole in the fabric of Underworld. The fires of the barn and slaves' quarters met and spread across the horizon, voraciously consuming everything in their path. The perimeters of Silas's domain ruptured: the crucified souls of those who had tried and failed burst free, their withered bodies popping like a string of grisly, ethereal firecrackers, giving up the ghost.

The tremor reached all the way to the tiny shack, the earth splitting open beneath the *nganga*. As it began to sink, Silas lost his footing; Lucas seized the opportunity and shoved him in. Silas screamed as his soul released like a tumor, tearing from the black, suppurated web of his heart.

Stripped of his power base, Silas grabbed at the first safe harbor he could: Daniel Duke Custis, his new heir apparent. As he reached up, Silas cried out plaintively, and Duke took his hand.

And that was all it required.

Silas's spirit form exploded in a vile rain of pus as the *nganga* sucked it greedily down. Duke's soul shriveled like a slug under a magnifying glass as the dark and twisted essence of that which was Silas entered him, rocketing through ganglia and neuron, through muscle and marrow, to violently wrench away all control. In the space of one seized heartbeat, Silas had taken possession. In the next, he turned, ready to feed upon fresh and innocent blood.

But the child, and Lucas, were gone.

Raging, his unearthly kingdom in ruin, Silas stepped over the twitching, now-dying Eli as he fled the island.

And the *nganga* boiled with infernal fire toward meltdown.

43

Lucas felt the night air on his skin as he carried the little girl. The swamp lay behind him, wooded fields before. As he walked, a faint breeze wafted, bringing the smell of cut grass, mixed with the barest hint of magnolia and dogwood. How long had it been since he had breathed air untainted by the stain of ceaseless pain and suffering? He could not clearly recall. He only knew that the air felt good. That the tiny form huddled in his arms felt good.

And that, but for one fleeting moment, he felt free.

The little girl stirred and shivered, her dark eyes fluttering open and gazing up at him like a lost and woozy lamb.

"What is your name, child?" Lucas asked gently.

"Ally," the girl replied in a tiny, frightened voice. "I want my m-mommy."

"Shhh," Lucas soothed. "You'll see her soon."

The child closed her eyes. "I had a bad dream," she murmured.

Lucas nodded. "So did we all," he said.

And so he carried her through the fields toward the road. And for that time he felt something almost like joy. Almost like victory.

And then the pain came from deep within, registering itself with each passing step. As time itself, so long held in abeyance by his purgatorial sojourn, crept back to take its due.

Kevin and Doris had just rounded the bend in the Land Cruiser, ostensibly heading for the plantation but in actuality completely lost. The road was dark and tree lined, not a house or billboard or road sign in sight. Kevin was wired and worried, mumbling under his breath as Doris attempted to navigate from memory.

"Are you sure it's around here?" he asked.

"I think so," Doris replied uncertainly. "It's been so long . . . Maybe we should have turned left back there . . ."

Kevin cursed as suddenly the headlights illuminated a figure shambling onto the road, bearing a small bundle. Kevin braked and swerved, barely missing the man, then pulled onto the shoulder of the road. They jumped out and saw what appeared to be a very young child in the arms of a very, very old man.

"Jesus, mister, are you okay?" Kevin asked. "I swear I didn't see you . . ."

The man was clad in a loose white shirt and black breaches, his onyx skin astonishingly withered, his once-regal features drawn cadaver tight around the bones of his face. He looked at Kevin with blues eyes at once piercing and infinitely kind, and handed him the little girl.

"Her name is Ally," the ancient black man said in a voice that sounded like dry leaves rustling. "She wants to go home."

Kevin took the child in his arms, speechless, as Doris rushed to open the rear door. As Kevin placed the girl gently on the rear seat, Doris called back. "Please, do you know the way to Custis Manor?"

Lucas looked at her and nodded, a strange half smile on his raisined face.

"Yes, I do," he replied.

But when they turned back to him, there was nothing left but dust.

In the grand ballroom, the reconstructed puzzle of the mirror glowed as the ragged survivors clawed their way back into the world of the living, coughing and gasping—Joya and Louis helping Zoe, then Seth helping Amy and Caroline, and lastly Josh. But as they collapsed shivering and spent on the floor, Caroline looked back to the portal.

And Mia and Justin were not there.

"No!" Caroline cried, falling to her knees and feeling the surface of the glass. For a moment she thought she saw the faces of Mia and Justin smiling through the void. Then the mirror went cold and inert. And they were gone.

"Something's wrong!" she said. She reached out, and the pieces of mirror scattered to her touch. Caroline freaked as her friends looked on, horrified. "We've got to get them out!"

"We don't have time!"

They turned and saw Louis, who was looking at the detonator. Seth rushed over and saw the numbers clicking down: *00:59 . . . 00:58 . . . 00:57 . . .*

"Oh shit," Seth muttered, then looked at the others, aghast. "We gotta go. Now!"

Caroline tried to protest, to no avail. Seth grabbed her and herded them all out. They spilled through the front doors and stumbled down the broad porch steps, staggering down the winding drive, driven by adrenaline and sheer will to live. Putting as much distance between themselves and the manor as possible. As the timer in the ballroom ticked down to *00:00.*

And Custis Manor exploded.

Silas looked out to see the house evaporate in a massive fireball, followed moments later by a cascade of flaming debris. And as the vast corona of light and heat belched skyward, reality visibly glitched as lightning flashed and the spirit world bled through to the physical one. He could see the maypoling pillar of light, streaming up to the heavens above the flaming manor, refracted through churning smoke and ash.

Underworld was burning. His earthly realm was burning. Worse yet, the barrier separating the real from the unreal had breached as the *nganga* itself became like a vast cosmic drain, sucking the tumult in and sluicing it into the earthly world. Though the beacon of light withstood the onslaught, the roiling storm of warring souls was drawn inexorably in, then blew through with hurricane force, ripping the shack to kindling as it spilled out into the placid Virginia night. And burgeoned upward, into clear and unsuspecting mortal sky.

And Silas Custis, his power waning, his soul housed firmly in the all-too-mortal body of Duke, could do nothing about it. But run for his miserable life.

"What the hell?"

Jackson wrenched the wheel of the cruiser and felt the vehicle lurch and skid on the flat black macadam of the road. One moment he was approaching the sign announcing WELCOME TO CUSTIS MANOR, the split-rail fence demarcating the grounds slicing by outside his passenger window, strobed by the red and blue glow of the police cruiser's light bar, the next he was witness to the Dresden spectacle of the historic mansion incinerating before his eyes, the blast shaking the ground, the car, and Jackson's back molars. Jackson swerved and regained control of the car . . .

. . . and suddenly found himself engulfed in a billowing black fog that enshrouded and obscured the road ahead and behind and everything in between. Jackson slammed on the brakes and slalomed, tires screeching as his heart pounded wildly . . .

. . . and around him he could see the forces that would not release, the souls so deeply moored in their rage and pain that it had come to define them entirely. The ghost riders—and the slaves locked in conflict with them—appeared within the storm, a great whipping force that blew across the estate, escaping from the boundaries of the plantation. And heading straight for town.

The storm blew past and disappeared down the road as Jackson roared to a stop and grabbed the handset, frantically calling it in. His hands were shaking. There was no code for this. As the dispatcher's voice squawked over the static, Jackson bellowed, "Just shut it down! The whole strip! Now!"

There was another blast of static. Jackson yelled his orders again, then jumped out of the car. He was so panicked and consumed in the chaos of the moment that at first he did not register the sound behind him. Then instinct kicked in and Jackson turned, reaching for his gun. Just a moment too late.

"Officer?" Silas Custis said.

And thrust his hand into Jackson's heart.

44

Friday, August 29. Stillson Beach, VA. 9:55 p.m.

The police car was easy to steal, by comparison. In the chaos surrounding his kingdom's demise, it was barely noticed. Silas commanded Duke's body to drive, and drive it did, heading to the edge of Stillson Beach, then ditching the vehicle and taking off on foot, heading to the heart of the boardwalk.

The bars and clubs all up and down the beach were being shut down, as Chief Jackson's message had quickly translated into virtual martial law. All in a vain effort to keep the lid on.

The orders were vigorously, zealously enforced. Tempers flared as young blacks and whites alike were herded out of bars and nightspots and into streets by police, then ordered to go to their hotels, go home, or go to jail.

At Titillations, Clifton Webb looked the wrong way at his evicting officer and took one last defiant swig of beer. The officer attempted to arrest him. Clifton fought back. Two officers joined in. Clifton started swinging. His friends came to the rescue. Two more cops joined in. Nightsticks flashed. Skulls cracked. More friends, more fists. A free-for-all ensued. Someone pulled a knife as the ill wind blew.

And the ghost riders hit town.

The melee became a riot, and the riot spread like wildfire: a centuries-old reservoir of violent energy touching off already-charged emotions like match to powder keg. On Pacific Avenue, a freewheeling cadre of baseball bat–wielding skinheads in a pickup truck took off on a terror spree, viciously beating a mixed-race couple and carving swastikas in their victims' squirming flesh. Shops were trashed and looted, cars overturned and burned. The war clashed and fused on both planes, amplifying the frenzy. There was simply no stopping it.

Silas stood in Duke's body, trying not to be seen. But he was covered with mud and blood from his trek through the swamp. And he was stuck with Duke's instantly recognizable, media-saturated racist face.

He didn't make it half a block.

In the mob of rampaging black youth that descended upon him, Clifton Webb was the one closest to Silas's face. And as the mob proceeded to literally tear his host body limb from limb, Silas made one last-ditch leap for survival.

It took every last ounce of spirit strength he had to invade and possess Clifton Webb in the seconds before Duke gave up the ghost forever.

Silas reeled down the boardwalk, surrounded by hatred and chaos. Before him stood the massive bronze heads of an anonymous man and woman, their blank eyes staring implacably inland. Silas collapsed against the monument and turned to see the spirit storm raging past him, sweeping across the boardwalk and beach, then blowing out across the vast and indifferent sea. The surf crashed upon the shore and swept back again, taking with it the increasingly distant sounds of horses and sabers and unearthly screams.

And there in the middle of it all was Silas Custis, now forced to take refuge in the body of a black man, less a different race than a different species to his way of thinking: a subhuman, the likes of which he'd

251

worked like beasts; the likes of which he'd put to death, over and over again.

But those days were gone forever. His power was broken, his empire in ruins. So when he saw the group of white men advancing, he momentarily forgot and let out a sob of gratitude as he staggered toward them.

It wasn't until he saw the terrible cold in their eyes that he realized the magnitude of his error.

But . . . ! he screamed as the first truncheon came.

But . . . ! as he sagged to the concrete, felt his ribs crack and shatter beneath the assault.

BUT . . . ! he cried through bleeding, punctured lungs.

And then the Great Night winked out forever, leaving behind a legacy of hatred as old and as vast as the nation itself. Leaving behind its blight, its stain.

Leaving behind just another dead black man.

On the streets of America.

45

Custis Manor. Underworld.

Justin lay dying on the ruptured ground. Above and around them, the spirit-fire raged. And Mia was there by his side.

We can't make it back, he said weakly, and she knew that it was true. He was too far gone, and the way was forever closed.

It's okay, she told him. They gazed out at the shining pillar of light, felt its inexorable pull. It was not easy to trust after all they'd been through. It was not easy to trust in a Creator who could sanction such horror. But the lines could not have been much more clearly drawn.

I love you, he said. *I'll love you forever.* Mia nodded and kissed him one last time.

Then, together, they surrendered. Releasing all ties, except to one another . . .

. . . and as their soulfire began to glow deep within them, they gripped each other a little tighter. There was no pain, only sensation. Their clothing began to smolder, then burn. As they clung to each other, their flesh ran like tallow, flowing together as the fire consumed them. The flame glowed bright as their spirits merged and melded.

Then together they flew upward.

Into forever night.

Visit the author on the World Wide Web at
www.craigspector.com.